The Reckoning

The Galatian Exchange, book 5

Pepper Pace

Contents

Part Three

A Word From The Author

If you have made it this far in the series, then you already know what I am going to say, but it bears repeating: The Galatian Exchange is an ongoing story, therefore, there is no end. Think in terms of a soap opera where storylines are resolved while the series continues.

The Galatian Exchange first appeared in Amazon's Kindle Vella. With nearly 120,000 thumbs up and over 5,000 story follows, it remained a top "faved" story, consistently appearing in the top 25. Each "season" is the resolution of a storyline, but keep in mind that the entire series has over 870,000 words, which means we are only half through what appeared on KV!

Unfortunately, KV was not available outside of the United States —and even within the States, not many people were familiar with the platform. Which is why I am pleased to release this series in book form in order to give all readers an opportunity to enjoy this epic journey.

Please remember that the series should be read in order, and that it is intended for mature readers as it contains adult content such as sex, language, abuse and racism.

©**Pepper Pace Publications**

In the Aftermath...

In the wake of the catastrophic clash with the Black Masks, Rafe's crew is shattered, separated across continents by loss and betrayal. As war grows closer, old wounds are torn open, and long-buried secrets rise to the surface, threatening to unravel everything they have fought for.

Now, the conflict takes an unexpected turn—onto the human stage. With enemies gaining the upper hand, Rafe and his scattered family must reunite as their fate now hinge on their ability to outmaneuver enemies old and new, in a conflict where every choice carries devastating consequences.

Part One

Chapter One

"You didn't have to come with me," Daya said shyly.

Paris gripped her hand. "Of course, I am going to be here with you. I am your transportation." Daya opened her mouth, but before she could protest or concede, he continued. "...as well as your man. There is no place I would rather be than by your side."

She smiled and gave his hand a tight squeeze. They were in the military medical center waiting to be examined by a physician. She was very thankful for Paris. He had gotten her seen within day instead of weeks. And best of all, he said the doctor was one of the best regarding reconstructive surgery.

Daya was nervous, but strangely, it had nothing to do with fear of pain or even a successful surgery. The truth is she didn't want to show the extent of her injuries to anyone but Paris. And even he had never seen her completely naked. He'd touched and kissed every inch of her body, but only from beneath her gown.

Once, when he had made to remove it, she had completely frozen, and it took a while before she could continue making out with him. She knew it was ridiculous for her to be shy about such a thing when he saw nothing but beauty when he looked at her. She knew this with every inch of her fiber. And yet, it had nothing to do with him but with her. She was damaged—and not just physically.

And now, this doctor would have to look at every detail of her body to repair it. It made her feel sick.

Paris raised her hand to his mouth and gently kissed the back of it. "Don't be afraid, Daya. If you don't want to do this—"

"I do," she replied quickly. "It's just a lot to deal with."

He stared into her eyes and spoke slowly. "Listen to me, my Daya. Many people love you just the way you are. I am, of course, top on that list."

My Daya. That term lightened her heart as she had not imagined that anyone would claim her in such a way.

"And I love you for that." Her eyes became hooded with emotion. "My mother and father have loved me no less since I got hurt. But it's hard for them to look at me like this. People who love me understand what it's like to deal with others who don't feel the same. I know you accept me wholeheartedly. If only the rest of the world was as evolved."

He smiled orange. "Then why the nerves? I can feel your heart beating, slamming through your fingertips."

She just leaned forward and kissed his lips.

The door opened, and a nurse stepped into the room. She came to an immediate stop the moment she set eyes on the odd couple. Her mouth opened and closed as if she had to stop the gasp of surprise ready to leave her lips. She forced a tight smile.

"Miss Daya Porter?"

Daya nodded. "Yes."

"Please come this way. Dr. Brookstone will see you now."

She and Paris came to their feet, and the nurse looked up at the nearly seven-foot-tall alien.

"Oh... you can stay here. We're going to do a full examination."

"It's okay," Daya said. "He and I are together."

The woman looked confused, which clarified when Paris placed his hand on the small of Daya's back, and the two walked into the doctor's office.

Dr. Brookstone was a tall white man. He wasn't just Caucasian but evidently had albinism. His hair was like snow, while his pale skin had patches of pink the way some humans tanned.

He reached out to shake her hand, his smile easy and polite. "Miss Porter. It's nice to meet you." He gave Paris a quick look, evidently accustomed to Galatians. "Lt. Frenchman."

"Dr. Brookstone," Paris replied. "I appreciate you agreeing to work with us."

She should not have been surprised he said "us," but she had to learn to suppress her smile of pleasure, or people were going to think she was demented.

The doctor looked at her again, but this time, he was examining her skin, easily separating the individual from the case.

"I'm happy you contacted me. I rarely see burns this severe—especially ones that haven't been repaired." He shook his head, and a look of disgust came over his face. But she knew it wasn't directed at her but at the institution that would allow someone to suffer in a body like this when it was possible to fix it.

She liked Dr. Brookstone immediately. He probably captured a great deal of attention with his looks, too. She considered herself rather well-educated, and she had never seen anyone so white. Daya wondered why no one had caught on to his condition, given the many tests that were given pre and postnatal to weed out such conditions and to make sure the rich gave birth to the perfect baby. Unless he wasn't born rich. Had he pulled himself up by his bootstraps just like she had?

Dr Brookstone examined only the exposed areas of her skin and, thankfully, didn't require her to remove her clothes. After several comments and the typing of notes into his computer, the doctor sat on the edge of his stool and sighed.

"There are several ways for us to address this. Unfortunately, there will be significant pain involved in any scenario." Paris made a quiet sound, and his demeanor changed, although it was hard for Daya to determine if the kaleidoscope of colors meant anger, disappointment, or sadness.

Daya didn't so much as flinch, though. "I understand."

"How far do you want to go with this, Miss Porter? We can focus on the visible areas—"

"No," she shook her head. "We can start with my head and hands, but I'd like to work on my entire body. I know it might take time, but time is something I have plenty of, Dr. Brookstone."

"Well, that's the good part. We have the technology to progress fairly rapidly. Your first option is to utilize artificial skin. It is very aesthetically pleasing. Cutting-edge technology would allow you to mimic the looks of any individual—including your old self. Of course, we'd have to have photos. There is also minimal scarring, although you'd have to take anti-rejection medicine for the lifetime of the transplant, but the success rate is very high.

"However, there are certain cons. For instance, you'll never age—and maybe that's not a downside," he smiled. "This surgical option would cause a person who ages to seventy to still have the face of a thirty-year-old. However, the artificial skin might only last twenty years, even with maintenance." He shrugged. "But it is a popular choice.

"The biggest downside is that because the dermis is artificial, you would lose almost all of your sensation wherever we replace the injured flesh. That's why we suggest using a mixture of artificial with transplantation of your own skin. The latter would involve regrowing the dermis. A benefit of that is it will repair any nerves affected by being burned."

Daya's brow gathered. "I would regain sensation in the places where I lost it?"

"Absolutely, but I must warn you that regrowing your skin won't create a flawless result. Unlike artificial skin, there would be significant scarring, and much of your success would be the results of a cosmetic surgeon. The hardest part would be your face, which would have to be re-sculpted in much the same way an artist would. But because your skin will change with healing, additional trauma, or any number of things—the visual results are unclear. But it won't reject, and you would regain sensation."

She looked at Paris; her teeth captured her bottom lip momentarily. "So, I could look perfect but lose the remaining sensation I have, or I could regrow my own skin but maybe look like a patchwork quilt."

Paris was very still when he spoke. "Or you can decide not to do either. This is not something you have to do, Daya."

Dr. Brookstone looked from him back to Daya. Maybe he was just now beginning to realize their relationship was much deeper than what was normal. "These are just options. You really should take some time to consider—"

"How long would it take if I wanted my own skin?"

"Three months to grow and to place the new dermis and then another six months to a year for healing. Complete healing could take as long as two years, but we are developing ways to hasten that."

Daya licked her lips, feeling the tight skin along the corner of her mouth stretch. She was looking at the doctor as she reached for Paris's hand and squeezed it. She addressed the doctor but was also speaking to Paris.

"I'm not afraid of the pain. Burns like this come with lots of pain and not just physical ones. The one drawback to any of this is putting my life on hold. I just found a job I love—"

"Your job will be waiting for you," Paris said. His mouth parted after saying those words, but then he closed it. Daya nodded and then gestured with her head.

"This is my boss, so if he says it's so, then it's so."

Dr. Brookstone chuckled. "Then, with that out of the way, how would you like to proceed?"

Daya bravely explained that while she wasn't looking for beauty, she would like to have her own skin and regain sensation. She asked him to replace the skin on her entire body.

She could tell he liked her choice when he sat back on his small stool and crossed his hands on his lap. "You have probably seen individuals with missing limbs that are re-growing them. Generally, you see it on the hands and feet, where it appears like baby limbs. But we can also regrow body parts like noses or lips. My colleagues and I work with Doctors Without Borders, and we have assisted many children who were born with birth deficiencies.

"I'd like to see a world where all people are treated for their illnesses and injuries without thought of money and status."

She nodded. "If I'd been rich, my doctors would not have used techniques that were outdated a hundred years ago." Dr. Brookstone looked down and nodded.

"Change is slow."

"I like Dr. Brookstone," Daya said as they flew the transport back to the school. At first, she had been terrified to fly in the mini spaceship until Paris explained that for him, it was no different than driving a car—except he was less likely to run into another slow-moving vehicle.

"I met him while working with refugees we initially thought were rebels. He stood up for them when we were prepared to cut them down—he stood up to us. Rafe took to him, and so did I. The Galatians have been funding his efforts ever since."

"You have a lot of stories like that," Daya commented. He gave her a curious look. "Humanitarian missions. You know, if the Galatians talked more about all the ways they help people, then I promise you'd be more popular. I think the rebels just see you in one light because no one has taken the time to show the other side."

"I don't know if I agree with that. Helping the humans has been our purpose since the beginning. It's no mystery. Some humans would rather die and be pirated off to predators than accept that we are their origins and that we only want to help."

Daya stared at him. "I don't think you're telling the right story."

"What do you mean?"

"You're telling your story. But you're not telling Dr. Brookstone's story or M, or even mine. The Galatians have helped a lot of poor, street people. They've helped orphaned kids and marginalized individuals." She looked out the window as the scenery below moved swiftly past. "And there are a lot more of *us* than there are of the rich."

His tail observed her for a long time.

Chapter Two

When Daya and Paris returned to St. Aloysius, he helped her down from the transport, and while they were close, he whispered in her ear.

"I have to show you something. Give me a few moments and then I will return for you."

"Do I have time to get a snack from the commissary?"

He told her he'd meet her there and then quickly moved in the direction of the soldier's barracks.

She watched him curiously for a few moments before heading from the transportation bay to the building.

Several soldiers nodded in greeting. They were polite, but she couldn't count any as her friends. There was Miss Keyes and several of the teachers and teacher aids that weren't quite as formal, but with the exception of Miss Keyes, none were what she could consider a true friend.

She hadn't had one of those since being injured. This made her think deeply about Dr. Brookstone's treatment plan. Of course, she wanted to have her injuries repaired. Who wouldn't? There was the constant pain, and she was prone to injuring the delicate skin. She had lost so much sensation on her face that sometimes it was like wearing a mask. She couldn't feel tears on her cheeks, snot on her nose, or drool that might run down her chin.

Of course, she wanted to fix those things about herself. But there was the other side of the coin. She wouldn't always have to *show* people that she wasn't scary despite how she looked. She wanted to meet people and make friends. She wanted to be like everyone else.

Was that why she was willing to go through this torture? She did not doubt that it would be painful. She still remembered the agony of being hospitalized the first time. Being burned alive had been bad, but being healed had been horrific. She had been placed in a medical coma so they could strip away her cooked flesh.

And after all that pain, she had been left with no nostrils, no ears, no hair and skin that rippled over itself in a way that skin had never been meant to look. At least after this pain, she would be healed—maybe not beautiful in the eyes of the average human, but at least whole.

Daya closed her eyes briefly. She actually wanted to go through that pain again? Yes. To be normal—to be passably normal, she'd do it again.

Paris thought it was a terrible idea. He didn't say it. He didn't have to. When you understood your loved one, you didn't have to exchange words in order to communicate. He didn't think of her injuries the way others did, because he found them beautiful. But would he still desire her without the intriguing scars? His consort was flawless, and he didn't desire her...

Daya sat at one of the empty tables unable to even take one bit of her sandwich. Others nodded politely when they saw her, but then quickly averted their eyes as they continued their conversations with each other.

Daya just looked down at her hands and waited for Paris.

He arrived about ten minutes later, and even she noticed her body straightened the moment she saw him. Having someone love and respect her meant so much to her, and she was happy she had put her trust and love into such a good man.

Paris came to her table and offered his hand. She placed hers into his and stood. Daya noticed but didn't acknowledge the others in the small room, that had discreetly turned their attention to Paris.

Ignoring them, he led her out of the room.

"Where are we going?" she asked in a low whisper.

"You will see."

He kept hold of her hand as they walked down a back corridor, at ease with the romantic contact even when he passed the soldiers who served beneath him. Soon, it became apparent they were heading to the soldier's quarters and then beyond it. He was guiding her to the new Galatian Warrior outpost. It had been built to house the newly assigned warriors after Paris had left to go on his secret missions.

Daya looked at Paris as he opened a door into one of the large barracks and led her inside.

What was he doing? He basically lived in her room now. So why was he returning here? She looked around curiously. The room resembled a cavern, and unlike the barracks of the human soldiers, it had a large pool right in the center of a grouping of rocks and stones.

She knew it was man-made. It hadn't existed even three months before today, but it looked like a real cave, including dim lighting and the soft trickling sound of water as it somehow ran down the stone walls.

Her mouth parted. "Wow..."

He paused and looked around. "This replicates our homeland."

"You lived in a cave back in Galatia?"

"No. We lived in the city center where there were many constructed homes. But my family had access to a cavern near the sea. It is the way some humans have... vacation homes. Come." He led her closer, and curiously, she looked down into the spa-like depths. The water was in constant movement. In some areas, it churned rapidly, while in others, it steamed like a sauna.

The aroma was strange and pleasant. It reminded her of Paris, clean but with an underlying spice that her index of smells was just too limited to identify.

"Galatians like bodies of water," she commented while looking down into the swirls. She remembered there being one in M's house where her father had been trapped like a caterpillar in a cocoon.

"We can make do with any body of water, but it's these waters we want from Galatia." He released her hand and began to undo his rigging and then placed his harness on a hook against the rock wall.

"Oh. Going for a swim?"

Paris stooped down to undo his shoes. "The pool is where we shed our waste, where we relax, and where we revitalize. The latter is the most important. We can shed our waste anywhere, but the special Galatian waters consume waste matter and expel medicinal minerals."

When he finished taking off his shoes, he set them neatly in the corner and then unbuckled his rigging and unfastened his skirt. These he also hung on a hook next to his harness.

Daya watched, not sure why she was still so surprised that he undressed so easily. Each night, he stripped completely before going to bed, and he never showcased his body, nor did he try to shield himself. There were other cultures like his where nudity wasn't sexual but natural. Her culture just wasn't among them.

Her cheeks heated as she watched him. It was still early in their relationship, and looking at him completely nude still sent tingles through her body.

Even though Galatians only wore a harness across their nude chests, the rest of their form was covered by long, leather-like skirts and thick black boots. This is why she could never have imagined the sheer perfection of a Galatian male. Although lean, their muscles were evident beneath their beautifully patterned scales. With a torso which was more elongated than humans, it gave them height that easily averaged seven feet—and there were some even taller.

Beneath the skirts were massively strong legs which matched their rippling arms, shoulders and chest. Some would consider the other *attribute* to be their best; and that was their generous "endowment". At a foot long in its flaccid state, Daya could attest that their penises grew to unimaginable proportions when aroused—proportions that she had not become intimately acquainted with as her body was much too delicate for even a small amount of friction.

And while those were the attributes that most humans appreciated, there were others that humans generally found far less appealing; such as their sharp claws, talons and teeth. And with slitted amber or green eyes, humans found them to have an "evil" appearance.

Long elephant trunk tails were mostly hidden but "peeked" from beneath the pleats in the back of their skirts. Most unsettling for many was their lack of expression. Because Galatians had no true facial musculature. Their brows and lipless mouths were all that easily moved, allowing only their scales to express their emotions.

Paris turned and took her hand. "I want you to get into the pool with me."

Daya's attention jerked back from his beautiful form to his words. She glanced over at the whirling water with concern. "It's deep," he added, and she heard amusement in his voice. "But I promise not to let you drown."

"I'm not worried about that."

He seemed to smirk. "I realize humans think our pools are dirty, that you are swimming in sewage. And it might be that way if this was a human pool using Earth water. But the enzymes in the Galatian waters are very hungry, and they devour the waste."

She thought about the number of Galatian Warriors that used the pool as a toilet. And not to be indelicate, but encountering a massive turd left behind by a giant was far from ideal.

She felt the subtle movement of his body that indicated he was chuckling.

"What are you thinking, Daya?"

She gave him a stern look. "Are you making fun of me? Humans were conditioned to think such things are dirty." But beyond that, she was susceptible to infections. When your skin split and bled because you smiled too hard, it was difficult to reconcile everything Paris said.

Another thing is she would have to take off her clothes, which meant stripping down in broad daylight right in front of him.

Daya looked down in embarrassment, and Paris placed the crook of his finger beneath her chin and gently lifted it until she met his eyes.

"I am having a bit of fun with you. But there is a reason I want you to swim in these waters. You see, I spoke to Dr. Brookstone, who said it would help to condition and prepare your body for surgery. It will also help to heal it after your surgery. Daya, if you are going to do this thing, then I want it to go as smoothly as possible. Dr. Brookstone has confirmed this would be beneficial even to someone with your injuries."

His tail swished, and his eyes softened. "Now, as far as the sanitary quality, know that any waste deposited—including yours is drawn to the bottom of the pool by a strong current where it is quickly absorbed and purged. Just like a filter, the water is purified. That means we *can* and *do* drink it—although I do not believe the taste would be to your liking."

She reached up and began to undo her blouse. Paris's head cocked to the side as if in surprise she so readily agreed to enter the pool. She didn't reply; she just thought if he said it was so, then she believed it.

When her blouse was undone, he slipped it from her shoulders and quickly hung it beside his items.

Daya slipped off her pants and shoes, and Paris retrieved those as well. When she was down to her underwear, she hesitated.

"Keep them on if you wish. But I cleared the room so no one will enter." He paused before continuing. "No one will be here but us."

She nodded and then reached behind her to undo her bra and then swept off her panties. She turned to hang them up herself, mostly because she needed a moment to get over her nerves. When she turned to face Paris, his eyes were on her face, although she noticed his tail had moved to the side and was observing the rest of her.

She had her arms crossed over her breasts. She might be tall and lanky, but she had generous breasts and hips, as well as a rounded rear. She watched his face and expression but used her peripheral vision to check out his prick—much the same way he used his tail to take in her body.

It lay dormant, thick and long, but not erect. It gave her a bit of worry he might not find her as attractive now that he got to see the entire thing. She inhaled and bravely lowered her hands and then turned slowly so he could see all of her. Her feet didn't have scars, and there was minimal scarring on the skin behind her knees. Sometimes, at night, she ran her hands over these smooth parts of her body.

Daya kept her mind blank as she slowly rotated, and when she faced him again, his prick was as stiff as an iron bar.

She looked at it openly before meeting his eyes in surprise. His scales had brightened with a deep blue hue (In desire? Embarrassment? Both?). He reached out to take her hand and then guided her carefully up the large, smooth rocks. Once they reached the ledge, he turned and opened his arms.

"Place your arms around my neck, and I'll place mine around your body. Then we will drop into the water safely." She nodded and followed his directions. His erection was stiff beneath them and she thought she could feel it throbbing with a life of its own. But he didn't acknowledge it, so she tried to ignore it as well, although it wasn't easy to do.

A moment later, he stepped off the ledge and she clutched him tighter as they smoothly hit the water feet first.

Paris kept a firm hold of her, but she still made a whooping sound. The water covered her head momentarily before they immediately broke through the surface.

"Okay?" He asked as she pressed her face into the crook of his neck. She inhaled quickly and nodded. She blinked her eyes and tasted salt when she licked her lips.

"Can you swim?" What a fine time to ask her, she thought, but nodded. He slowly released her, making sure she remained no further than a hand length away.

As Daya gracefully kicked her feet in order to stay afloat, she realized the water was fizzing around her but not around him. She stared curiously as her flesh began to tingle in certain areas, like the inside of her elbows, behind her knees, between her fingers, and beneath her breasts.

"What the-?" she began.

"The waters are cleaning you. I am not saying you are dirty," he added quickly. "But it will find what it wants to consume, and in return, it will give something essential and healing in exchange. Let the waters do their job."

She nodded, digesting his words. She gently rubbed beneath her breast where it was beginning to itch and thought about those little fish that ate the dead skin from people's feet. Was that happening to her now?

Paris turned and swam to a corner where the water bubbled like a Jacuzzi. "This will help with the itching. There isn't salt water over here."

She swam after him. "What do you mean there isn't salt water over here? It's one pool, isn't it? Won't the water just mix?"

"No, not when the current goes in different directions." Daya reached what she now considered "the Jacuzzi", and as she took a moment to float in place, she was pleasantly surprised the itching stopped.

"Tell me if it's too warm," Paris said.

"This feels nice." She forgot all about this pool being a glorified toilet. Daya smiled, and he moved to gently pull her into his arms, being careful he didn't hurt her now that her skin was softened. He waited for his kiss and received a deep French one where her tongue filled his mouth. His sweetheart was not at ease about revealing herself. He never felt the need to encourage her to do what didn't come easily because he had time, and in time, he knew she would realize he would never hurt her.

Daya relaxed in his strong embrace. Paris made her feel like the best *her* possible. She was kissing her man out in the open and fully nude. Was this really her? She pulled back enough to look at him.

"Thank you, baby."

He just leaned forward where he nuzzled her cheek. One day, she would realize that thanks between them was never necessary.

But then he felt something brush his prick and realized it was her hand. He sighed. This was the only form of thanks he wanted.

He was surprised and pleased she had initiated sexual contact, and he showed it by kissing her again. He wanted her every minute of every day but held back more than he desired as he didn't want her to ever misconstrue his interest in her for merely sexual.

As his erection grew, Paris felt her fingers wrap around his shaft while trembles rocked his body. He couldn't stop the gasp that fell into her mouth. She suddenly pulled back.

"I can hold my breath for a very long time."

He blinked in confusion. "What?"

Daya slipped down until her head was under the water. He suddenly felt her mouth on the head of his prick. They had done a lot of kissing and touching, but she had never gone down on him.

Paris closed his eyes. The air left his body as if someone had hit him in the gut with a pipe. He tried to control himself as she stroked and sucked him. Paris wanted to hold her head in place, to pump into her mouth. He wanted to let go and make love to his woman with abandon.

But he couldn't.

And it made him feel bad for wanting to do that when he knew he couldn't—not ever. Her skin was as delicate as tissue paper—now even more than ever since being submerged in water for so long.

He would tear her.

Paris felt Daya suddenly release him and break through the water, where she promptly sucked air into her lungs.

She couldn't believe what she'd just done! She'd gone down on her boyfriend. It was a first for her, and it was everything she had fantasized about the sensation of him filling her mouth, the hardness against her tongue. Even the taste of his creamy precum. She felt like every other normal woman that could satisfy her man. For the first time in her life, Daya Porter felt sexually empowered.

She wiped the water from her face and eyes and then looked at Paris with pride. He cupped her face, and he leaned into it, but then he gently ran his thumb against the corner of her mouth. He then showed her his thumb, and it took a moment for her to recognize what she saw there.

It was her blood.

Her mouth had cracked in the corner and was now bleeding. She reached up and quickly wiped it away, feeling suddenly embarrassed and self-conscious.

"Oh!" she exclaimed. "I didn't feel it." The tingling sensation from the water must have masked the injury... "

"We should get out." Paris swam to the ledge and quickly got out. He then reached down to offer his hand. He was careful as he helped her out of the pool, allowing her to do most of the work so he wouldn't hurt her. He was worried at the sight of her puckered flesh, and it made him feel even worse at the spots of blood dotting her body, which now ran in thin rivulets.

He felt suddenly guilty. He'd done this to her. She hadn't wanted to get into the pool, and now she was bleeding.

Daya quickly hurried over to where her clothes hung. She didn't bother with putting on her underwear and just quickly pulled on her pants and blouse, still sopping wet. She just wanted to return to the building where she could shower and get changed. Mostly, she wanted to hide away for a while.

Paris's erection had disappeared.

Chapter Three

M ayva strolled through her new penthouse apartment in the heart of Manhattan. There were two levels, exquisitely decorated, and even though it wasn't the province of Illis France, she felt the accommodations were suited for someone of her status.

A new set of soldiers had deposited her personal effects. She was pleased those hateful assholes were out of the picture. She was half starved from fear of eating fouled food. She had subsisted on packaged tuna and soup. And when she was thirsty, she drank from bottles of wine. She didn't even trust the water that ran from the fountain—sure that they had shit or pissed into her reservoir.

It still angered her Ragna had allowed this. But this apartment certainly went a long way to make up for that.

As she looked through each room, Mayva was surprised she didn't see a den with a cavern and pool. She tapped a long nail against her cheek as she thought back to Ragna's words. She had said she would send her a man who would match her surgical enhancements.

Since she had been enhanced to pleasure a Galatian, Mayva had just assumed that is who she would have been assigned to. She didn't think any humans could be a physical match. Although, if there was, then it could be amazing.

She was frowning, though, as she returned to the large bedroom. There was only one bedroom. Mayva had said her sex slave/partner would have to live with her. But she had never said they would need to sleep in the same room—in the same bed.

He would just have to sleep on the couch—at least until she decided how proficient he was as a lover.

Mayva was grinning in anticipation. She decided to unpack her wardrobe as she waited for her lover.

An hour later, the front door opened. It annoyed her the visitor hadn't bothered to use the intercom to announce his arrival. She strolled out of the bedroom with a stern expression on her face.

But as Mayva reached the loft overlooking almost the entire first level, she gasped, squinted, and then clutched the front of her blouse.

"Who are you? What are you doing here?"

"I am Pod," the creature said. "Queen Ragna said I am here to pleasure you, Mistress."

Ragna took a step back in revulsion.

It was a blob. The creature was as gelatinous as a tub of gelatin. It was grey and no taller than four feet high but was also almost four feet wide, which meant he would almost have formed a circle had it not been for his cone-shaped head.

There was not an ounce of hair on the creature's body—and that was easy to see since it also wore no clothes. She should have been able to see its sex organs, but it had none. What it did have were teats that sat atop its rounded belly. The thing had no legs but had no problems with moving about. In place of arms were flippers that looked like they might be comfortable on a penguin.

The creature had large black pools for eyes, which seemed artificial in such a gelatinous face. In the place of a nose were two small holes and a gaping, lipless circle for a mouth.

"What the fuck are you?" she managed in a voice that had turned as soft as a whisper.

"You would not be able to pronounce my species with your limited voice." He suddenly made a guttural squeak and whistle sound that made her want to cover her ears. Thankfully, it ended quickly. "In this tongue I would be called Keengalese.

"My kind has been very useful to the Interplanetary Collective. Because of our boneless form, we can infiltrate even the smallest spaces. Our kind can pass through locks, air vents, and seams. We can also change our shape to penetrate any orifice."

Pod raised an arm flipper, and it quickly elongated. Within seconds, it had taken on an obscenely large phallus shape. Pod's mouth hole opened, and out came the long length of a tongue. It waggled suggestively.

Pod moved forward toward the stairs!

"Get the fuck out of here! This is some mistake!" Mayva blubbered.

"No mistake, Mistress," Pod replied, his voice surprisingly nice—even containing a sexy, masculine tone. He continued forward until he reached the stairs, and Mayva took a step back.

"Get out of here, I say!" she screamed.

"I am sorry, Mistress. But I do not take my orders from you. My Queen has bid me to pleasure you." Pod paused in climbing the stairs. "My kind is known for our sexual abilities. I can fill any orifice. I can ripple and massage. I will make you feel good, Mistress. But... it can go the easy way, or it can go the hard way. But it will go—in your mouth, in your pussy, and your ass—so says Queen Ragna."

Mayva turned and ran to the bedroom. She slammed the door shut and then looked around for something heavy to push in front of it. She spotted one of the bedside tables and was about to retrieve it when she heard a shuffling noise.

When she turned, to her horror, she saw a stream of slime sliding between the tiny crack between the door and the floor. She remembered Pod's declaration that his kind could infiltrate any opening.

She backed up until she hit the bed. Mayva looked around and picked up a lamp. She threw it at the blob forming on her side of the bedroom. It bounded harmlessly off the gelatin.

"I'm going to contact Ragna..." she stuttered. "I'm going to get this straightened out! Wait a minute!" She screamed. "Don't touch me!"

Pod became fully formed. He reformed a giant prick and stuck out his tongue, once again waggling it.

"I do not take orders from you, Mistress," he spoke perfectly from the same mouth. "It is up to you if you would like to do this the easy way or the hard way."

Mayva tried to make a mad dash across the room, but something looped around her ankle. When she looked around, it was to see that Pod had reached out to grab her with a long, rope-like appendage.

"The hard way, then," he spoke casually.

Three women sat on the paved patio between their homes. They drank tea and watched their children. Karma was reminded of being a child, and her mother, as well as the other women in her old apartment building, were sitting on their stoops or pulling up chairs to watch their children playing after school before it was time for dinner. She remembered looking around to see the mothers with scowls or grins as they discussed the most recent important occurrence, smacking their palms on laps and enjoying each other's company even when the stink of overflowing garbage filled the street and the voices of vendors rang out loudly advertising their wares.

There were places in the world where people lived in villages, and while she had never thought about it before knowing the Galatians—before having friends, this was now one of Karma's biggest desires: to raise her children and to live happily within her tribe.

Before Maddie had been sent away to consort school, she remembered being a little girl who always gravitated to the kitchen. That's where the help communed, laughing and joking; brown, beige, and tan faces with warring accents and dialects, and in the instance of her Hispanic Nanny, there were even different languages.

The kitchen was alive, unlike the den where father watched the news or stocks through his virtual headset while mother kept up with fashion and gossip using her own headset. If she went into the den, she felt as if she was alone, even with them sitting right there with her.

When she was very small, she remembered Nanny urging her forward with a cookie when she appeared in the doorway, and not the ones she made for her mother and father, but spiced cookies with a sharp but sweet taste. The servants would drink mysterious hot beverages she was too little to have, but Nanny always gave her half a cup of warm milk with cinnamon and chocolate.

Those were the best times when everyone laughed, joked, and told stories. But as she got older, the help would grow quiet and make excuses to leave whenever she came around. Eventually, she stopped, knowing that while she had every right to be there as the little mistress, this was *their* territory. The kitchen belonged to them, and she wasn't one of them.

When Karma came, the sisters began to gather daily—at first to teach Karma, but eventually, it was just a way to commune with each other. That feeling she had lost so many years ago returned—even when Auras and Polat (May the Great Guardian rest their souls) were being contrary, it took her back to those days of her childhood. She had never wanted to miss a day in the gardens with the ladies, even if Drago's dinner included a challenging recipe or if she had a meeting with the school board that might go on for hours.

Being here with Karma and Kemistry, a mother, a mate, and a friend, was a life she had never dreamed of having, but one far better than what she had been conditioned to desire. This was what it felt like to truly belong.

Kemistry gazed out into the field of wildflowers and watched her children playing. *Her children...*

When Drago and Maddie added Rex to their family, he became the little boy she thought she would never have. She loved holding him even in the beginning when he cried so often. There had been discomfort in his healing, and she had been able to understand that. But once he healed, he became content even in just observing the world around him. Kemistry found love through her relationship with Drago.

But she had never thought she could ever grow to accept the over-sized Galatian. He was so stoic and just big—so big it didn't make sense! And he was so powerful he could unintentionally injure her just by not minding his tail!

But one day, while they were training together—still new to the other's species, she connected to him and was slammed with all of his doubts and misgivings. Some of them were even about her.

I can't do this! She is so little I'm going to hurt her!

As time went on, she read his insecurities, some about upcoming missions but some also about her:

Will she think I am strange if I touch her pretty feathers?

What happened to her mate? I wish I could kill the Tybernees that hurt him... she looks so sad.

She is kind. I will protect her.

Can she really read my thoughts? I'll keep my mind blank. Don't let her-

Drago was one way on the outside but something else on the inside. Her heart immediately warmed towards him. Once they became friends and she eased his concerns without exactly revealing that she had read his private thoughts, he opened up and became her brother. He had learned not to broadcast his every emotion, but, in some ways, she missed seeing his insecure speculations.

There was more to Galatians that could never be uncovered just by sight. She had assumed that they were heartless warriors who only cared about winning. She soon learned their hearts were as tender as their heads were hard. Once under their protection, they would die for you—even for a stranger. Kemistry had known Galatian warriors, physicians, and simple spouses and it was always the same. They had a sense of honor unmatched in any species she'd ever read—and as an empath, she had read many.

And then Maddie came along to ruin the entire dynamic... only it didn't. Just as she had developed preconceived notions about Galatians, she had them about consorts. But Maddie was brave even when she quaked in fear internally.

Most Galatian Warriors said goodbye to their Japoxillian when they entered the Exchange. But Rafe's team was different. Their missions were so deadly that the bonds they formed ran deeper than most Japoxillian-Galatian relationships.

By unspoken agreement, the Japoxillian agreed to stay together until the Galatians were returned to their bound-mates. Then, they would truly feel that their mission was complete.

Kemistry had grown thankful for her friendship with Maddie. Because of Maddie and Drago's matting, Kemistry had learned just how badly the Galatian men had been treated at the hands of their Queens.

These consorts made the Galatians question. It began with just one defiant act: facing forward during mating while rejecting the elixir.

Kemistry had "read" him when Drago realized he loved Maddie in a way that he could never love Isyss. Through their connection, she realized with shock that he had been groomed to think it an honor to be mated to someone with the prestige of Isyss—someone as old as his mother! And even though the two had mated many times, Drago never realized how much he could enjoy it until it was with someone he desired. Drago had fallen in love with Maddie and through him, Kemistry learned to love Maddie, as well.

Kemistry had learned a lot in since her many years of being

linked to Galatians. She would stand by the unpopular opinion that the females were just as honorable but also just as stubborn when it came to their beliefs.

But her human friends were not ready to hear that—especially Karma, who was still trying to reconcile the loss of one child at the same time she had gained another. The poor girl was a horrendous mix of opposing emotions. It would take time, and this little piece of the world where they could laugh, talk, and live their best lives together was the balm that would help heal them all.

But this was just a reprieve from the impending danger. They all knew it, but no one wanted to talk about it. A war was coming. None of them had come this far to lose something as important as their right to live their own lives. But for now, they would relax. They would commune, and they would live their best lives.

Kemistry's eyes followed the laughing children. Kelsie was able to keep up with her friends for the first time in her life with the use of a hovercycle. She skimmed several feet into the air, never reckless and never hitting the ground which might dangerously launch her through the air.

Dorf had been against it. But when he saw the longing on her face as she watched M and Bain running under the bright sunlight, he relented.

But the hovercycle was just a bandage on the bigger problem. Kelsie was dying. Even the act of laughing and talking weakened her and could send her into a fit of coughing.

The doctor said a lung transplant was the only remedy.

And because child-sized lungs were not in easy supply, she would have to grow new ones. For months Kelsie would wear a special device over her chest where her lungs would grow outside of her body. As they became functional, she would have two sets of usable lungs. And for the first time in a long time, she would know what it was like to breath normally—but not only that, she would have a much greater lung capacity than the average human.

Some would then consider her an enhanced human.

But right now, she was just a little girl that wanted to play with her friends.

"I wish I could braid Kelsie's hair," Kemistry said. She turned to Karma before she could speak. "I know you can do it for her, but I wish I could."

Karma nodded. Runnar was in his hoverseat facing Rex. As usual, Rex, who was in his own hoverseat, was calm but intrigued with the other baby. Runnar, on the other hand was straining to reach the other child. He gurgled and stretched, letting his wants known.

"Sometimes I wish I had scales. Runnar's nails are only going to get sharper and he's still too young to understand that even hugging me could slice me open."

Maddie looked at her. "I want Runnar and Rex to play with each other—"

"But they can't touch," Karma finished.

Upon hearing his name, Rex looked at them. Sometimes it was like he could understand more than any six-month-old should. Drago had instructed the physicians to enhance Rex's brain so even though he had Down's syndrome, he had none of the effects of the disease. He too would be a super human.

"Runnar has more skin than scales," Karma continued. "So, my hope is he will learn from experience that his claws and teeth can cause pain. Unfortunately, my poor baby is probably going to hurt himself before he hurts anyone else."

"How long before his claws are razor sharp?" Maddie asked.

"Rafe says it won't happen until after he's a year old. But Runnar isn't exactly like a Galatian. It might be sooner or it might be later."

"Don't let it worry you, dear," Kemistry said while reaching out to pat her knee. "Runnar will heal and he will learn."

Karma nodded wondering if she was doing this right. She wished for the hundredth time she could talk to a Galatian mother.

Kemistry flapped her wings and rose into the air by a few feet. "Okay, children! Don't be so rough." M and Bain had pulled Kelsie to the grass and they were rolling among the wildflowers. The kids stopped to look up at Kemistry and then Bain stood and offered his sister a hand up and he and M helped her back onto her hovervehicle.

"Sorry, Mom," Bain called.

Kemistry's eyes grew big and glassy with unshed tears. She loved those children so much. It had only been two days but the children were in awe of their new life away from the regulations of the orphanage. They still had a long way to go, but they had also come a long way—and that included her and Dorf.

Chapter Four

Karma floated on her back in the water. It wasn't quite a leisurely swim but therapeutic. Since first being introduced to a Galatian pool, Karma's swimming skills had strengthened a great deal. She could now swim with confidence from one end of the pool to another—of course avoiding the arctic and sauna temperatures which always seemed to be positioned in back.

It seemed that the front of the pools were always mild causing her to wonder if it was done with the human consort in mind. Obviously, the consort would need to keep maintenance of their mate while he was molting or during grooming.

She smiled to herself. Rafe took more care of her than she ever had him. That would change now that she didn't have a rapidly growing belly that got in the middle of everything...

Karma touched her flat belly and closed her eyes. She quickly shook away her thoughts and dunked her head beneath the pool. Half a minute later when she broke through again, it was to see Rafe standing by the ledge.

"Guardian! You're so quiet!" she lurched back.

"I didn't mean to frighten you." He was turning a soft orange of amusement. "Are you here as an invitation to mate?"

"Uh... what?"

She saw him chuckle. "Because you know the water will ease our coupling. You are sore still, are you not?"

"Oh. There's no pain," she replied. At least there was none as long as his foot long prick wasn't buried inside of her to its base! They hadn't had intercourse since that first night. Rafe came to bed each night, spooned her and then fell asleep.

As his consort—his wife, she would not have denied him. But in her defense, it had been a tiresome few days and she had retired to the bedroom each night exhausted and barely conscious by the time he arrived.

"We can mate anytime you desire me, my husband." She replied honestly. "But you did push it all the way in that first time, so it did hurt," she whispered the last, her face warming.

He leaned forward. "It won't hurt so bad the next time. I had to set your cervical opening in the right position to accommodate me. Unfortunately, you did not have the proper training."

Her face still held a hint of a frown at his description of exactly what he'd done and why. "I'm no virginal consort. I don't need training..." she smirked as her feet kicked gently in the water. "I do the training, as you may remember."

Rafe sat on the ledge; one leg high on a rock while the other stayed on the cavern floor. Had he been naked, she would have seen that his prick was stiff. But he was still completely dressed.

"Indeed, wife. You excel as an instructor." His tongue flicked briefly from his mouth as he watched her. "What I meant is that your body did not receive dilation training after your surgery. Of course, I could have helped "train" you while you were in a coma. But... somehow that seemed invasive. And in truth, I may have enjoyed it too much."

"Rafe Sigur, you wouldn't!" That reminded her of the old folk story called <u>Sleeping Beauty</u> where Beauty had awakened after her long slumber to find that she was suddenly married and having born several children.

"Of course, I wouldn't. The doctor's did leave a dilator in place for several weeks just to prevent things from reverting after surgery—and I do believe your coma allowed you to avoid a great deal of discomfort... with the exception of assuring that you fit my prick."

"Damn. I had no idea all that was involved in making sure human women could fit with a Galatian."

He nodded. "It is one reason consorts receive a lifetime of support—or so the Queens rationalized."

"But we know the truth," Karma said unable to keep the bitterness from her voice. "The surgery was just to make sure we didn't pose a threat to their position."

Rafe took a deep breath. It was as if he was trying to avoid becoming angry himself. She swam to the ledge and placed a hand on his skirt covered knee and he covered it with his own hand, his temper quickly dissolving.

"If you aren't here as an invitation to mate, then have you grown fond of my pool?"

"Oh." She held up her left arm. "I'm here healing from our son's scratches."

Her forearm had several light abrasions—nothing deeper than what she might get from one of the thistle bushes in the garden back at the hotel. It wasn't even enough to draw blood, but it did sting and it happened every time she held her baby.

Runnar's claws might be considered soft but when he held onto her, it came at a price.

Rafe reached for her arm and examined the marks. Some had already healed considerably. His eyes scanned what he could of the rest of her body. Before she knew it, he was pulling her from the pool. He perched her on the ledge where he examined her torso and found more scratches on her neck, chest and shoulder.

"Karma... I didn't realize."

She hadn't wanted him to know. As it was, he always took Runnar from her arms whenever he grew too playful just to prevent this exact thing from happening. She wore long sleeves to protect her, but it did a good job of also concealing her injuries.

"They're just scratches."

He cupped one of her breasts, and for the first time ever, there was nothing sexual about it. After examining it he met her eyes.

"He hasn't bitten you yet?"

"No," she had prepared herself for when that happened. Unlike human babies, Runnar was born with tiny little teeth. She swore she wouldn't drop him. She wouldn't scream and she wouldn't yank away. She would squeeze his cheek until he released her. She might be in tears, but he was just a baby and didn't understand. And it wasn't his fault he had a frail human as a mother.

Rafe blew out a long breath. "I'll have a sleeve built for your arms. But he will have to be taught to go against his natural instinct to grab and hold with his claws."

"Rafe—"

"He must adapt, Karma. Soon we will have a toddler that can easily kill anyone in this household." Rafe looked away in deep thought. "He could be surgically declawed—"

"No!" She glared at him in shock. "We are not going to maim our son!"

Rafe blinked. "No. I would never hinder our child. I am sorry for even..." he ran a hand over his head and she saw the stress Rafe had been put through for these last three months."

"Rafe, honey. Take off your clothes and get into the pool."

He nodded and rose, quickly shedding his clothes and boots but being sure to keep them neat on hooks and within the proper shelves.

She returned to the pool, and a moment later, her mate dove in with barely a splash. He moved for a minute beneath the waters, and when he broke free, it was in the heated waters of the sauna. He looked at her and then dove again and, this time, broke free right next to her.

"Are the children still outside playing?" she asked.

"Dorf and Kemistry are giving them their lessons."

"And Maddie?"

He shrugged. "She returned to her own home."

Karma placed her hand on the rocky ledge of the pool, her back to Rafe. She turned to look at him over her shoulder.

"And Runnar?"

Rafe reached out to run a light finger down her spine. "You are in the perfect position for me to confirm that your cervical opening is properly aligned..."

Karma grinned. "That's going to depend on Runnar and how long he naps."

Rafe moved behind her so his pelvis was against her ass. "There is a nanny..." Rafe pushed his prick down so it bounded up between her slightly parted thighs. He held her in place as he rolled his hips so his shaft slid along her parted lower lips.

Karma moaned as he skimmed her clit.

"Nanny is good for many things," Karma said breathlessly, "but not for feedings. Runnar prefers his milk from the source."

Rafe's free hand was on her breast. "As do I." He squeezed firmly, surprising her, but then she looked down and saw a spray of milk shooting from her nipple. Rafe was no longer behind her, and like a creature that felt as at home in water as he did on land, he skimmed forward until he was on the side of her. His mouth locked around her nipple and areola while his hand continued to squeeze, forming a cone he drank from.

He released her breast after a few seconds. After all, he had to save some for his son. Karma moved so she could wrap her arms around his neck. Her legs wrapped around his body, and they kissed for several minutes, her tongue picking up the sweet milk that now coated his mouth.

Rafe moaned, and it gave her a pleasant thrill he still found so much pleasure in kissing. She loved him so much. He was such a good and caring man, and he'd been so patient sexually. She knew he desired to mate every single day but had willingly gone without so she could adjust to her new life.

"Never again will I make you wait..." she whispered into his mouth. "Take me every night for the rest of our lives. Every night we're together."

Rafe's breath came out in a harsh grunt. "Fuck..." he groaned.

"Promise me."

"I promise... " His voice shook. Suddenly he grabbed her ass and hoisted her up so their foreheads touched.

"Put me inside of you."

"From the front?" she asked, her lips seeking his mouth again.

Once again, he groaned. "We'll go slow."

Karma did as he instructed, finding his hard prick easily as it was resting against her rear. She wrapped her hand just below the head, feeling him throb with anticipation. And then, leaning forward so her head now rested over his shoulder, she guided him into her opening. He went in smoothly with the aid of the water.

She heard his growl, and a moment later, his mouth had captured the lobe of her ear. She felt his tongue teasing it, and she pushed another inch of prick into her canal.

She felt him kneading her ass. His hands pushed and massaged the two rounded spheres as if it would coax his prick in further. And perhaps it did because even though his massive girth filled her as she pushed him inside, inch by inch, there was nothing but satisfaction.

Rafe had to concentrate all of his will not to jackhammer up into his woman's tight depths. He allowed her to control how far he went and was incredulous when his testicles finally rested against her. He was in completely!

"Karma..." he cried. "I don't know how much longer..." he needed to pump.

Karma squeezed and winced. "Slow, babe."

Rafe could only nod. He pulled her close against his body and slowly pulled his pelvis back, withdrawing two inches of shaft. He slowly pushed forward with agonizing gentleness.

"Yesss!" Karma clung to him. His thickness applied delicious pressure behind her clitoris. "Ohhh. Do it again, Rafe..."

He did. Repeatedly. Soon, he could speed up and apply a bit more force.

"Am I hurting you?" he remembered to ask when he felt the engorged head of his prick graze her cervical opening.

Karma wanted to answer truthfully, but the truth didn't make sense. It hurt deep within her in a place where she had never felt pain before. But it was a pain that increased the pleasure he brought each time he slid out of her canal. His withdrawal applied pressure behind her clitoris, where she didn't know there were pleasure receptacles. It was as if he massaged her clitoris from the outside, but the sensation spread throughout her entire canal!

He would withdraw and immediately push forward, creating a rocketing pain and pleasure that intermingled into one sensation of ecstasy.

"Don't. Stop." It was her only answer. Karma opened her mouth and bit his cheek. Hard.

Rafe felt the bruising bite, but it didn't cause him pain or injury. He even understood it—giving pain if she felt pain. *But she had said not to stop...*

Rafe pumped into her tight pussy, wanting to explode but needing her to do so first.

Cum Karma, cum, he silently begged. Rafe reached out and sank his nails into one of the rocks on the pool's ledge.

Karma felt Rafe's fluid movements become staccato. He was going to cum, and as amazing as it felt, the 'edge' that would push her into an orgasm hadn't happened.

She put her mouth to his ear, although she knew she didn't need to. "Cum, Rafe," she whispered. "I need your cum to push me over."

Rafe froze for a split second. The next second, he plunged into her depths and, with animal cries, orgasmed deep within her belly.

His hard thrust and hot release was just the catalyst Karma needed in order to finally climax. Her hands gripped his sleek, hairless head as she cried out and blindly clamped her teeth down once again on Rafe's face.

Rafe pumped his seed into his woman's body as she bucked and cried out, her teeth eventually releasing his face.

If she was going to bite, his face was the best place as his scales were small enough not to cause injury to her. If she bit him elsewhere where the scales were larger, even though he kept them tightly closed, it was possible for her to lift one enough to slice through her mouth.

When he felt her orgasm ease, Rafe placed his mouth over hers. She breathed heavily into his depths, periodically kissing and licking him. He inhaled her cries and then slipped his spent prick from her body.

There were lots of intermingled fluids that flowed free to feed the pool. Rafe cradled her in his arms like a babe, allowing her to rest from trying to float. Her eyes closed.

"Every night, you say?" he asked in amusement at her limp form.

Karma managed to open one eye. "If the other consorts can do it, then so can I."

"I accept," Rafe replied. "However, perhaps I'll just lick your pussy for the next few days." Karma's body jerked reflexively, and she moaned as her clit lurched. He grinned a blue and pink tint.

He lifted her out of the pool while she turned to snuggle against him. She had no fear of being dropped, even though it was no easy feat climbing out of a deep pool with a grown woman snuggled in your arms.

Of course, her man did have a tail to help him. He carried her back to their quarters, and instead of running her a hot bath, he placed her in the shower. There, he cleaned her, washed her hair, and then placed a kiss on each buttock.

But normally, when he would carry her to the bedroom to apply lotion and oils, this time, she grabbed the brush and began to scrub his scales. Rafe groaned in pleasure, but before she could give him a full oil treatment, little Runnar Sigur was awake and hungry, and M and Bain were ready for their weapons training.

The two could only smile as they quickly dressed to meet their new domestic duties.

Chapter Five

M and Bain were bounding off each other as if they were overflowing with energy despite the fact that it had been a long day.

Schooling was complete for the day. Dorf and Kemistry had opted for an upscale online school where normally an AI interface was assigned per household. For obvious reasons, they had opted not to have the robot teacher.

Kemistry particularly enjoyed the hands-on approach to educating the children herself, while Dorf generally ended up playing online games.

Rafe and Karma knew they couldn't ask for better teachers than Dorf and Kemistry, and although the three children missed Miss Porter, they certainly didn't miss the overcrowded class.

Kelsie had lost interest in playing, and she joined Kemistry in the courtyard. She could barely keep her eyes from the beautiful turquoise creature and still couldn't believe this kind of individual wanted to be her mother. Kemistry always seemed to brighten up when she looked at her and Bain. But it was more than that. Somehow, Mom and Dad could make them feel...at ease. It had been like that even from the very beginning.

They had explained their special abilities to link through a bite where they could communicate and share without words. But neither she nor Bain had been brave enough to do that, and Mom and Dad hadn't insisted.

Kemistry smiled when the little girl's hoverbike stopped next to her chair. She was perched on a papasan chair, finishing up with the input of the day's lesson.

"How are you, dear?"

Kelsie gave her a tired smile. "Fine."

Kemistry noted that the little girl's eyes drooped. She reached out and stroked her cheek with a fur paw and thought she seemed a little warm. Kemistry turned off the virtual computer and spread her wings.

"Come. Sit with me."

Kelsie turned off her hoverbike. The three steps it took to reach Kemistry left her breathless. She spread her wings, and Kelsie happily sank into her soft embrace.

Poor child. She was exhausted!

Kemistry rocked her in the papasan chair and hummed a soft melody. While all Japoxillian had beautiful voices, she couldn't match Dorf's. And yet Kelsie thought it was the best song she had ever heard. The little girl felt herself yawn and tried to stay awake so she wouldn't miss any of the singing, but soon, her exhausted body succumbed to the comfortable fur and feathers and the soft lullaby.

When she was asleep, Kemistry kissed her warm forehead in concern. The hoverbike was supposed to make things easier for her. But maybe it had the opposite effect. Maybe it made her more active, which caused her lungs to become over-taxed. Whatever the intent, Kemistry feared Kelsie was worse off than when they'd brought the children home.

The surgeons had scheduled her transplant to take place once the biopsy tissue had multiplied sufficiently. She could only pray she wouldn't lose strength in that timeframe.

She frowned, wondering if she knew what she was doing. They had taken on two human children, and one was dangerously ill. Maybe...maybe it would have been better if Karma and Rafe had taken them.

Dorf walked beside Rafe, pleased he was included in the training. With Drago floating in his pool still in the middle of ecdysis, Rafe would definitely need the extra help. He didn't understand just how rambunctious three kids could get.

Dorf didn't know how that teacher handled having a classroom of fifty or more kids.

Not that he was truly complaining. He was proud of the accomplishments all three were making with their lessons. M found things more challenging, but he understood her schooling prior to St. Aloysius, had been virtually non-existent.

Bain was bright but didn't participate. What he wouldn't give to link with the boy and to try to reach him nonverbally. But Kemistry said they shouldn't push it, and he knew she was right. It was best if he opened up on his own. But it was obvious that although he had settled in rather quickly, he was still a troubled little boy.

Kelsie was very smart—perhaps even gifted. She enjoyed reading and could spend hours devouring information on the computer if they didn't regulate her screen time.

At times, it haunted him how easily his new children could have become lost in the system. It bothered him just as much thinking about all the other children that might not ever be rescued. For now, he could only focus on M, Bain, and Kelsie.

"You know, you could have asked me before this to help with combat training," Dorf said.

Rafe spared him a glance. "You were too busy trying to capture Kemistry's attention."

"Aye," Dorf agreed.

Rafe was in his weapons room, considering what weapons training they would begin with.

"Swords?" Dorf asked.

"Haru would murder me if I did that without him."

"I've always been a crack shot." Dorf reminded him.

"Laser's than?" Rafe asked.

"Mmm. That may be a bit too dangerous for newlings." Besides, he still didn't feel exactly comfortable handling that particular weapon. He still sometimes felt his missing wing, especially at night.

"Well, we have plenty of bullets."

"Okay. Let's do it."

They collected the guns of choice and carried them outside.

"How are you getting along as a father?" Rafe asked.

Dorf's chest puffed up. "You know I love M and Runnar."

"Yes."

"But having absolute responsibility for children changes everything." Rafe nodded in agreement. Dorf looked up at him as they walked. "I already know I would kill for them."

"Meh. You have killed for less. But I understand."

"True. But killing has never come with ease—not for my kind. But for them, I'd throw myself into battle and destroy without a seconds thought."

"That is what it is to be a parent, a spouse. My life changed completely."

"Yes."

They went outside and spotted M and Bain on a hill away from a grove of mature trees where they had room to play. M was showing Bain the fighting stances she had been taught by her uncles.

Rafe nodded in approval. She still had great form. It would certainly be wise to send her to military training. The children were the right age, but he would certainly miss her.

But he would cross that bridge at a later time.

Dorf stopped walking. "Aww," he purred. He was looking at Kemistry and Kelsie napping together, curled up in one of the outdoor chairs.

Rafe stopped to look as well. "I gather she is taken to being a mama."

"She has. To think I was scared about telling her."

"You did right, Dorf. I was wrong."

That wasn't easy for Rafe to admit. He didn't mind changing his mind, but being absolutely wrong meant he had to second-guess all his decisions. And that wasn't something one could afford to do when they were at the head of a Special Ops team heading for a major war.

Dorf just gestured with his head. "Come on. Let's get our children trained to be warriors."

Dorf watched as the two children came to a stop once they saw them approach. He felt a wave of excitement coming from them both, which fired the excitement in him. It was their first training, and all M could talk about since her two best friends had arrived.

Training had been the least item of importance for all that needed to be taken care of. First and foremost was the question of Kelsie's health. She was seen by pediatric doctors and surgeons. Next was getting them settled into a new home.

He and Kemistry had been quick to add the new members to a household that still wasn't complete. They worried the kids wouldn't like that their house wasn't as polished as the homes in the Washington Hotel.

The homes in the new compound were large enough but relatively rustic with no servants—except in the case of Runnar's nurse. They had a vendor for the kitchen, but it was one of the first models. And while the kids had been given virtual televisions and computers, they hadn't had time to purchase gaming units all human children used.

Their bedrooms were just furnished simply with none of the décor that appeared in the fashion logs. They were Japoxillian and didn't have a use for human décor, and yet they merged their likes and needs with those of a human.

Somehow, their sweet kids were very forgiving and appreciated even the smallest things, from not having their own individual bathrooms and the child-sized nests that might have been a bit too juvenile.

Kelsie and Bain thought the perches and scratching posts in the main living area were fun and didn't mind that items had to be adapted to the height of a Japoxillian.

The little chairs and low tables fit them perfectly, and the high lofts that Kemistry used could have caused everything to appear strange, but the kids just stared at everything in awe. They took pride in their humble home and lack of servants. Bain even picked up the stray feathers and bits of fur that always seemed to be lying about. And Kelsie was intrigued with the vendor and wanted to prepare dinner as soon as she saw it.

Their family was perfect in Dorf's eyes. And now he would teach his son the family business. He was a warrior, and that would be his legacy, their tradition. Too bad Kelsie was asleep and missing this moment. But as soon as she was healthy, they would practice together.

"Are you two ready?" Rafe asked as they came to a stop before the two anxious kids.

We been ready, Papa! M said while jumping up and down.

"Bain," Dorf said, "You are being taught by the best band of warriors known to the entire Galatian special forces. It's hard work, and it can be dangerous. Are you sure this is a path that you want to follow?"

Bain quickly nodded. "Yes. I'm sure. I want to be a Protector like you and uncle Rafe."

Dorf grinned proudly. "Well, it doesn't begin with fighting. It begins with respect. Respect for your craft and your weapons."

"True," Rafe agreed. He sank to one knee and peered at them at eye level. "I can teach you to fight or to defend yourself. But to be a top Galatian Warrior goes beyond that. It's about instinct. Our senses are also our weapons.

"I taught M to trust her ability to do the impossible. And once she saw someone else do it—me and her uncles, she knew those things were no longer impossible." Rafe took a moment to peer into each child's anxious eyes. "Nothing is impossible, young ones."

Rafe spread out a cloth on the grass and then opened his gun case while Dorf eyed possible targets in the distance. This should be fun for them, he thought.

But no one saw Bain stiffen. Rafe lifted one of the pistols, and Bain's breath froze in his throat. He took a step back, and M glanced at him, wondering why he was walking in the wrong direction. She couldn't wait to hold the pistol!

But he had a funny look in his eyes.

Bain held up his hands as if an animal was lunging at him.

Rafe noticed the boy's reaction and the way he was staring at the pistol. He looked down at the weapon, not understanding what Bain saw that alarmed him.

Dorf was still looking off into the distance, searching for possible targets. He knew the soldiers had paper targets, and he should have thought to get them-

He felt something bump into his shoulder, and he turned to see Bain backing away. The look of horror in the boy's eyes instantly alarmed him.

"Son?"

Bain looked at him, his mouth opened in terror. Now, he was backing away from him, as well.

What Bain saw was a memory of his dad pointing a gun at him.

Bain! Come back here!

Bain turned and ran. His father was chasing him, and he could almost feel the bullets hitting him in the back. Bain sprinted through the forest as Father called him to come back. It only made him run faster!

Two soldiers were coming towards him; their camouflage uniform was something he was used to seeing since they'd come to the school. But then he noticed the rifles pointing in his direction.

Bain screamed and pinwheeled back, falling on his butt before scrambling up and scurrying away again.

Bain! Come back! His dad was calling, but Bain just kept running.

"W ait!" Dorf placed a halting paw on Rafe's wrist. "Don't chase him. It will make it worse."

Rafe ran both hands over his head. "Damn, Dorf. What did we just do...?"

Dorf stared in the direction that Bain had run. "I need to go to him." Dorf went down on all fours and moved nimbly into the forest.

Papa? M stared up at her father with wide eyes. **What's wrong with Bain?**

Rafe placed a hand on her shoulder. So, he never told her about his past.

"M, did Bain ever tell you why he came to live at St. Aloysius?" M shook her head.

As a Galatian, Rafe was a firm believer that some truths could only come from the mouth of the owner. He did not own Bain's story. "I am sure your friend will explain when he is ready. Come. Let's go home."

Can I help find him? Bain trusts me.

"He is not lost, daughter. This compound is large but well-secured. He won't be able to leave, and it is probably best if his father locates him. Dorf can...communicate with him better than any of us."

M looked down forlornly, and a moment later, she felt her father's arms around her as he embraced her. She placed her head on his shoulder and cried a little for her friend.

"It will be okay, little one. We will get your friends the help they need." She looked at him and nodded, wiping the tears from her face.

Rafe collected the weapons, and they headed down the hill towards home. When they reached the clearing where Kemistry and Kelsie had been napping, it was to see the Japoxillian helping her daughter onto the hoverbike. Both looked at the approaching figures, their smiles falling away at the expression on M's face.

"What's happened?" With a few flaps of her wings, Kemistry quickly flew to M and Rafe.

"Bain ran away," Rafe announced. "We were going to begin weapons training, but when he saw the pistol..."

"Oh, Guardian..." she said in a faint voice.

"Dorf went after them—"

"He may not find them without his wings!"

"There are guards stationed—"

"Guards with guns! Make sure they don't unholster them! I'm going to find my child!" Kemistry took off into the air, soaring high so she could see the world below her.

Rafe was instantly on his communicator, relaying her orders while M headed to Kelsie, who was sitting on her hoverbike with fear in her eyes.

"Bain ran away?" Her voice was filled with confusion. "I don't understand. I thought he liked it here. He said he did."

My papa says it has something to do with what brought him to the school. And I think it also has to do with the guns we were going to train with. Do you know what happened to Bain's parents?

Kelsie was shaking her head. "No. I need to find him—"

M took notice of her friend's peaked features. She was sick. It was easy to recognize. It happened when she did too much by herself, and it had been getting worse as of late.

Recently, while they were still at school, Kelsie would jerk awake at night, and when M asked what was wrong, she would say her breath got stuck in her chest. So sometimes M would watch, and sure enough, Kelsie would stop breathing for a while until her reflexes kicked in and woke her up.

That was something new, and the next day, she would tell Bain that Kelsie had to take it easy.

It seemed to M, that even taking it easy wouldn't keep Kelsie from getting worse. She had a bike and didn't even have to walk, and she was still struggling to breathe.

We need to go back to the house and wait for him. He's going to need us when they find him.

Kelsie looked out into the nearby forest. She drew in a great breath, and while it hurt her chest, her head cleared.

"Okay," she finally said, and M led her to her new home—which, in M's opinion, was much nicer than the other ones—even the ones at The Washington. She helped her into her nest, which had more turquoise feathers than Bain's, which had more of Dorf's feathers, and then she tucked a blanket around her even though the weather was comfortable.

What do you want to drink? M asked instead of *if* she wanted something. She knew her friend by now, and she never wanted to be a bother, so she would deny herself. Kelsie asked for ginger ale, and she got them drinks as well as a couple of snak-ums cakes.

The two girls ate and speculated about Bain.

"Do you think they will send us back?"

No!

"We're a lot of trouble. Maybe more than they want." She placed her head tiredly into her hands. "I don't want to go back to the orphanage. I love it here, M."

They won't send you back.

Kelsie lifted her head and met M's eyes with her own tired ones. "It happens all the time, M. The grownups realize they aren't cut out to being parents or they want different kids. I don't know, just that sometimes the kids come back, and it's really bad for them when they do. Because they knew, just for a while, what it was like to be wanted."

M smiled at her. **You worry about the wrong thing. You and Bain aren't going back to St. A. We need to worry about how to help him.**

Karma rushed into the house with Runnar clutched in her chest. When she saw the girls, she relaxed.

"Are you okay?" She asked.

"Yes," Kelsie replied. "Did they find Bain?"

Karma came forward and placed a hand on Kelsie's head. "No. Rafe will let me know as soon as they have word." Runnar watched with uncharacteristic calm, intrigued by the new environment and activity that had distracted his mother. He didn't even reach for the turquoise feathers that lined the nearby nest.

Bain was out of breath but kept running until the stitch in his side turned into a fist that slammed into his gut. He went down onto his hands and knees and then, with barely a pause, crawled until he reached a large tree surrounded by a cushion of fallen leaves. He collapsed there, fighting to catch his breath.

He was covered in a cold sweat, his eyes glazed, and his vision cloudy. As he lay there, Bain could only see images from the past: Dad chasing him. Dad's gun was pointing at him. Dad. Dad. Dad.

Bain pulled himself into a sitting position and made himself into a tight ball with his head tucked into his arms and his knees drawn up to his chest.

And that was how he was when Dorf found him.

Dorf's heart was going a mile a minute. What if the guards hurt his boy? They wouldn't mean to—maybe they wouldn't understand. But in his mind, he kept seeing some horrible accident. Maybe Bain would fall and break a bone—or even worse. Earth had snakes and other deadly rodents the child hadn't been trained to avoid.

Dorf knew the boy's life hadn't always been an easy one, but he wasn't made for this. He was used to a roof over his head and regular meals. He had routines and not... No. That wasn't true. This boy was adaptable because he was a survivor. Hadn't he proven that even now?

Damn, his useless wings! Dorf just continued to follow Bain's scent. It had begun as the dark, acrid odor of terror, and now that odor was laced with exhaustion.

As he closed in on Bain's location, Dorf heard the soldiers that had surrounded him. They were quiet and, thankfully, had remained out of sight, or Bain might still be running. What he knew was the boy was no longer on the move and wasn't exuding the acrid funk of exhaustion.

As he moved forward, he concentrated on Bain's emotions and realized it wasn't just fear but included remorse, anger, and regret.

Bain's song came easily to Dorf, but it was an intricate one as it wasn't just his mourning song, it was his anger song. Dorf had never made a song such as this one.

He began the melody softly like bird-song. It was Bain's song and not for him to add lyrics. As it grew in intensity, he knew Bain heard it but wasn't running. He felt grateful as he carefully approached, the song growing in intensity as his voice warbled and moaned and cried out in anguish.

Dorf heard a ruffle, and as he sang, he saw the blond-haired boy standing several feet away. He was watching Dorf, his mouth agape.

"Stop," he spoke. "Please, stop. I can't..."

Dorf immediately stopped.

He saw tears streaming down the boy's face. "I'm sorry, Mr. Dorf... I didn't mean—"

"Son, don't be sorry. Don't ever be sorry for how you feel. No one gets to dictate that for you but you." Bain wiped the tears from his face with dirty hands. "Can I come closer?" Dorf asked. Bain nodded slowly.

Dorf approached on two legs, and when he was face to face with the boy, it was to see Bain staring at his sneakered feet.

"Do you want to talk about it?" Bain shook his head almost imperceptibly.

"Are you ready to go back home?" Bain finally met his eyes, a question in them. Did he mean home as in St. Aloysius or the home of Mr. Dorf and Mrs. Kemistry? "I'm sure your mother and sister are worried, not to mention Rafe and M."

Bain's mouth parted. Did that mean they still wanted him? He nodded and walked to Dorf.

"I'm sorry," Dorf said before leading him home. Bain didn't respond, but there was a question in his eyes. "I'm sorry I frightened you. I didn't mean to, Bain." Bain looked at the ground again. But Dorf just smiled. So, he didn't want to use his words. But this was a conversation they had to have.

Dorf held out his paw. After a moment, Bain placed his hand out to be held, and Dorf leaned forward and sank his teeth into the pad of the boy's hand. Bain jumped with a look of alarm. But instead of jerking away and trying to retreat, he just looked at Dorf with an expression of defeat.

It's okay, son. Your head will feel strange for a moment, but that will go away.

I understand. M told me. Bain's eyes opened in alarm as he looked at Dorf. *Wait...You really can hear me. And I can hear myself think.*

That is how it works with our kind. Not only can you hear thoughts, but Bain, you can sense emotions. Can't you?

Yes. Bain nodded in surprise as he stared at Dorf. *That song you were singing. It wasn't your song. It was mine. I thought...*

Ahh. So now you understand that you can keep some of your thoughts private. But while we are linked, we can talk easily. But you still have your privacy. Does that make sense?

I understand.

Now I see that you have many doubts. But you don't have to doubt me or Kemistry. You and Kelsie will always have a home with us because we have already accepted you as our own. Now, you see that once this happens, it cannot be reversed. You are our emotional chil-dren, which is just as important as being biological ones.

Bain nodded, for he did see he hadn't pushed the Japoxillian away. But he had filled him with anguish, and for that, Bain was ashamed.

Don't be ashamed, my son. Dorf sighed. *Let me show you something.*

Dorf opened his thoughts to Bain in a way he'd never done to anyone, including Kemistry. He showed his joys but also his fears and vulnerabilities. If he had revealed what scared him to his new wife, then she would have tried to fix him, which was not what he needed from her.

He worried about his limitations now that he was without an eye, ear, and wing. He worried that he wasn't brave enough or capable of caring for children. He worried he would let Kemistry down as he had let down Karma, M, and Rafe. He wondered why he had survived when so many good Japoxillian hadn't.

When he finally closed off his thoughts, he released Bain's hand and took a step away, not meeting his eyes.

"You see, Bain. We all have insecurities."

Bain reached for Dorf's claw. He brought it to his mouth and bit.

"Ow!" Dorf pulled back and rubbed his sore paw. "It doesn't work that way." He took Bain's hand again and bit down.

Sorry. Can I be...like you? I don't think I'm cut out to be a warrior.

Do you mean you want to be an empath?

Bain nodded.

No, son. But I can help you find who you're supposed to be. Maybe it's not a fighter. Maybe it's something else. But I thought you were excited about becoming a Guardian.

Bain closed his eyes. *I ran away and left Kelsie and M. I just ran without thinking about anybody.*

Dorf was quiet. But in that quiet, he tried to give him a feeling he'd had—one that had shamed him. It was a feeling he'd just recently experienced.

Relief. Relief he wasn't dead.

When he was able to meet Bain's eyes, he saw the boy staring at him. He opened his mouth.

"C-can we go home…Dad?"

Dorf removed his teeth from Bain's hand, but instead of releasing it, he felt Bain grip his paw. Dorf's eyes felt moist, but he cleared his throat and nodded, neither feeling the need to speak as they walked hand in hand back to their home.

Kemistry was watching from where she had perched in a tree. She was sure that Dorf knew she was there, but he said nothing.

There were times when she thought he was too distant from his emotions, but now she saw he was this way for a purpose, and it wasn't for her to "fix".

Once they were out of sight, she took flight to beat them home.

Chapter Seven

Mayva lay on her stomach, eyes closed, arms and legs splayed out. It didn't much matter if she folded herself into a ball or hid under the covers. That... that... *thing* could have its way with her from even the smallest opening.

She knew it was on the end of the bed, pulsating, watching her. She felt it move, and she tensed. It moved closer until it touched her leg with its strange, moist gelatin skin.

"Go away," she managed past a throat sore from crying and screaming for the last several hours.

"I cannot," he said in a maddeningly calm and masculine voice. "I haven't fucked your mouth yet."

Her eyes widened, and she suddenly came to life. Mayva quickly sat up and scrambled to the far corner of the oversized bed, not concerned with her nudity or the various body fluids that were now drying on her body.

"No!" She suddenly slapped her hands over her mouth, trying to form a tight seal.

"Mistress," Pod said merrily. "I think you will be pleased with my array of semen flavors. Do you prefer a strong or a light taste? I can also fill you until you overflow..." He slid close, leaving behind a trail of grey slime.

Mayva began to gag behind her hands. Tears came to her eyes as she began to scream into her palm.

Paris turned the doorknob and met resistance when it didn't open. He listened for a moment and heard a soft sound.

"I-I'm going to get showered. Can you come back later?" Daya called.

"Yes." Paris paused and then retreated downstairs. Several of the soldiers greeted or saluted him, but he barely noticed. He went to his office and sat down behind his computer. He tapped his nails on the desktop before bringing up a screen so he could make a call.

"Paris?" Rafe's face was suddenly on the screen in front of him, floating as the hologram projective above the desk. "Is everything okay, brother?" He'd obviously noticed Paris's purplish tint.

"I am confused."

"You? That surprises me." Rafe considered Paris to be the most thorough member of his team. He never had a care about taking an unpopular opinion and was unflinchingly unapologetic. "Well, what can I help you with?"

"It is about...relationships. With humans. Romantic ones..."

Rafe's eyes widened. He looked behind him. "One moment. Let me go to my office." The screen went black for a moment, and when Rafe returned, he was in a different room. "Ah...I'm back." He looked uncomfortable as he paced. But knew things must be bad if Paris was asking for his advice on relationships, as he had nearly destroyed his own. If schools for consorts were necessary, then schools for the Guardians were imperative, especially *when* things between humans and Galatians became equal.

Paris ignored his Commander's obvious discomfort as he pushed forward. "Daya is angry with me, and I don't know why."

"You should ask her."

Paris cocked his head. "Should I?"

Rafe thought about it. "No, maybe not. Sometimes, you should know without asking, and perhaps this is one of those times."

Paris sighed and nodded. "I think you are right, but it is not one thing. It seems as if it culminated, and now she has locked the door to her bedroom—the one that we have been sharing."

"Sometimes humans need space just as we do."

Paris was already nodding again. "But it's not just her anger. She is sad. I made her sad."

Both men remained quiet.

"What did you do?" Rafe reluctantly asked.

Paris explained the doctor's appointment they had gone to.

"It sounds as if it will be torture."

"In essence, it will be. I do not want her to go through this, but her mind is made up." He then explained, inviting her to the Galatian pool.

"Good idea," Rafe agreed. "It should help with her pre- and post-surgical healing. How did she accept it?"

"Once I explained the benefits, she got in readily."

"And she didn't appear angry with you at this point?"

"No. In fact, she responded... um... positively. But injured herself when she tried to accept me into her mouth. Her skin is so fragile, Rafe. It began to split and then bleed. It was my fault. She was in the water much too long, and she is so delicate. It was after that in which she became angry. And now I am unsure."

Rafe thought about it. "She got hurt, and now she is angry. It is obvious she blames you for hurting her. You should apologize."

"But I didn't hurt her. She hurt herself when she took me."

"Hmmm. Then, I do not have an answer. Why would she be angry at you if she hurt herself?"

Paris's shoulders went up. "I do not know."

Rafe sighed. "In these matters, I am no expert. Perhaps you should speak to Karma."

"Speak to your woman about my romance?"

Rafe shrugged. "In honesty, it might be best. Let me get her. One of Dorf's children ran away earlier, and she is with M, reassuring her."

"Wait. One of the children ran away!" Paris exclaimed.

"Oh, he is fine. Dorf retrieved him, and all is well."

"But why? What happened?"

"We were going to begin weapons training with the children. Bain saw the hand pistol, and it apparently brought back memories of his father's attempts to murder him."

Paris closed his eyes and then ran both hands over his face and head. "Daya is going to be devastated."

"Why?" Rafe asked. "All is well now that Dorf connected with Bain and made him understand he is safe amongst us."

"I will need to tell her."

"Yes," Rafe agreed. "Humans must be made aware of everything."

Rafe rolled his shoulders. Maintaining a human household was no easy task. He needed to do the right thing for M even when she didn't want to do the right thing. He and Karma had come a long way, but he knew that soon they would need to speak about Ragna and how she would be made to pay for the murder of their child. Even Runnar, who was both Galatian and human, had to be raised to understand both sides of his nature. It was a great deal of responsibility.

Paris was staring at him. "I think you are probably right. I should speak to Karma."

Rafe nodded in relief. He hurried to M's room, where both human females looked up at him expectantly.

"How are you two?" he asked.

I want Bain to be okay, M replied.

"We can visit them in the morning, honey. Bain needs time with Dorf and Kemistry," Karma explained.

"I need to borrow your Mama. Why don't you take your bath, and we can watch a movie later." M's eyes lit up.

Okay, Papa

He took Karma's hand and led her to the office, where he explained that Paris was almost desperate.

"Oh, my Guardian. What's happened now?"

"Daya is angry, and he is confused. I thought it might be best if he got a human perspective."

When they got back to the office, it was to see Paris pacing on the hologram. He perked when he saw Karma.

"Hello, Karma. I am sorry for interrupting. I understand there has been an incident today with Bain. Is he alright? I am invested in their well-being, as is Daya."

"Only time will tell, but I think he is on the right track. But what about you, Paris? I hear you are having some trouble. How can I help you?"

She liked Daya and felt bad she hadn't reached out. After all, she had helped with M when she had been out of commission. Also, her circumstances with Paris were similar to her own. As they weren't consorts, they were both humans who were in unsanctioned relationships with Galatians. It might have been generations since the last time a relationship such as this had occurred.

They needed to connect and grow their friendship. She should have done that a long time ago.

"I want to understand Daya," Paris explained. "I love her very much, and I don't want to lose her again."

Karma suddenly liked Paris a great deal. "I'll help you however I can. Tell me what happened."

This time, when Paris recounted his story, Karma stopped him frequently to ask questions. Some questions seemed redundant until she explained that Daya was a grown-ass woman who didn't need someone else to think for her.

Paris and Rafe just blinked.

Karma sighed. "Paris, you need to try to see things from her perspective. What if you had to go through life being physically compromised? And if there was a way to repair your injuries, wouldn't you?"

"Yes," he answered without hesitation. "But I am a warrior. I cannot be compromised."

She gave him a grim look, and Rafe stirred. "I think my wife is not happy with your response."

"But why? Is it not true?" Paris asked.

"And there is that superior attitude Galatians have." She rolled her eyes. "It is true that you are a warrior. You did create humans. You are more intellectually advanced. And none of that matters when humans have to navigate a world that thinks you aren't good enough. I've had to do that. Daya's had to do that. So, to have another person come along and second guess our decisions about what is best for us is belittling."

Karma turned and looked at Rafe, who watched her in surprise.

Paris hid a smirk as it was evident that Karma's comment wasn't just aimed at him. He quickly neutralized his color when she turned her attention back to him.

"When you do that to Daya," Karma continued. "You are telling her that you are better than her. And I am sure you are aware of who else does that: the Queens."

Rafe exhaled, and he and Paris looked at each other. He could not argue Karma's assessment. She was right that the Galatian males and females weren't very much different.

Paris was thinking deeply about Karma's words when she prompted him to continue his story. Rafe was correct she was insightful, or maybe a human understood humans best. If that was a rule, he would change it. He wanted to understand his woman best. But more importantly, he wanted to honor her.

"I invited Daya to the Galatian pool at the school."

"Why?" Karma asked.

"I wanted her to be well, and I knew the pool would help."

Karma smiled. "Okay," she replied as if she didn't completely believe him.

Paris opened his mouth and paused before continuing. "I also wanted to show Daya she could trust me. She is still very embarrassed about her burns. Even though we sleep in the same bed and we share intimacy, she has never completely undressed in front of me. I wanted to show her she is beautiful despite her injuries and that she can open up to me. I love the way she looks, and I desire her just as she makes me feel desired and loved."

Karma encouraged him to continue with a nod. "And that didn't work?"

"It did. But she stayed in the pool too long, and when she...uh... well, the skin on her mouth split and began to bleed. When I told her she was injured then, she wouldn't look at me again. That's when she returned to her room and locked the door behind her. I don't understand."

"Oh, Paris. Daya is embarrassed. You saw her fail at seducing you."

Paris shrugged. "I always desire her. She knows that."

"What we know doesn't always match our insecurities. Look, Paris. I am sure Daya loves you just as much as you love her. But her injuries aren't just on the outside."

"Ah." This is something Paris could understand. "Her anger is misplaced."

"Maybe. And maybe not. But I believe Daya is dealing with a lot more than you know. And if you two are going to make it, then she will have to open up more. You two need to talk."

Paris nodded. "I thank you, Karma. Your words ring true. How can I make her open up to me?"

"By remembering that you should never *make* her do anything. You can only be honest about your feelings and thoughts while respecting that she might think differently. But it's her right. Just be there to support her."

"I want to talk to her. I will leave you now. Good night, and thank you."

"Good night and good luck."

Paris signed off and headed to the door. Luck would have nothing to do with it. They would both need to learn.

Daya was putting lotion on her skin when she heard a knock on the bedroom door. Tensing, she wondered if she could find the right words to ask for some time alone. She didn't want to debate with Paris. She was desperately in love with the man. But she hated her body. She hated the way she looked, and she didn't want him to look at her as if he preferred her broken than whole.

"I am sorry, Daya," he said from the other side of the locked door. "Can we talk?"

They needed to talk. He needed to move back to the barracks, and then maybe things would go back to normal. Why did she ever think she could be like a normal woman? She was still a mess, not just because of how she looked but because she couldn't even feel good enough with a man who loved her unconditionally.

She drew in a shaky breath and made sure her robe was tied securely over her gown so there was barely any skin visible from the neck down.

He heard the door unlock and felt relief when he saw her, completely covered as if she was prepared for a winter's night instead of sleep. She stepped aside and allowed him inside. He closed the door after him.

"Are you angry with me?"

"Paris," she gushed. "I'm not angry with you, but I am mad and disappointed and just so fucking tired!" His tone moved through a rapid series of colors. "I want to be normal. I just want to look like everyone else! I'm tired of being different. I'm tired of my split skin and... "

She turned away, her anger falling away in shame.

Paris looked down and nodded. "I think you should get the surgery if it will make you feel better. It is just that I don't want you to be in pain. But... I know you already are."

She turned and looked at him and then rushed forward and hugged him. He held her as tightly as he dared. He surprisingly pulled back first but took her hands in his.

"I cannot tell you how you should feel. I am learning I should not even try. But I can only tell you how I feel, just as I encourage you to always open up to me.

"You see, I think you are absolutely beautiful, both inside and out. Don't misunderstand. I do not have a preference for scars over skin. I find both beautiful. But I think Galatians are intrigued by opposites: my impenetrable flesh vs. your delicate one. It is no secret I am very attracted to the way you look, just as I am to the person that makes you who you are."

Daya's eyes glistened. She knew this. Of course, she knew this.

Paris continued. "But, Daya. I am not attracted to your pain. It hurts me to see you hurt, and to see you bleed is...difficult. But I won't let my own fear hinder your healing."

She hugged him again, clinging to him. "I know you love me the way I am. If that's all I needed, then I would be the happiest woman on Earth." She pulled back enough to look up into his face. "I want to share myself with you without shame." She touched her chest. "I can't do that right now. I can't."

He nodded. "Okay." He rubbed her shoulders, being extra gentle. "We will do nothing that makes you uneasy. If I do, then you tell me."

Daya nodded. "I'll try."

"Daya. I am not human—as if I need to remind you of this. I only mention it because I don't think like you. I don't know the things that come naturally to you. In time, I believe that I will learn the ways of humans. But until then, how I react might not be as you expect."

"I know, Paris. I'm trying to understand you, as well. I love your attitude and your honesty. I won't doubt you, how you feel about me, your attraction for me. I need that more than I can ever explain. With you, I've come further than I ever expected. I never thought I'd tell a man I loved them. I never thought I'd want to have...sex. I want you, I just..."

He touched her face. "Tell me?"

"I just wish that I was someone else."

He lowered his head until his forehead touched hers. She noticed his scales growing pale. This was different than when he'd gone through a kaleidoscope of hues. But this she thought she understood.

"Paris?" He didn't respond.

She rubbed his arms. His scales were smooth. He didn't speak. But her heart felt his, and she knew.

"Babe, don't cry. I'm okay. We're okay."

"Just get better, Daya. Please get better," he whispered.

She knew she had to do that and no longer just for herself. She had to do it for all the people who cared about her.

Chapter Eight

Daya was supposed to get dressed and then make her rounds to check on the children, as she had been doing double duty as both a teacher and housemother. But Miss Kaye had agreed to take over the house mother duties while she was incapacitated. So, she was convinced to take the rest of the day off while Paris pulled the mattress to the floor and they got comfortable, stretched out while Daya snuggled in his arms.

"Aren't you bored?" she asked with an embarrassed smile. "You've been all over the universe, fighting pirates, going on missions and just lying here has to be dull."

He made a half *hmph*, half chuckling sound. "I do not need those things." And then he closed his eyes and cradled her closer to his side, his face moving to rest carefully on the top of her head, where he placed his mouth to kiss her.

She smiled and wondered, *why am I like this?* Correction, she knew why, just why she couldn't be completely happy in her own skin. She had a job she loved, a relationship that, while not quite normal, was better than any she could have ever wanted. She felt blessed despite the abducted man in the basement beneath her and of course, the pain of her scars.

"Paris?"

"Yes?"

"What is our future like when you picture us together?"

He relaxed his hold while still keeping her close to his warmth. "I do not think very far ahead. It's not practical for..." he stopped.

Daya sat up slowly and looked down into his face. "For a soldier?" she completed.

He nodded. It was deeper than that. He was at the top of his field, which meant that his team took more risks, but also had the support of their commanders and the Collective, who afforded them with almost complete autonomy when it came to dishing out justice.

Over time, he had buried his ability to empathize with his opponents. He saw injustice and reacted swiftly. But now...perhaps retirement was a good thing. He saw his life through the eyes of a human—through *his* human, and it was ugly.

He reached for his woman and pulled her back into the comfort of his arm.

"I've read stories about humans and their family units. I wish that for us. A family; children, my brothers and their families, all communing and supporting each other."

"That's beautiful," she murmured. "I've learned to find support in my community when I couldn't find it in the government."

He thought about her words, and it jogged something in his mind, but it swiftly disappeared as he thought about the steps that would need to be taken for any of that to become reality.

"Do you think the Queens would leave us alone to live like that?" Daya asked as she stroked his chest and listened to his heartbeat. "I mean... the part about having children, they definitely won't do," she said shyly. "But would they leave us alone to just live our lives together?"

"It won't be up to them. The Collective will make the determination."

She tilted her head to look at him. "The Collective needs you. They're going to rule in your favor despite all of the propaganda about species mixing that's all over the media. That's coming from the rich people who aren't in touch, who don't know what the Guards can do to help *all* people and not just to line the pockets of the rich." She relaxed against him again. "Shit trickles down, but you have the Collective in your pockets."

"Eh," he agreed, amused at her uncharacteristic use of profanity but enjoying the fact he was learning all angles of her. "But anything can happen, and we are prepared to fight for our emancipation from the Queens."

"I'm just happy that The Collective is on your side. They have to rule in your favor."

Thoughts began to swirl in his mind as if Daya's perspective was a lubricant that loosened something stuck in position for far too long. He wasn't the same Paris Frenchman who had jumped into battle without a care because his future meant nothing. It was as if he had been a machine; a killing machine.

He had killed, maimed and tortured hundreds upon hundreds of beings without a care. But now he knew love, it seemed that the actions of his and his team might have been harsh.

And if that was the truth and The Collective was supposed to be the hand of justice, why then did they allow it? Paris's mind moved deeper as he realized thoughts he'd never had before about treachery in the highest corners. That change couldn't just occur within the Galatian race it had to happen up high where The Inter-planetary Collective ruled the galaxies unchallenged, where they deemed entire species unintelligent and therefore less important. His humans were one of those races, and there was no way that anyone could deem Daya or any of the other humans he had watched over this last year to be categorized as a lower life form. Why had they never questioned that?

The puzzle pieces finally began to slip into place. The answer, of course, is that The Collective needed lower life forms in order to enslave. And if not for the direct connection humans had with the Galatians, the human race would have been wiped out by forces like the...

Paris sat up. What if they weren't the true hand of the Collective? What if it was the Tybernees? They continued picking away at the humans. Retired Elite Ops members were supposed to train the next generation, but why retire them when they had reached their peak in performance? To be at their peak when they were tied to their bound-mates, to propagate their species?

No. To be out of the way.

Paris's brow drew down.

And while the men were out fighting for The Collective, perhaps the Queens had gotten into their ears. Maybe they had their own side deal to keep the males under control.

Which meant The Collective wasn't in their pockets, but the pockets of the Queens.

Daya sat up, her brow dipping. "What's wrong? Are you okay?"

He smiled, turning a pale orange and pushing those thoughts to the back of his mind. He would give them more consideration later. But for now, he was with the one person he would change his world for.

"Yes. When I am with you, I am at my happiest. I cannot say that has ever been the case when I was tracking space pirates."

She leaned in to kiss him and felt his tongue as it explored the depths of her mouth. It stoked the embers that had been ignited by her earlier disappointment. She heard a sound like a soft purr vibrating from his chest. He had removed his clothes but was under the blankets, and when she looked down, she saw that his own 'embers' were coming to life.

Paris was studying her face when she once again met his eyes.

"Shall I make you cum?" he asked politely.

"Uh..." Daya's face warmed. "Yes, please." She loved his blunt manner. But it was more than that. It turned her on. Her body grew hot and slick in places that hadn't felt an inner flame for such a long time. His aim was to please her in all ways, as a friend but also as a lover. She needed to be the same with him.

She placed her hand on his chest when he leaned forward to share another kiss. He gave her a quizzical look.

"I'd like to make you cum. I tried, but it didn't go so well."

Ah. She wanted him in her mouth. He suddenly understood she wanted this. It wasn't just to please him, but to please herself. Paris groaned internally, his prick stiffening. He lay back on the mattress, not removing the blanket from his lower portion. He would allow her to control this action, just as she had tried to do while they were in the pool. Ah...his poor human had tried something new, and it had failed.

But not this time.

He placed his arms beneath the back of his head, an unspoken invitation for her to do whatever she wanted.

Daya drew in a shaky breath. Once upon a time, men like Paris Frenchman were just tall green aliens with scales for skin. But her eyes could no longer see him in that way. All she saw when she looked at him was a beautiful man with a gorgeous body and a magnificent prick.

She ran her fingertips down his torso, beginning at his collarbone until she reached the blanket bunched and tented at his hips. No hiding that massive thing when he was turned on. She had to swallow back the naughty thought as she slid the blanket off.

His belly tensed, and she heard a soft sigh moments before the huge green appendage snapped back into position inches from his belly. The pale green prickhead glistened. His shaft, slightly darker, was lined with veins. By comparison, his testicles were small and perfectly hairless. She had never wanted to suck anything more in her life.

Momentarily ignoring his throbbing prick, Daya leaned forward and placed her lips gently on his balls. She was thrilled when he moaned and felt brave enough to pull one into her suckling mouth.

She lapped it and felt Paris move. She glanced up and saw he had thrown his head back.

Her heart raced as the slick juices of her desire slipped from between her thighs. She released his testicle with a soft 'pop' and moved to the next. His hips began to move in slow rolling circles, and she was mesmerized by the graceful yet decadent movement of his pelvis and hips.

That is what it will be like when he is balls deep inside me...

Daya released his testicles, her eyes on his thick shaft. She wrapped her hands around the base, but they weren't anywhere near to closing.

Paris's hip gyrations stopped, and he seemed to freeze, waiting for the next move on her part. She didn't make him wait. Daya leaned forward and kissed the exposed shaft as she gently squeezed his base.

Paris gurgled something like a moan and an exclamation. Instinctively, she knew his shaft needed to be wet to do what came next. So, she licked him like a lollypop, moving higher until eventually reaching the head of his prick. It was pulsing, and precum was streaming from the opening.

She used the slick precum to lubricate the length of his shaft, and then she began to jack his prick using long but rapid movements of her fist.

Paris's hips rose from the mattress, and she saw his head whip from side to side. She quickened her movements and used her other hand to gently massage the mushroom-shaped head.

"Ahhh!" Paris yelled. He fisted the mattress, and it shredded beneath his claws. That didn't make her slow her movements. In fact, it turned her on all the more. She was doing this. She was making him feel good! Paris began to thrust into her slick fist. She had plenty of lubricant in the form of the copious amounts of semen flowing like a fountain from the pulsating hole at his very tip.

Her mouth watered for it, but she was mesmerized by the rolls and thrusts of Paris's hips as he simulated fucking her fist. He was so graceful, so sexy in his movements. His moans had become fuel to her burning flames. She quickly leaned forward and began lapping at his fat prick head.

The taste of his seed filled her mouth, and it was her time to groan, experiencing him by smell, by touch, and now by taste.

She could tell he had slowed the thrusts of his hips. He now moved in slow circles again, his moans telling her she was doing this right. She sucked and licked her man, and he was careful not to injure her delicate mouth and lips.

"Daya!" he spoke from gritted teeth. "If you don't want me to cum in your mouth, move now!"

She just probed at the opening of his prick with her tongue as if inviting him to give her all he had.

Paris threw his head back and called out something in his native tongue. Cum shot into her mouth, and he fought not to pump into her. He had to dig his feet for purchase and cling to the mattress with his claws to hold back, but jet after jet of his cum shot into her mouth.

He looked down when he realized she hadn't released his prick head. Her mouth had formed a seal. She was swallowing him.

He said a few choice phrases that amplified his orgasm as he pumped his seed into her.

It seemed a long time before the tension left his body, and he relaxed back onto the mattress. His much softer prick slipped from her mouth, and he heard her belch. He opened his eyes lazily and looked at her. Her expression had gone aghast as she quickly covered her mouth.

"Excuse me!" she said, embarrassed.

"Damn." He whispered. "You took it all."

"Isn't that what I was supposed to do?" she asked curiously. She certainly wasn't going to allow him to dribble from her mouth, no matter how much effort it took to swallow him down without choking on all the cum he was feeding her.

Paris propped himself up on elbows. "Wait. You've *never* done that before, not even with someone else?"

"Never."

His eyes probed hers. "Daya, I know the asset in the basement never... but *no one?*"

"I never... " Her face felt heated.

He pulled her into his arms until she was in his lap. "I have been so cavalier about mating and nudity and this has all been very new to you."

Daya shrugged as she relaxed against his chest, her head tucked beneath his chin. "You're my man. This is what we're supposed to do."

"Not at my pace," he said adamantly, "but at yours."

She smiled. "I don't have a pace. This is all so new."

Paris kissed the top of her head.

"Paris." Daya looked around. "Uh, did you see the mattress?" It had been shredded from the talons and claws on his hands and feet until there was nothing much left but fluff and springs.

He chuckled. "I will get rid of it tonight once everyone is sleeping. But first, shall I pleasure you now?"

Chapter Nine

"*Bain! Get back here!*"

Bain shot up in his bed, still hearing the voice of his father in his ears. It had been so long since he'd dreamed of his parents. Those were bad times. He'd grow quieter than normal, haunted by images he'd seen—as well as those he hadn't. His PTSD had caused an almost permanent retreat into himself—that is, until a bald little Black mute girl with fierce dark eyes captured his attention.

Bain looked around his darkened room. His new mother and father had created a comfortable bedroom which would be any child's dream, but the corners felt too dark and the sound of his father's voice still echoed distantly within him.

Bain jumped out of bed and hurried out of the room. Dressed in pajamas that seemed too formal, he felt the silky shirt sticking to his back, and his hair was plastered to his head despite the coolness of the house.

When he opened the bedroom door, his breath froze in his throat as he prepared to see his father jump from the darkness of the hallway. Of course, the hall was empty. He still didn't feel relief as he hurried to the end of the hall where Mom and Dad's bedroom was located.

But before he could pull the latch to open their door, he heard the soft sounds of a beautiful melody. The harmony was exquisite, two sounds from two voices that complimented the other. He was reminded of the beautiful song Dorf had created just for him. It had worked like a lifeline that pulled him out of his anxiety. So now, when he was once again filled with terror, he sought Dorf and the balm he so easily elicited.

But Bain drew back after realizing that Dorf and Kemistry weren't simply singing to each other. They were making love. This was *their* special song. He didn't know how he knew this, only that since allowing Dorf—no, not Dorf but *Dad* to connect with him, he seemed to better understand the Japoxillian species.

Bain backed away. He backed down the hall until he was even with Kelsie's bedroom. Pausing, he listened for a few moments, hearing the soft swooshing sound of her breathing machine. He opened the door to her bedroom and slipped inside. He could clearly see the slight lump of Kelsie's slumbering form because of the breathing machine she'd been using since moving here. It was next to her bed and had a button that emanated a soft yellow glow.

He felt instant relief and tipped over to the nest Mom and Dad had situated throughout the property. They used them as gaming chairs, reading nooks, and, at times, for impromptu naps.

Bain snuggled into the soft feathered and fur cushions. When he inhaled, he thought he could smell Mom and Dad, so he buried his nose into the cushions even though the feathers tickled his nose. Peace engulfed him and his lids soon felt heavy.

"Bain?" came Kelsie's soft voice from her bed.

"Yeah," he whispered. "Sorry. I didn't mean to wake you up."

"Are you okay?"

Bain paused, nearly as long as he had back when the words wouldn't (couldn't) come from his mouth. "I had a nightmare."

Kelsie sat up in bed. "About your father?"

"Yes," he whispered faintly.

She didn't ask him about his nightmare or assure him everything would be okay, she simply pulled back the covers and scooted to the side.

"Come on. You can sleep here."

He shook his head even though she probably couldn't see. Correction, he had blond hair, so she probably could see it even in the mostly darkened room.

"I like the nest. I can almost feel Mom and Dad in them. Do you think that's why they built them?"

"I think they built them because they're so comfortable. But you could be right." She pulled the covers over herself again and the two friends grew quiet, but not from a need to sleep.

"Why didn't you ever tell us about what your dad did—me and M?"

He sighed. "I try not to make it real. If I pretend hard enough, then I can almost forget." M and Kelsie helped him to forget, and soon, he was able to open up to them and to other children and Miss Porter. Kelsie didn't reply and it suddenly dawned on him she had secrets, too. She never talked about her past and because she was always so optimistic, he hadn't thought much about it.

But he did know that if she was keeping something terrible buried inside, then there was the perfect vehicle to release it.

"Have you linked with mom or dad?"

"No!" she seemed alarmed at the idea. "I don't need anyone reading my mind!"

"That's what I thought, too. But it's nothing like that." Bain stretched in the nest and got comfortable again. "It's just another way of talking, but without words and with emotions. Also, it's not one-way. I can see...no feel, Dad's thoughts and emotions. He really cares for us and not like the school has to care, or the government, but like family cares."

"Wasn't it weird?"

"At first. It was like my mind had to adjust, but it didn't last long. Also, they don't see all of your thoughts, just the ones you... broadcast." He didn't know a better way of describing it. It was the secret voice in his own head that Dad could hear. And, of course, his emotions. You couldn't help but broadcast your emotions.

Bain decided that communicating in this way would keep everybody honest. No one could harbor secret plans to murder their family...

"You know, I wish everybody could always speak with their minds. Dad told me there's a belt that can be used between linked individuals. He uses it for Uncle Rafe when they go out in battle. Then they can talk without words and without the bite." He wished he was a Japoxillian. "You should let mom or dad link with you, Kelsie."

"Why? I am fine, using my words."

"You think like a scientist. Aren't you curious?"

He didn't see her frown. "People share what they want to share."

They were quiet for a while before Bain spoke what had been nagging at him. Once he and Dad had returned home, Mom had fussed over him, making sure he wasn't hurt and putting salve on scratches he had on his cheek and arm.

But he had avoided Kelsie's concerned look. He felt guilty. M had come over to check on him and it was the same thing. It was hard to meet the eyes of his friends.

He'd left them.

"I won't leave you again."

"What? Are you talking about running away? You better not do that again. I like it here and even though I doubt they'd send us back, I'll have to work doubly hard to make everything perfect."

"Huh? What are you talking about?"

She just sighed. "Go to sleep, Bain," she said softly. "I'm tired." She looped the tube over her ears so the medicated oxygen flowed into her nostrils. Her lungs opened a little and she could catch her breath. She wondered distantly if it would be okay if she used the oxygen all day...

Kelsie heard Bain get out of the nest. He padded over to the bed and climbed in beneath the covers next to her. She sat up long enough to give him one of her pillows.

"Goodnight, Kelsie."

"Goodnight, Bain."

Chapter Ten

"I hope I'm not bothering you," Karma spoke into the communicator.

"No bother at all," Daya smiled. "I've been meaning to reach out to you since...well, since everything." Her smile faltered at the mention of things that might have been better left unsaid.

Karma just nodded. "The same here. I've wanted to thank you for all that you did for both M and me. I remember you stood with me in that attack."

Daya simply nodded solemnly and quickly changed the subject. "Paris said that Bain had some issues. I planned to speak to Sir Dorf and Kemistry, but...well, life."

It was Karma's turn to nod in agreement. They talked about Bain and the other children for a few minutes before Karma's brow dipped. She had seen Daya's picture before the burns, back when she helped Maddie with the teacher's interviews, but didn't think she knew her. But wouldn't it be something if their paths had crossed?

"We're the same age. Where did you live as a child?"

Daya was lucky and had grown up in a small rented house. Her life would have been considered 'privileged' compared to most people of color. But there was no doubt her family struggled. Food was far from plentiful, and presents were non-existent. Her parents had explained that having a roof over her head was present enough.

She explained where she lived and went to school, already knowing the two had never met. She would have remembered someone as beautiful.

Karma listened quietly. "I don't know if you know this, but I'm no princess or exotic daughter from a wealthy family. I grew up in the projects right here in this city."

Daya sighed. "Yes. It's been broadcast by the rebellion." They were saying horrible things about Karma being part of a spy network intent on overthrowing the government through male Galatians. Daya knew enough about Karma's history with the Exchange to dispel that completely. Lt. Sigur had been tasked with investigating her himself and had found she had been used by the previous head of the exchange so he could kidnap the original consort.

Unfortunately, only one side of the story was being broadcast, and it put Karma and Lt. Sigur's team in a bad light.

"We're the same age, but our paths probably never crossed," Daya stated.

"It's a shame. We could have been good friends. It's not too late now."

Daya smiled. "I'd like that. It's been a long time since I've had a friend—well, except for Paris."

"He really loves you."

"I know. Why does that feel so right? He's an alien, and yet he's more human than many of the men I've dated."

"The Galatians are aliens, but we're also part of them. I think that we're more alike than we realize."

Daya nodded in agreement. "Sometimes it feels as if there is a master plan to put the male Galatians in a bad light—to make them seem untouchable. But I know that they will go out of their way to help those in need. They are nothing like we were taught—how the media portrays them."

"You're right. I wish the Guardians would take more control of the dialogue."

Daya gave her a grim look. "Since you've been asleep, it's been terrible. Have you been watching the media? That woman Mayva Heath has so many lies about you and the Exchange."

Karma sighed. "I've seen a bit of it."

Daya tilted her head. "You seem pretty calm about it."

Karma's eyes flashed momentarily. "I'm not. But some things can't be rushed." She smiled again. "You know, you and Kelsie will be having surgery at about the same time."

"Yes. I'm so happy she's getting the medical treatment she needs."

"What are your plans for your rehabilitation?"

Daya shrugged. "None, really. Paris has agreed to be my support person after I leave the hospital. By then, I'll be able to manage."

Karma was shaking her head even before Daya finished speaking.

"Hear me out, Daya. I think you should move to the compound."

"Oh. I couldn't—"

"There's a lot of pros about doing so. Kelsie is going to have a medical specialist in organ transplants to help her. Your skin is an organ—the largest on the body. You two can be treated by the same physician. More importantly, I can help."

"Karma. I appreciate it, but you ladies already have too much on your plate."

Karma's smile fell away. "I'm not saying this lightly, so think hard before you reject the offer." Daya's mouth fell open into a large "O" at the suddenly serious tone in her new friend's voice.

"We are family, the Galatians, their mates, our children. And we are all under attack. We can't stand alone—that's obvious by what happened to my unborn child. I wouldn't be standing here now if not for the aid of my brothers, sisters, and, of course, you. We need each other. I don't want Paris a hundred miles away if the Queens come back to finish what they began. And if Paris's bound-mate should get an idea he no longer wants her because he wants you, then you should be with us. Our men will fight better to protect us if we're all together."

Daya's heartbeat thudded. One of her unspoken fears was just what Karma had voiced—Paris's bound-mate coming for her.

Daya looked at Karma earnestly. "Another way to look at this is that you are a dangerous woman to be associated with."

Karma nodded, not feeling offended. "I'd be more worried if The Council wasn't involved. The Queens have stayed away for a reason. But you are right. I'm dangerous—probably more dangerous than they know. But Daya, don't you feel that the males need us? Not just a human influence, but us in particular? You and me? We have a sensibility and survival instinct the consorts are just beginning to hone. But you and I know that it's not just killing that's going to win this battle. It's also cunning...which is something the Galatians lack. I need you here to be a voice of reason and to be a sounding board. In Rafe's heart of hearts, he just wants to annihilate Ragna and Mayva. But I want them to pay."

Daya's breath was caught in her throat. Did Karma know about Mr. Conrad in the basement? It was as if she could read her mind.

But no. Paris swore he hadn't told anyone, not even Rafe. Karma did make good points. She didn't think the Queens would prevail because to do so would be the end of the Galatian's relationship with The Council. But the Queens would know this, too, which is why they were working so hard to put so much anti-Galatian information out through the media. No one needed to tell her that the Queens were behind it—even if it didn't exactly put them in the best light, either.

"It is something to think about," Daya admitted. "The school is loud, and the children would be curious. I don't think seeing me without skin would be the healthiest thing. Also...there is a matter of the pain. It will be...bad. I might, well, make sounds, and they could be loud. I don't want to traumatize the children—but the same goes for M, Bain, and Kelsie."

"The difference is they know and love you, Daya. I'd like you to stay here—at least while you're healing. Afterward, you and Paris can always leave. But I want to help care for you. Please consider it."

Daya nodded. "I promise to talk to Paris about it. It's getting late, and we've talked for nearly an hour. I'm sure you have lots to do."

"Rafe has been staying close to home, and we have a nanny for Runnar. But there is always something to do. Let's talk again soon?"

"Yes. I'll call you in a few days and tell you my decision. And Karma, I really appreciate the offer."

"It's me who appreciates you—especially what you've done for Paris."

"The decision to separate our families wasn't made lightly," Rafe said. He and Karma were touring the compound. She wanted to select places where homes could be quickly built. A functional and beautiful home could be put together in a day's time, furnished, and ready for habitants within a week. She had watched in awe as the walls and roof were placed on Dorf and Kemistry's home while an existing house had been remodeled for Maddie and Drago within a day or two.

She was excited at the prospect of having them together, and that included Justina—although she might not mention that until after Daya moved in with Paris. She was certain Daya would understand the necessity. Just as she knew that if they didn't do this, then there would be dire consequences.

It had become clear to Karma after speaking to Daya. She didn't know how she knew this, but the knowledge that things had to be put right rang through her, and the first step was to gather all the players.

But how did she explain that to Rafe? Did he operate on 'gut' feelings? She would try reasoning with him.

"Drago made the decision not to move his family with ours—and I'm not saying I find fault in that. But he's the one who reached out to you to live with us again. He knows it's the best way to keep his family safe."

Rafe listened quietly. Karma was right about one thing: they were always better together. In fact, knowing that as mated retirees, they would be forced to follow their consorts wherever they wanted to live had been hard for Rafe to reconcile. He had molded them into a single, fighting organism, and it never seemed right that they would one day take off to the far corners of the Earth. He was just happy Karma had shown up and pointed out that there was more for them to accomplish beyond being warriors.

"You're quiet..." Karma prompted.

He reached for her hand and smiled a soft orange. "I can only leave it up to them."

"Then let me reach out to them."

He looked at her. "You want to speak to my men?"

"You don't think they'll listen to me?"

Rafe resumed walking. "They respect you, Karma. It would be nice to live with Kendrick and Paris again."

"And Haru."

"No. Not him. His mission is too important for him to return to us."

"And what does he tell you?"

"About leads to finding Ragna."

"Hmph."

"What?" Rafe asked.

"You can draw her out pretty easily. There's one surefire way, and that's learning about Runnar's existence."

Rafe gasped. A rush of air exploded from his lungs. "Karma!"

"Relax, honey. I'm not suggesting it. I'm saying that we have to think outside of the box."

"What do you mean?"

"I don't know, Rafe," she shrugged. "That's why we need our family. We have to strategize—and not just you and your warriors. We *all* need to figure this out."

Chapter Eleven

"I'm going to carry you back," Rafe said matter-of-factly, but he was scanning the surrounding area instead of looking at his mate.

"What?"

He finally turned to her. "You're limping."

"Oh." Karma reached down to rub her thighs as they walked. She had noticed the tingling sensation in her legs, but not that she was limping. Since awakening from her coma, her legs routinely felt numb the longer she stood. And if she ignored it too long, it could become painful.

But Karma didn't complain. She'd mention it to Sanjay when he eventually contacted her to ask about Runnar. She really wanted him back as her personal physician. She had nothing against the Galatian surgeon who had saved her life, but Sanjay was who she knew and trusted.

"Karma." She looked at Rafe, realizing he had spoken. "How long has this been going on?"

She waved her hand dismissively. "Since waking. But it is getting better. I just need movement and exercise." Karma smiled and gripped his hand again. "Don't worry about me. We have plenty of other things to worry about."

He inhaled. "There isn't much I find more important than you, my love." He swooped down and swiftly lifted her into his arms. Once they were face-to-face, he stared into her eyes.

"Is there anything else I should know?"

There was a lot he should know. But intuitively, she knew that now was not the right time to talk about each of her concerns. Rafe had become wonderfully understanding in light of keeping so much back from her in the recent past, but what she needed to broach was a topic that needed to include all of the players.

So, instead of answering, she placed her head on his shoulder and snuggled in contentment within his strong embrace.

"I'm fine. Let's go home. It's time to feed my son." Her full breasts, as well as Runnar's appetite, seemed to work in sync. Her heart swelled just thinking about his sweet face and the way it lit up when he saw her. Despite being just a few months old, Sanjay had confirmed that his development was more in line with a Galatian child's and he was progressing much more rapidly than a human. Again, she longed to know a Galatian female she trusted but doubted it could ever happen.

Rafe placed her back onto her feet and then knelt on bended knee before her. "Climb onto my back, and I will give you the ride of your life."

"You did that last night," she joked. He paused, and she felt a trembling chuckle move through his body as she climbed onto his back.

"I love when you make crude humor," he said while hoisting her up high. Karma easily wrapped her legs around him. She placed her arms about his neck with her head close to his and prepared to ride her husband in a manner she'd never ridden him before.

Rafe went low on his haunches and ran at a moderate speed. It was much faster than she ever could have, so for Karma, it was as if they were in a vehicle. But she grinned, thrilled at his speed and strength.

He saw a tree and headed for it.

"What are you doing?" she called anxiously.

"Hold on," he warned.

She tightened her hold, and a moment later, they were scaling the tree. He used his tail instead of the claws on his feet since he was still wearing boots and soon was high in the air with Rafe taking in the land that made up their community.

"Oh! There's our house," she gestured with her head, not daring to loosen her grip on his neck. "I'd like to see Paris and Daya living just before that ridge."

"That's close," he commented.

"Daya will need to be close for us to care for her after the surgery."

"Aye."

Karma turned and looked further down the valley. "We'll put Justina there. Far away. She might be okay with the situation between Paris and Daya, which doesn't mean she wants to see it in her face whenever she looks out her window. Besides, Justina has always been a private one.

"You have many ideas, Karma Sigur. And what of Kendrick?"

"He should be close to Justina. And Haru should be close whenever he returns. We should have a place ready for him in case it happens sooner than later."

Rafe tilted his head. "You believe that to be a possibility?"

She shrugged. "It's a contingency. You make them yourself, or you wouldn't have this secret place all ready for us, including a shadow crew."

"Aye." Rafe climbed back down the tree, scaring her as he went head first before leaping to his feet and racing forward on all fours.

"Hello, Justina." Karma spoke to the ex-consort via communicator.

"Karma!" Justina was beaming in a way Karma had never seen before. She actually looked happy. "How are you? Oh my goodness! The baby! How is he so big!" Runnar was propped in Karma's arms, staring with intrigue at the holographic form. He was used to it by now but still reached for the pixelated image.

"Oh, Karma, he's so adorable! He looks like you. He's got hair, and he's brown. But I can see Rafe there, too." Justina saw the Galatian aspect in the set of his eyes even though she couldn't see his scales with his jumper on. But she was being honest in thinking the baby was adorable. In honesty, she hadn't known what to expect. She was just happy when she learned there had been another baby after the first was lost.

She gave Karma a soft look. "How are you? I'm sorry I haven't called. I didn't know if you'd be up for it." Justina didn't say that they were never the closest of friends. And that was her own fault. She had been so miserable for so long.

"Things have been hectic but also wonderful." Karma filled her in on what was happening at the compound, including the new edition of the children.

"I'm sure your little girl likes that."

"The kids are doing well, but the big change is with Dorf and Kemistry. They were in a..." Karma shook her head. "I'd call it a dark cloud, but the children brought them out of it."

Justina's smile faded as she thought about Laylay. She missed that red-feathered, German-accented little soldier who watched her so critically. It had taken a while before she trusted her to care properly for Paris. Near the end, they had come to a grudging understanding and possible friendship.

Her death had allowed her to finally see the humanity in Paris. He was devastated, and Laylay's death had taught her how deeply a Galatians emotions ran.

Because of his and Laylay's shared link, Paris had experienced physical pain along with his mental anguish. It had lingered causing him to become despondent. And it had been up to her to coax meals into him and to lead him in and out of his pool. It was also her that brushed and oiled his scales when he quaked with unshed emotion.

When his pain mirrored so much of the anguish she experienced, Justina could do nothing less but to reach out to him.

"How are things with you and Paris?"

"There isn't anything with me and Paris. You know he is now with the teacher." Karma just held her breath as she watched and listened. But soon, Justina's words softened. "I think he is finally on the way to being happy again...well, if Paris had ever been happy. Ever since he entered my life, he's been nothing but a twat." But she laughed. "But so was I."

"Do you like being single?"

Justina beamed. "Let's just say that I like being independent." Karma nodded in understanding.

"And how does that work with Kendrick?"

"He's not my mate, so he doesn't make demands. He comes by each day for a meal, and we have good conversation. Did you know that Kendrick is funny? I mean, he could be a comedian. And he likes watching movies and listening to music. And best of all, he enjoys human food. I can cook whatever I like eating, and he enjoys it too."

"Even pork?"

"Especially pork! If I didn't know it, I'd think he was a human in a Galatian costume."

"I see...is there something special between you two?"

"Guardian, no! But he is a friend." Justina didn't feel the need to explain that no male could ever hold a 'special' place in her heart. That was her business... although she somehow suspected Paris understood this. She had worried that Kendrick would get the wrong idea with Auras being dead. But he never seemed sexually interested in her. Despite knowing that Paris was *with* another, Kendrick treated her as if she was still his brother's mate. She respected him even more because of that.

"Well, I'm happy so much is going right," Karma said seriously. "But this isn't just a social call."

Justina's expression instantly became serious. "What's wrong?"

"A lot is wrong. I'm sure you've seen the media and all the anti-Galatian Guard rhetoric being relayed."

"It's ridiculous. Just because we're going to win this thing between the Queens doesn't mean they should allow all the hate. That bitch, Mayva, knows none of this is the fault of the males. They've done nothing but treat her decently despite the fact she's a murderous psycho-bitch!"

Karma huffed mirthlessly. "Psycho-bitch. I like that. Well, what makes you think we're going to win against the Queens?"

Justina blinked. "I mean, it's obvious. The decision is with The Interplanetary Council, and the Galatians are the Council's right hand. They wouldn't dare rule in the favor of the Queens. The Queens can't do shit for them."

Karma found Justina's frank manner of speaking to be refreshing. She liked this new Justina.

"But don't you think it seems too easy?"

Justina shrugged. "That's why they got that psycho-bitch as their mouthpiece. She is very popular among the conservatives. I heard she's going to be hosting the next North American Galatian Exchange.

"What?" Karma's heart leaped into her chest. "Are you sure?"

"Yes, it's been in the news. That bitch has gotten so popular. I hear she's jet-setting all over the world: lunch in the Paris province, weekends skiing, hob-nobbing with movie stars. She is living her best life."

Karma's eyes narrowed. "That's in line with what I want to talk to you about. I want the Galatians to get their freedom from the Queens, but I also want to see the people who killed my baby be brought to justice. I need your help for that to happen."

Justina nodded without hesitation. "Finally, someone on our

team is being proactive! Both of those psycho-bitches have to pay. What are we going to do?"

Chapter Twelve

Mayva's eyes were closed. She kept her breathing even. She was very practiced at being deceptive. It seemed she'd had to be this way all of her life.

Pod was asleep next to her—or whatever that thing did when it rested. It certainly made sounds as if it slept: soft snores and grunts like a typical male.

She slid smoothly from the bed without seeming to make a big deal of strolling to the bathroom. She didn't trust that alien. He might only be pretending to sleep.

But as she reached the bathroom door, she noticed his breathing hadn't changed. Mayva went inside and softly closed the door. She had made it a habit to do this twice a night, even when she didn't have to pee. Initially, the creature made it his business to calculate how long she stayed in the bathroom. And she always made sure to give it at least three minutes but no more than five. She'd return to bed and pretend to sleep until the creature returned to its own slumber.

She carefully but quickly lifted the lid from the back of the toilet where she had stowed money. Not knowing what to expect when she'd initially joined forces with the Queens, she had stock-piled some necessities, including some of Heinrich's money.

It was in a small plastic bag, and she quickly rolled the bills into a tight bundle, returned it to the bag, and then inserted it into her vagina. A lady had a built-in secret compartment, and only the most unscrupulous would ever search her there.

She also had money stashed in other places. She'd done that after killing Heinrich. But she had enough, for now, to get to the real money.

She intended to disappear. To hell with the Galatian Queens and their promises of fame and wealth. And especially fuck that bitch, Ragna. She'd treated her as if she was a common street human! And after all, she'd given up in order to fight for her team. She'd turned on her friends, given up her chances with a real male in the form of the next Galatian Exchange.

Now, she was being assaulted by a hideous creature that forced her to cum because of its relentless attention. She didn't mind cumming. She did, however, mind that it was at the touch of that blubbery blob!

Yes, Ragna had tricked her well by pretending to give her something she wanted, but she would get the last laugh. Who would do their commentaries when she was gone? And when the Queen's Council found out she'd fled under Ragna's watch, then she suspected that the ugly bitch would have hell to pay.

Mayva nearly laughed, but she quickly got the clothes from the hamper and put them on, including suede sneakers. She would have to do some walking, but she was strong—stronger than some would give her credit.

She tied her hair into a quick bun and then slipped on the camou-flage-colored cap. She quickly flushed the toilet, turned on the water momentarily to simulate washing her hands, and then opened the bathroom door with her breath held.

Pod was still sleeping, snoring his hideous snore and laying like a lump on his side of the bed.

She strolled to the door, walked out, and then did the same at the front door.

She knew there were cameras that watched the outside of her apartment, as well as the building, just as she knew there were more homes than hers in the multi-home complex. They were thankfully empty. She couldn't stand the idea of having a witness to her degradation. Well, she was sure she did have a witness in the form of her guards. Even though it was a new team, she was certain they watched everything that happened to her and laughed about it.

Tears pricked her eyes at how far down she'd come. She should have never trusted the aliens.

She'd done some "innocent" exploring since arriving. She walked along the well-maintained gardens with no person visible except Pod. She'd once rudely told a soldier who was standing guard that she didn't want to see his face and to stay out of sight. He'd been pissed, but evidently, she was still enough of a boss he had done what she'd asked.

That had been step two of her plan. She didn't want soldiers standing around observing her. They would have to do it by monitoring the cameras, and she was convinced that humans were so lazy that staring at cameras wouldn't hold their attention. She was sure that no one expected her to run away—they were only present to keep her safe from prospective kidnappers. So, if she did get caught trying to escape, she'd simply explain she needed a walk and to leave her alone.

She was on Earth now, and this was her domain. Mayva grinned to herself, although she wasn't safe yet. But she couldn't help thinking that if Ragna had been smart, she would have never turned her into an enemy.

Mayva walked with confidence down the empty corridor until she reached the stairs. She didn't dare utilize the elevators. So far, everything has been going smoothly. She saw the front door and knew this would be the real test. She wasn't sure what to expect once she opened those doors.

But then she heard the soft sound of something sliding. It was a thick yet slick sound. She looked over her shoulders and saw that slime was gliding across the floor from a crack beneath the security door.

Her mind screamed in alarm. Pod! She thought about running, dashing out the door and down the street, but Pod could stretch like an inchworm and was quick. She knew that from days of her useless attempts to run from him.

Instead of running, she stood and watched his gelatinous form come together. Once it had, it observed her momentarily.

Well, she thought. Make your flippant remarks, and then go run and tell Ragna. She'd rather die than stay here as some alien's prisoner!

"You won't be able to get away without my help." Mayva blinked. Wait...what did he say? "I'm no rapist, mistress. I do not like what I've been asked to do to you. I give pleasure, not pain. So, if you want to get away from this place, then I will help you."

Was this a trick? His voice was soothing and masculine. Actually, it would have been nice had it been attached to an acceptable body.

"Do you desire freedom?"

After a beat, she nodded.

"Fine." And then Pod rose up, growing bigger, his form lengthening. And before she knew it, he had grown nearly seven feet tall and had taken on the form of a Galatian.

Her mouth dropped. With the exception of his lack of color, Pod now looked like a Galatian, including the rigging, skirt, and boots.

He nodded at her look of surprise. "Yes, I could have done this earlier to ease your discomfort, but Queen Ragna requested I make myself as...unappealing as possible. Now, if you want your freedom, follow my instructions."

Chapter Thirteen

At this point, Ragna was more annoyed than worried. But that wouldn't last.

How dare this human refuse my calls! She had given her a few days of quiet to adjust to her new circumstances, ignoring the many calls. She had enjoyed listening to the messages of the human begging, finding it amusing when the begging became thinly veiled threats.

Ragna couldn't help smirking to herself. Yes, she was getting a taste of her own medicine. As much as Mayva Heath thought herself superior to other species, but rape could not be condoned. Trafficking in sexual favors was, at times, a necessary evil but still distasteful.

Ragna strolled out of her cavern as she considered what lengths she was willing to take to ensure the continuation of her way of life. It didn't mean she didn't know the difference between personal and social justifications. When it came to securing the future of the Galatians, nothing was off limits.

Take Rafe, for instance. She wouldn't force him to be the powerful man he could be, a ruler who could stand by her side when all he wanted was to be a fighter. But she didn't force him. Simply put, she found his lack of drive unappealing. But more unappealing than a man who didn't realize their potential was a man she had to force.

However, she was willing to live her life in the manner she wanted and to allow others (as wrong as they may be) to live theirs.

Perhaps that is why the Queens got along so well with The Interplanetary Collective. Each member of The Collective represented a species that had their own individual...vices, and the Queens understood that. Farming out the most prized Galatian males to do their bidding had been a sacrifice but had ensured the discretion of the Collective.

Ragna walked across the rocks, floral, and fauna before she reached one of the large grottos. Already nude, she stepped into the naturally heated waters, reveling in the sure success of her plans.

Amalia had made huge mistakes, mostly by taking responsibility for their current success when everyone knew it was due to her efforts. Placing the human as the spokesperson for the insurrection had been her best idea yet and was the move that would allow her to finally overthrow that blow-heart to be the next Most-Exalted.

She swam to the edge of the pool after only a few minutes of bathing, a niggling worry impeding her thoughts. Maybe the human had figured out a way to kill the Keengalese. They were tough to kill with their gelatinous outer body, but not impossible...

Once back inside the cavern, Ragna was in a more serious mind frame when she called Pod.

No answer.

She cursed to herself and immediately contacted the head of security.

"Queen Ragna—" began the anxious human voice

"What are they doing?" she demanded.

"Uh..." the man stuttered. He didn't ask any more questions as he immediately turned to a subordinate and had them pull up the surveillance camera in the penthouse apartment.

Ragna could see the image the security cameras captured. It was plain to see that the rooms of the penthouse were empty.

"Where the fuck are they!"

"Uh..."

"I will fucking destroy you if you say 'uh' again!"

The head of security quickly began to type commands until he brought up an image outside of the building.

"Here!" he announced. "The mistress is being led by a Galatian. This is at 0330 hours—"

"You idiot! That's not a Galatian!" The soldier simply blinked at her. "How many gray Galatians have you seen?" The man's mouth opened and closed like a fish out of water. "No one thought to question why the prisoner was being led away from the premises?"

"Queen, no one questions the Galatians. Ma'am," he added as an afterthought.

Ragna closed her eyes. Her scales darkened but then lightened as her rage was replaced by fear. If she lost the human, then Amalia would have a way to discredit her! "How long ago was this? And don't give me your military time! How long?!"

"Uh...seven hours, ma'am."

She pointed her finger at the subordinate who was busily typing into the computer, obviously thinking ahead to track the whereabouts of the escapees.

"You!" The man stopped and pointed to himself. "Shoot your Commander in the head. You have three seconds, or I will wipe out your entire team."

The young man gulped and looked at his Commander, whose eyes were practically bulging. The commander shook his head as he sputtered while backing away. But the younger soldier pulled his firearm and shot his commander in the head.

"You're in charge now," she announced tightly. "Find them. I'm on my way." The younger man's face had grown white, and while he couldn't find his words, he nodded in acknowledgment. Ragna signed off and stormed to her wardrobe to get dressed.

She was going to have to go to her least favorite place: Earth.

Dr. Garry Brookstone patted Daya's hand. "I think we're all set. We have the cultures and will begin growing your new skin. Give it about two weeks, and it will be optimum for the transplant."

Daya smiled and nodded. "Thank you, Doctor, for pushing everything forward so quickly."

Garry looked at the hulking Galatian that stood beside the examining table where Daya Porter now sat draped in a cotton gown. It hadn't been his idea alone to push things along as quickly as possible. When a Galatian bellowed, everyone listened.

Not that Garry was afraid of Galatians. He knew what most didn't, which was that as long as you stayed on their good side, they were fair and not completely dangerous.

But in truth, he would have taken this case even if Lt. Frenchman hadn't used his considerable influence to force him. Garry could never say no to an individual in need due to some tragic occurrence no fault of their own.

Take his albinism. He'd been made fun throughout his entire youth. There was a surgery that had fixed his eyesight, although he still had issues with nystagmus, which caused his eyes to move back and forth like an old-fashioned typewriter, no matter how intensely he stared at an object.

There were products that protected his skin, and the rest no longer mattered. He no longer hated his white hair, pink eyes, and the patches of pink on his skin. How could he when he treated so many unfortunate beings with untreated disorders that destroyed their lives? Daya Porter was one of them.

He'd done some research into her case. She'd been attacked and set on fire. Although it was sadly something that happened often, he had never treated anyone with such damaging burns. She was lucky not to have lost her limbs, fingers, or toes.

No. Looking at her, Garry would not consider her lucky.

"I'm happy to take your case. And don't worry, I will do whatever is necessary to give you the best results," he said honestly. "You mentioned that you don't want to stay hospitalized for the duration of your healing. I don't know if that's a good idea. While you won't need around-the-clock care, for a while, you won't be able to do anything for yourself."

"I will be with Daya," Paris said. Daya looked at him with apprehension before squeezing his hand and giving him a tentative smile.

"There will be Paris, but also, my friends have invited me to stay with them, so I'll have others who will help."

"But I will do most things," Paris announced.

The doctor nodded. "I will also look on you as much as possible."

"Yes," Paris said. "We will utilize the holographic feature of the communicator. I will have one issued to you immediately, as frequent visits to the compound will be inefficient."

"Oh no. That's not good enough," the doctor said before Paris barely completed the sentence. "I will need to be a constant presence during this time." Paris looked pleased.

Garry patted Daya's hand once more, then stood and headed to the door. "Why don't you get dressed, and I will get some literature for your caretakers to go over."

"Thanks again, doctor."

When she and Paris were alone, Daya sighed in relief, but her brow gathered, belying her relief.

"What troubles you?" he asked intuitively.

"The asset in the basement."

After Daya and Paris left, Garry went into his office and pulled up the old news reports. He re-read some of the articles about Lt. Rafe Sigur's fall from glory. Once a hero responsible for putting a stop to the Tybernees invasions, he was now considered to be an alien whoremonger that fetishized humans, wanting to farm them out for the purpose of over-running the Earth with hybrid human-Galatian beings. The reports stated he and his team meant to over-run the Earth, taking human women for their own pleasure.

Lt. Frenchman and Daya Porter were a couple, and he knew for a fact she wasn't a consort. Those who ran the Exchange were too short-sighted to include people based on their merit instead of an idealized perception of Caucasian-American perfection.

Even in places like the Asian provinces, no one but White people were ever included in the Exchange—and by people, he meant biological women. No trans woman and no male had ever been allowed an opportunity to serve.

Garry sighed in frustration. You couldn't believe the media. They had their biases. But how much truth was in these reports? He knew Paris Frenchman was a part of Sigur's team. He was evidently romantically involved with Daya Porter and had even mentioned her being cared for at the *compound*.

"Damnit, Paris. What am I about to get in the middle of... " People were searching for Sigur and his men, and now Garry was about to know exactly where to find them.

He wasn't in the business of turning over innocent people, even if it meant pleasing the authorities. But he also didn't believe in the exploitation of human women. Doctors Without Borders was just one aspect of his duties; another was helping to put an end to human trafficking, and while Daya and the other women that might be involved with Sigur's crew weren't being trafficked, if they were being harmed in other ways, it was his business to put a stop to it.

Chapter Fourteen

As Paris and Daya drove back to the school, she once again broached the subject of Mr. Conrad. Now was the time to think of him by his human name and not simply as an asset.

"I can't care for him while I'm healing from the surgery. Plus, I don't know how long I'll be away from the school."

Paris was contemplating the road as he drove. He looked at her. "I don't give a damn about that creature in the dungeon. He can rot down there for all I care!" His voice was fierce, and his eyes bore into her, never going back to the road.

Daya was about to tell him to watch where he was going before she realized he was. He was using his tail to see the road while he faced her. She calmed, but her expression became stern.

"Are you accusing me of giving a damn about him? Because I can assure you that I sleep quite well knowing he's in the basement paying for his crimes against me as well as those that I'm sure he committed against other women."

Paris shook his head. "I am sorry if my words made you feel that way, but it was not my intent." His voice had gone soft. "What would you like to have done with it?"

Paris refused to consider the prisoner as "him", as a person, or any being that had intelligence. Animals like him are what he had been trained to dispatch with no second thoughts. Once an enemy of The Interplanetary Collective, creatures like him were hunted and annihilated by the Galatians, who had been given full autonomy to be the judge and jury.

Daya placed her hand over his, and his grip on the steering wheel became less of a stranglehold.

"I'm sorry, sweetheart. I know you didn't mean it that way."

He tilted his head before looking back at the road. *Sweetheart.* He liked that word. His heart was cold and unfeeling for most, but not towards Daya. And she knew she was getting the best of him.

"I have previously said I'd place a Galatian Guard in his care, but I no longer think this would be best. He should interact with no one but us. We can leave him where he is. I'll come once a week to give him food and water. Enough to last the week."

Daya gnawed her lip. He knew she did that when she had a nagging thought.

"None of the other Guards or soldiers know about his existence?" she asked.

Paris took some time to respond. "I'll put it this way: I've never told anyone. But I would consider my crew inept if they have not put it together. However, I have not told them, and I would like to keep it that way."

She nodded in agreement. What those soldiers must think of her. Maybe that is why they weren't so quick to befriend her, and it had nothing to do with her scars. Damn, at least the children didn't know.

"Kendrick is still heading the local prison system. We could pass him on to prison under his watch. But the problem is that with the Guardians falling out of favor, I wouldn't want to take a chance some human bureaucracy might rear up, releasing him, and then your involvement becomes known. Me, I have a built-in excuse to imprison him...but—"

"They wouldn't understand that I also have one, too."

He just nodded once. He inhaled and looked at her again as he drove. "Another option is to kill him, which is the safest for you. You do understand he can never be released now that he knows your face?"

"He has a family: a mother and father and maybe a wife."

Paris was shaking his head. "Such matters don't concern me." He looked at the road again. "I am concerned only with his actions and his deeds."

Daya rested her head on the window as she thought.

"I just wonder if he has regrets. Don't you believe in rehabilitation?"

"Yes," he said softly. "But he hurt you. And for that, there is no mercy. There is no softness in my heart for him. If you have a preference, I will comply. If not—then I will take care of him myself."

Daya opened and then closed her mouth. She honestly didn't know how she felt.

Martin Conrad sat on his blanket. Periodically, he would stare at the locked door, waiting for his daily meal. He would begin waiting the moment he woke up.

Time had no meaning. There were no windows, and with the exception of dull security lights, the room was almost completely dark. He had learned to survive in this hell hole.

Daya Porter was nicer and at least used the hose to fill his bucket with water once a week. But the alien just hosed down the room, hosed him down, and he had to scurry for his bucket to capture some of the water in it.

In the beginning, before he knew he wouldn't be given water daily, he was sure he would die of thirst. The alien monster would open the food slot and drop his slop onto the floor. He'd eat it hungrily off the floor, lapping it up if it was a stew.

At first, it was degrading. But that didn't last long. Hunger, thirst, and loneliness had turned him into a pathetic creature.

His clothing was nothing more than rags before finally disintegrating all together. He had tried to hold them together because it was a source of warmth in the cold cement cellar. Now all he had was the blanket which had become moldy. A rat had chewed parts of it. The rats came from the small hole in the center of the room where he shit and pissed.

Sometimes, he caught one, but instead of eating it, he had patted the little creature, stroking its soft fur. But once he let it go, the rodents ran away to the safety of the hole.

Martin watched the door and rocked. *Don't make her mad.* When she got mad, she didn't come for days until his belly burned.

Still, he would rather see her than the lizard-faced alien. At least when he looked at her ugly face, he felt some vindication that he had done that to her.

He just wished he'd done worse, got into her pussy. But she fought too hard, and then she was on fire. Martin Conrad smiled as he thought about her life as a freak.

He might be a prisoner, but so was she. And one day, he was certain he'd be free. But nothing would ever free her from her prison.

When the door opened, Martin scurried to the far side of the room. It was a requirement for the food slot to open. He bit his lip anxiously and saw Daya Porter's face in the security window.

He relaxed a little. She would leave his food loaf on the ledge instead of dropping it on the floor.

He heard a strange sound. It sounded like keys in a lock!

Conrad's brow quirked up as he stared at Daya's face through the slot. And then the door slowly swung open. His heart began to race as he looked at her, the open door and then the freedom beyond.

"Mr. Conrad. I am going to give you a choice."

He almost ran to the door. He would have knocked her down, maybe even stepped on her as he ran out of the prison to freedom. But then the alien-lizard man stepped into view, almost like a warning.

Martin's voice gushed out in disappointment.

"Are you going to let me go, Daya? Please have mercy! I've suffered. I've paid for my crimes. Please let me go!" He remembered the girl she used to be—pretty with a constant smile on her face. She was smart, too. He knew he'd had to have her. She was better than the street scum he was used to taking. Some didn't have to die, they did what he wanted and lived another day. But to be honest, he enjoyed lighting them on fire and listening to their screams....

"Mr. Conrad, being released is not one of your choices. I will never let you go."

His face screwed up, and he began blubbering as tears popped into his eyes. "Please, Daya! You are better than this—"

He saw her sigh, not in sympathy but as if she was tired. Martin glanced at the alien. The Galatian eyes bore into him as if Daya were his property.

Martin's eyes blinked. Oh my God...had Daya been reduced to fucking a Galatian? Is that why all of this was happening?

"Mr. Conrad, do you have any idea how long you've been a prisoner here?" she asked.

He just continued to stare at her. "Two years—"

"Six months."

His eyes bulged. "Six months. I don't believe you..."

"I have no reason to lie to you."

"I've been here longer! I've been here years!"

"Shut up," the alien growled and took a step forward. Martin scurried back against the wall. "What do you want from me?"

"You have a choice," Daya said softly. You stay here, locked in this dungeon for the rest of your natural life. Or I release you to die. I'll let you have that choice. But to be honest, it's a kindness that you don't deserve. You're an evil person. You laughed and cursed me when I screamed. You laughed."

Paris moved from one foot to the other in thinly suppressed anger.

"I... I was sick. I promise you I've learned my lesson. Send me to prison. I won't tell anyone. I swear it!"

"You have your choice." She closed the door. "I'll give you time to think about it."

"No!" he screamed and rushed to the door. "Please don't leave me here! I don't want to be here!" he began to sob. "Let me out, you bitch! Let me out, you ugly bitch! No, no, no, I'm sorry. I didn't mean that. Daya, you're better than this!"

Daya walked out of the dungeon.

Paris locked the door and turned off the overhead lights. He then took Daya's hand.

"Your heart is sweet," he said. "Martin Conrad has no regrets for his actions. And if he could, he would kill you."

"I know, Paris."

"I will dispatch him later. I will make it quick."

She turned to look at him. "Let him decide."

Paris sighed. "If you wish."

Dorf walked up behind Kemistry as she was preparing lunch in the kitchen. She was humming a familiar tune, and he smiled to himself. She sang that song at night when they made love.

She turned. "Dorf, I'm preparing hamburgers for the children and tuna steak for us. I don't believe our children like seafood as much as we do."

"They will learn to love it. Uh...Kemistry?"

"Yes," She suddenly frowned. "What's wrong, love?"

"I want to get my wing fixed and have my eye replaced." She just stared at him. "I know I was adamantly against it, but it's something that needs to be done.

"Oh, Dorf. You know you don't have to do that for me."

He pulled her into a hug. "I know. You've never asked me to fix my injuries." Kemistry just snuggled against him. "Because I only see perfection. You are Sir Dorf, warrior, father, husband and friend. But what has changed your mind?"

His brow gathered. "Bain. He ran away, and I didn't have wings to go after him. I am not the best that I can be as long as I'm like this."

"Oh, honey. Wings and eyes don't make you less of a Japoxillian!"

"I need to do this, Kemistry. I need to be in tip-top condition for our children." She nodded. "I understand. But you know this place will start to look like a battle hospital!"

"I know, but I'll wait until Kelsie is better."

A look of concern crossed her face. "I'm worried about Kelsie."

"Why?" Dorf asked quickly. "The doctor said the surgery is relatively routine. And she's a very brave little girl."

"It's not that. She's holding so much inside. It's like Bain's father trying to kill him and how he held that in for so long."

He nodded in concern. "I think one of us should connect with her."

"I think so too. But she said no, and I want to respect her rights not to be read."

"Do you think it has to do with what happened to her parents?" He asked. They had read the files for both children and knew their histories.

"I'm sure it does. But all we can do is be there for her so she knows she can trust us."

He pressed his forehead against hers. "I did not think it would be this difficult to be a parent."

"But it's also amazing. They make me so happy. They really appreciate us, Dorf. They like us."

"And soon they will love us."

Chapter Fifteen

By the end of the week, Kendrick, Justina, Paris, and Daya had moved to the compound. Justina said nothing when she learned that Paris and Daya would be living together close to Rafe and Karma's home.

Justina had a smaller cottage to call her own, and she decorated it to her own liking— although Kendrick offered to stay with her 'for protection purposes.'

She declined but offered to share dinner with him each evening, and he glowed with happiness thinking of juicy burgers, pot roast with the fixings, and noodle soups instead of the boring Galatian-style broth his previous consort made in abundance each day.

Daya was anxious about the prospect of living with a consort's ex-mate. When she raised the awkwardness of the situation, Paris simply shrugged.

"Justina doesn't care." Daya just stared at him until he knew he had to continue—although there wasn't much more to say on the topic. "Justina wishes to no longer be a consort."

"Ohhh."

"Of course, this is unheard of under current law. Some contracts have been signed. When the law changes, Justina will be free to pursue relationships of her choosing. I have promised her this—although she doesn't know this."

He thought about his words and felt they were sufficient. Anything more was Justina's tale to tell.

He moved close to Daya and inhaled her essence. She looked up at him and smiled, then placed her arms around his body. He leaned forward, and they shared a kiss. He sighed happily.

"It is a strange situation," he finally spoke. "But it is no one's fault. Karma speaks the truth when she says that we are stronger together. And I admit I like the idea of your new sisters coming to your aid."

"Sisters." She tested the words.

"Yes. That is what they are when you join our family. Just as the males are my comrades, but also my brothers. Now that you are my mate, they will be your brothers and your sisters."

Her breath caught at that precious word. Paris said they were mates. The words had flown so nonchalantly. His eyes widened slightly at her reaction.

"Did I misspeak? I assumed—"

"No. We are mated. It's just that this is far from what I ever expected. Even when I fell in love with you, I didn't understand that with you, I was also gaining an entire family."

Paris dipped down and then carefully lifted the tall woman, his arms settling beneath her ample backside (as she had been eating well lately and had gained enough weight to fill out properly.) Once they were eye to eye, he stared into her beautiful brown ones.

"They will be your comrades, your allies, sometimes annoyances, but always your family."

She nodded solemnly at the weight of his words.

"You are ready, Drago. You have vacationed long enough," Rafe said lightly. He stood nude on the edge of his brother's pool. Paris and Kendrick flanked him. Kendrick was holding Drago's nude son, Rex, while Rafe held Runnar.

While it was not necessary to stand on ceremony, this felt far from routine, and all males were in attendance at Drago's awakening. Bain and Dorf were the only males not present, as Bain wasn't exactly comfortable being nude, and Dorf didn't want his son to feel pressured.

Drago floated in his cocoon. He moved within the depths of the chrysalis, his newly vibrant scales visible despite the layers of old, dull scales that lay discarded within the cocoon.

"Besides, your son misses his da." Kendrick mocked. "Soon, he will be calling *me* da."

Drago jerked, and while it was clear Rex was comfortable in his uncle's arms, he knew the man that held him was not his father.

"Fine," Kendrick said and stepped into the pool where the water was at its most tepid. His weight drew him beneath the surface until, a moment later, he and Rex resurfaced. The baby knew how to swim and blinked the water out of his eyes and then made a rare laugh while inhaling past his held breath.

Drago's body swayed, and his cocoon moved closer to the edge, to his brother and son.

"You should be proud, brother!" Kendrick suddenly laughed. "Your son pisses like his uncle!" He lifted the babe from the pool, and sure enough, a great stream of piss arched through the air.

Rafe stepped into the pool with Runnar pressed to his chest. He blew into the baby's face who instantly held his breath and blinked.

This wasn't the first time that Runnar had gone 'swimming' with his papa. And although he was comfortable floating on his own, he had yet to actually swim, so Rafe was more careful than if the boy had been a full-blooded Galatian. A Galatian baby was born able to swim and just as comfortable on land as in water.

Paris dropped into the water next, and as he wasn't holding a baby, he swam to Drago, who had been resting in the sauna waters of the pool to help soak away the weakening cocoon.

Paris towed his brother to the cooler water and then began biting and shredding at the cocoon. Drago helped from within while the others watched while holding curious babies. A small piece of chrysalis floated toward Kendrick and Rex, and the baby reached for it as if it were a curious new toy.

Kendrick intercepted it and then offered it to his nephew, who promptly put it into his mouth. Kendrick wasn't worried. It was too big for him to choke on. But curiously, Rex soon began to kick his legs and called, "Dada! Dada!"

Kendrick looked at his nephew in surprise. Had they secretly incorporated Galatian DNA into the infant when they were fixing his brain? Because Galatian babies could identify the 'essence' of their fathers. But humans had no such ability. He released the baby, whose fat little legs began to kick as he swam to his father.

"That is very strange..."

What wasn't strange was that Drago began to struggle more, shredding his cocoon away as he sensed his son.

Runnar wanted to do the same as his older cousin, so Rafe released him as well, but the hybrid child simply floated in place despite kicking his legs and slapping at the water.

"Soon, son." Rafe murmured in pride. "You're only three months old." He wondered if his son would ever molt and, if so, if he would go into a chrysalis.

Drago quickly shed the final remnants of his cocoon, and he reached out and scooped up his happy son. Rex wrapped his pudgy arms around Drago's neck while happily gurgling words that included "dada". Drago kissed and hugged him, laughing tiredly when the baby's hands moved across his face. It was as if the child recognized that while his scales were different, this was still his father.

While Drago got reacquainted with his child, Kendrick and Paris collected all of the scales. They wouldn't degrade—at least not for centuries but would be dangerous to humans. So, they were collected and placed in a basket for safekeeping.

Drago climbed out of the pool with Rex propped on his hip.

"Thank you for bringing him to the pool over these few days," he said to Rafe, who was already out of the pool and wrapping Runnar in a thick towel.

"Eh," Rafe nodded and handed him another towel. Drago carefully wrapped his son, who was still clutching at his dad's face, mouth, and eyes while gurgling happily.

Rafe smiled. "He missed you."

"I missed him, too. And his mother. This was the worst..." Drago's voice held emotion, but he didn't say more.

Rafe placed his hand momentarily on Drago's shoulder. There was no good time to molt, especially if one had to leave their most precious commodities behind.

"Let's get the babies cleaned up. There's a meal waiting. The ladies made a feast."

This day had become a celebration of many things: Drago's return to the waking world with a vibrant suit of scales, the creation of a new commune, and the addition of new family members—which included Bain, Kelsie, and Runnar.

Bain and Kelsie watched in awe as the Galatian males sucked down giant spiders, popped handfuls of fat black bugs into their mouths, and crunched on the roasted beast that was as tough as leather.

None of that impressed them more than seeing M and her mother also eating *and* enjoying the spiders and bugs. Bain bravely took a squirmy bug by one thin leg and was about to pop it into his mouth when the 'bug' broke free and scurried down his arm.

It took all of his courage not to squeal in fear, but M captured it cupped in her hands before releasing it back to him.

*If M can do this...*He inhaled and popped it into his mouth, quickly chewing. He was about to gag before he realized that it tasted like... bacon. He looked at M as he chewed and then nodded.

"It's... good." He looked at his sister next. "You should try it, Kelsie."

"I'll just stick to the salmon. Mom, let me help her cook it," she announced proudly. Bain was sure to take a serving, although salmon wasn't his favorite.

As the day began to wind down, the babies went down first, and then Kelsie, who was completely surprised when each of her aunts and new uncles gave her a goodnight hug. Mom and Dad tucked her in, and although she was exhausted for a few minutes, she stayed awake in disbelief that this might really be her forever home.

Bain and M went down next after forcing themselves to stay awake while listening to the interesting stories the Guards told. Fighting their sleep with every ounce of their might, they eventually fell asleep in the comfy nests that Dorf and Kemistry had set out before the outdoor fire.

Rafe lifted his daughter and carried her carefully into her bedroom while Karma got the sleeping child into her pajamas.

Kemistry carried Bain, gliding through their home on turquoise wings, and gently placed him into his bed. Dorf put him into silk pajamas, thinking that his children certainly looked grand. They kissed him on his cheek and then went back outside, thinking that today was one of the best of their lives.

Daya was clearing away the dishes and stopped Karma when she tried to help.

"Karma, you're exhausted. Let me clean up. You did a lot of cooking today and teaching me how to prepare these meals."

Justina had wordlessly collected dishes, and she looked over at

Karma as she carried a handful back to the house. "Don't overdo it, sis. We can handle this."

"I'm plenty rested," Karma said dismissively. "Besides, I don't want to clean up yet. I'd like us to have a discussion." She eyed all of the adults present as they watched her expectantly. "It's about why I asked you all to be here."

Maddie's brow rose as she quickly added food to a covered dish. "Well, it's getting late, and I might be a little busy later..."

"Who are you fooling?" Justina snickered. "You and Drago have slipped away more times than a big man on an icy sidewalk!"

Maddie's face reddened, and Drago shielded his mouth in a human expression of amusement.

Rafe was a little more serious when he asked. "Is there something on your mind, my love?"

"Our survival," she replied sincerely.

Daya's attention was piqued—not she wasn't already hyper-aware of her own standing in this family. And yet, it hadn't taken long for her to relax. These people were truly nice and that even included Justina.

They didn't speak much, but when Justina did address her, she did it with ease and politeness. Daya thought she might become jealous if she saw Paris and Justina speak, but when it happened, she recognized that Paris was simply catching up with an old friend.

Things felt more at ease for her after that.

Now Karma wanted to change the easy vibe of the day into something certainly more serious.

Many might have thought this wasn't the right time to introduce serious conversations. This was their first full day in the compound and meeting new family. But all Daya could think is that if Karma felt the same pressure to act on their circumstances, then there was no time to delay.

This was a discussion that should have happened weeks ago.

Karma moved so she could see each of the people who were so important to her, the most important people in her life, because they were the ones who had already proven that they would fight for her continued survival.

But there was more to it than that because Karma Sigur had vowed that she would do what was necessary to bring each of these individuals the freedom to live and love freely.

Instead of thinking on the offense, now was the beginning of their attack against the Queens!

Chapter Sixteen

It was close to midnight, but the adults were gathered around the picnic table, a small fire still burned in the nearby firepit, which offered a backdrop of light along with the bright stars that sparkled in the sky.

Karma had taken a seat at the head of the table. And while there was a seat to her right, Rafe was standing at her side behind the empty chair. On the left sat Maddie and Drago and then Justina. Across from Justina and next to the empty seat sat Paris and then Daya. Kendrick took the chair next to them while Dorf and Kemistry sat side-by-side at the opposite end of the table.

Karma looked at the face of each member of her family. "Each of you has played an important role in why I'm still here today. I want to thank you again. I'll never be able to thank you enough."

She looked up at Rafe, who remained silent as he gazed at her. She knew he wanted to remind her that Galatians did not need words of thanks. But he didn't, and she smiled at him. A wave of love was exchanged between them. She knew without a doubt Rafe said nothing because this was her time, and he wanted her to know it.

She reached for his hand and hung onto it as she turned back to her family.

"I'm alive. We're all alive. But unless we take action, our lives won't be worth living."

The sisters watched quietly while their hearts sped up and dread fell over them. Their minds filled with all that they had to lose.

Both Dorf and Kemistry knew the emptiness of their recent lives apart. And now that they were together and had grown their family, neither could imagine losing it—especially to megalomaniacs like Ragna and Mayva.

Maddie thought about her love for Drago and what her life would be like if she ever lost him or Rex. Why would she ever want another man? A different child and a different life? If they didn't win this war, then Drago would have to go back to his bound-mate, and their family would be forever destroyed.

Justina thought about how much she loved her life now. She never wanted to go back to being a slave to either humans or aliens. She wanted to change the laws so that little girls had a say in their own lives and selfish adults couldn't force them to live a life that was worse than death.

Daya thought about the fragility of life. Land mines were every-where. And one misstep could mean the end of your livelihood—if not your life. One wrong turn, and she was going to go through the worst pain of her life...for the second time.

The men were also thinking. Their purpose was to protect—even Kendrick, who no longer had a consort. This was his family now, and without them, he would be on Galatia with Evora as his bound-mate. And while he had no issues against her personally, he didn't want the life of a retired Galatian who was no longer able to indulge in his love for the human culture. The Queens recognized nothing but their own wants, and as such, he would no longer be able to indulge in the pop culture of humans, groove out to the variety of music, or enjoy the diversity of the food.

"This is playing out on the human stage," Karma said. "And as

Guardians, you have fought in the skies, on the ground, and in water. You've had your battles broadcast across the galaxies, and you have been praised and vilified by all kinds of species.

"But this time, it is not just a vote from the Collective that's going to decide the course of our combined history. If it were, then that wench Mayva wouldn't be plastered all over the media talking about how vile I am." Rafe's nose flared, and Karma held up the hand he wasn't holding as if to apologize to the group.

"The thing is, The Collective is supposed to be deciding whether or not to emancipate the males. But all of a sudden, Mayva's supporters are picking up traction with rallying against the Guardians and inter-species relationship." She frowned. "The strange thing is, The Collective is allowing them the opportunity to rally this new support."

Kendrick and Paris exchanged looks.

"The Collective would hardly be on the side of the Queens," Kendrick replied. "We've worked with them for generations—"

Drago interrupted. "But it's the Queens who sit on The Council, not the Guardians."

"But that's only because they represent *us*," Kendrick replied. It was true and had never seemed odd. The men battled, and the Queens ran things. It had only been natural for Queens to represent the Galatian interests.

Karma nodded.

"Let me understand," Daya said before Karma could open her mouth. "The Collective make the rules for lesser beings—which include humans." Paris darkened but said nothing. Daya continued. "So why would they care if they're in the good graces of the humans?"

Karma gasped. "Yes! That's what I couldn't put my finger on! I don't think The Collective intends for us to win this. What if they use all of this hatred to justify ruling against the Guards, stripping you of your freedom while still requiring you to serve them?"

Kendrick smirked. "And who would enforce this? We are the apex."

"No," Maddie said. "The Queens are."

Rafe inhaled a long breath. "We are too self-assured in our superiority." He looked at his brothers. "But we aren't superior. We are fighting a battle where we don't understand the rules because it is on the human stage. My wife is correct. We don't understand this manner of battle—humans should know what they see instead of what a clearly biased individual says."

Maddie and Justina both chuckled humorlessly.

"It doesn't work like that," Justina took a sip of wine. "Humans would rather win the battle of words than cash money."

"Unless you've slept on cold concrete in the middle of a snowstorm," Daya said. She froze in embarrassment when Justina met her eyes.

Karma licked her lips as she looked from Justina to Daya. "And that is why I need each of you. We *all* have different outlooks and different viewpoints. There isn't just one human way of looking at things."

"True," Dorf said, feeling the hodgepodge of emotions that wafted from each of his family members.

"What if everything you say is true?" Kendrick asked slowly. "We should begin hunting for Ragna again! End her life for what she's done—"

"And then what?" Justina interrupted. "Do you think they won't know we're responsible for it? And then we'll force the hand of The Collective, and they really will be justified in killing this crew!"

"She will die," Rafe said matter-of-factly.

"Death is an easy end," Daya whispered.

"In time, death comes to us all," Paris added. "But maybe after a long, long time."

Karma stared at them as she gripped the hand of the man she loved.

"I have an idea. But I'm going to need your input—each of your input, and from every angle. Because we need to take action, like yesterday."

Everyone watched her curiously but with a great deal of anticipation.

Ragna glared at the new head of security. "How can you say that you lost them? Is this not your purpose? Your only purpose was to watch and protect the human!"

Seven men were in the room, watching quietly. The young man in charge streamed sweat, remembering what he'd been forced to do to the previous Commander.

But it wasn't just him. The other soldiers might be silent, but their thoughts of anger and even hatred ran deep. Of course, they were careful, never showing their outrage. They knew that Galatians had a nearly supernatural ability to 'sense' things.

But this particular Galatian didn't realize that humans had an uncanny ability to carry hatred without ever showing it.

The young soldier cleared his throat. "Queen, there is no way to track the transport vehicle used once they left Earth. We've located the stolen craft on the satellite site star Alcyonne, where we believe the Keengalese arranged for a clean transport vehicle. Ma'am."

Ragna was glaring at the boy for not providing the answers she wanted. But at that moment, her communicator sounded—which likely saved his life.

Amalia? What did she want?

Ragna ran her claws across the top of her head as her nerves began to pique.

She spun around. "Just find them!" She stalked out of the room, answering the call on the way outside. "Queen Amalia. How can I be of assistance?"

Queen Amalia's color was purple in deep annoyance. A hologram instantly appeared, showing the woman sitting on her throne.

She was evidently in the Queen's Council room with the heads of the femdom around her on their thrones.

"What do you have to say about that interview?!"

Interview? They had several months before the Heath woman's scheduled interview. More than enough time for the upcoming Galatian Exchange. Ragna cursed to herself. Did the Queen's Council find out the human was missing? If so, it meant they were spying on her!

"Well?!" Amalia bellowed.

"I...I'm not sure—"

"Rafe's whore is holding a press conference! It's been all over the media! Where have you been?! She's planning an interview, and I want to know what you're going to do about it?"

Ragna began to stutter. "I-I had no idea. I've been quite busy with our efforts—"

"What efforts?" Amalia asked. Ragna was quiet. "What are your plans with the Heath human? Push up the rally, and I want her to be prepared to give an interview right after Rafe's whore gives hers. Well? Why are you pale?"

"Uh... I need to look at the news conference."

Amalia sighed. "Contact me the moment you—"

Ragna disconnected. She ran at breakneck speed back to the penthouse that had once been Mayva's home. Her heart was pounding as her body shook. She turned on the large television.

She didn't have to change channels or go searching. Rafe's human was suddenly there on the screen. Her brown eyes seemed to burrow into Ragna's amber, lizard-slitted ones as if they were in the same room.

You should be dead. Next time, I will not miss my opportunity...

"I want to set the record straight." Karma's unwavering voice sounded across the room. **"For so long, the Galatians have controlled the narrative. You have been lied to. We all have. But the deceit is not from the Guards. They are just the face of that control.**

But the real culprits have fallen beneath the radar.”

Karma paused. **“Please join me for an Interview tomorrow, where I will reveal more information about what really happened the night of that deadly battle, the reason behind the battle, and why you are being manipulated every time one of Mayva Heath’s public announcements airs.”**

Suddenly, the screen flashed an image of Mayva holding a laser. It was clearly the footage from the security camera showing Ragna and Mayva’s attack on Karma and her family. The look of demented hatred had transformed Mayva’s beauty into a grotesque look of evil.

It showed the slow-motion sweep of the laser as she cut down the lives of the Japoxillian. And then it cut to a badly deformed Galatian Queen in a torn black skintight suit. It showed the Queen shooting Karma in an obviously pregnant belly.

Ragna glared at the screen, but her anger was laced with fear. This was bad, very bad.

“One day,” Karma said, her voice strong instead of tearful. **“What they did to me and my family might happen to you and your family, to your unborn baby, to your-your friends.”**

Karma’s eyes were suddenly glassy, and she swallowed past a lump, but her eyes never waivered, and her expression didn’t change. The screen went dark.

“Ladies and gentlemen, that was Karma Chambers, consort to Rafe Sigur,” a male newscaster stated. **“She has made some very strong allegations against Mayva Heath. Her interview will be televised globally and even inter-galactically tomorrow evening.”**

The co-host was a pretty and prim woman who looked upset. **“That was chilling.”** She turned to the man. **“We’ve tried to reach out to Miss Heath and the North American Galatian Exchange, but there hasn’t been a response—”**

Mayva threw a chair at the television, which was so advanced that it didn't break.

"As you know," the male co-host continued. **"Mayva Heath was recently embroiled in some controversy when she was kidnapped by the previous head of the North American Galatian Exchange..."**

Ragna stormed out of the apartment. She had to find Mayva!

Part Two

Chapter Seventeen

"Hello. Today, we have a special edition of News Across the World. I am Emily Chase, commentator, reporter, and former attorney.

"Today we have as our guest, Karma Chambers-Sigur. Full disclosure: Mrs. Chambers-Sigur reached out to our team two days ago and requested that we handle her very first interview. She indicated that there were no questions off limits."

The camera moved from the pretty, middle-aged woman to that of a Black woman with deep brown skin. While she wore very little make-up and her expression was passive, she carried an undeniable beauty, amplified by its simplicity.

"I am broadcasting from my London site, and Mrs. Chambers-Sigur is broadcasting from an undisclosed satellite space site," Emily continued. "As you well know, there have been very controversial acts that have taken place in the North American Province—mostly surrounding the North American arm of the Galatian Exchange.

"Mrs. Chambers—"

"Please just call me Karma." Karma's rich voice interrupted, and now the camera showed a split screen of both women.

Emily nodded graciously. "And please—I'm just Emily." The reporter once again began addressing the audience. "Karma is the first Black consort to ever be mated to a Galatian. In recent months, the Galatian Queens learned that the mating was unsanctioned and that Mrs... *Karma* had become pregnant with a hybrid child with Lt. Sigur, a decorated and high-ranking Galatian Guard.

"As per their law, they... " Emily seemed to search for the correct word. Karma provided a cool response.

"Murdered. The Queens murdered my unborn baby with the use of their secret team of assassins: The Black Masks."

Emily inhaled solemnly and respectfully before continuing. "After the killing of Karma and Lt. Sigur's child, The Interplanetary Collective was petitioned with a request to emancipate the Galatian males from the control of the Galatian Queens. The Interplanetary Collective, in fear of retribution on both sides, called for a cease-fire to prevent a civil war. They are still in deliberation on such a monumental case.

"Folks, history is being made, and at the middle of it stands Karma Chambers-Sigur. Welcome Karma. Have I gotten the facts right?"

Karma nodded. "You did as well as you could. But you said that I am the first Black Consort. In truth, I am the first *non-white* one. I think you will find that to be a much more significant issue."

Emily nodded slowly, marinating in those words before she continued. "Karma, you are being called the New Face of the Rebellion."

Karma's expression appeared amused. "I can understand why we don't want to discuss the big *white* elephant. It's too close to what the rebellion has been speaking of for years.

"The Exchange supports the Galatian Guards while they fight for freedom and justice across the galaxy. If only the rich can afford to enter the lottery, and those happen to be Caucasian Americans, then that is simply the game of chance." Karma squinted, "But that's not quite true. White men aren't the richest humans in the world. Some provinces have brown-skinned people who have purchased their way into the lottery but whose children have never been selected. Even in the Asian province, only whites are ever selected." Karma touched her temple. "But we aren't supposed to question the status quo." She sat back in her chair, her face once again passive.

"These are familiar arguments," Emily countered. "The Loyalists will say that white Americans have special interest groups that secure their...standing in the new order. Rather right or wrong, other racial groups should do the same." Karma nodded once as if accepting her words but indicating she had no "horse in that race."

"So," Emily continued. "Are you the new face of the Rebellion?"

A streak of surprise showed across Karma's face. "Are you asking me if I infiltrated the Galatian Exchange—with no special interest group backing me, with the sole purpose of becoming pregnant so I could disrupt the Exchange from within?"

"Some have suggested that rebels assisted you in gaining entry into the Exchange. Mayva Heath has stated on record that you are a spy for the rebellion, but such a poor one that they won't even acknowledge you."

Karma didn't respond immediately. She just stared at the camera until Emily opened her mouth to ask another question. But Karma finally spoke. "Then perhaps we should start with Mayva Heath."

"Yes, she is an outspoken proponent for the Loyalist Faction."

"She was supposed to be the consort for my mate, Rafe Sigur."

"Yes, but she was kidnapped by the head of the North American Exchange, Heinrich Tolbert. It is said he was secretly involved in a faction of the rebellion and, as such, was against species mixing, planted you, and...here we are today."

"I suppose there are people who want to believe that," Karma replied coolly. "If Mr. Tolbert's purpose was to destroy the Exchange from within, he would have chosen someone who would not have brought attention to his actions. In other words, he would have chosen a *white* woman."

"So, you are saying that you and Heinrich Tolbert were not working together?"

"Mr. Tolbert was my employer. I was a maid. I worked for his family for just under a year. I lived on Thirteenth Street and Sycamore in the poorest area of the city—at least when I could afford a cheap apartment to share with someone. When I couldn't, I slept on the floor of the train station with the other homeless, or I squatted in a vacant building. I had no time to be a rebel when my life was working twelve-hour days and then trying to find food and a place to sleep. Worrying about the lives of the top 1% has never been a poor person's priority."

Her words were stern, but her voice never rose.

"So, how did you get into the Exchange?" Emily continued with interest.

"I was blackmailed."

Emily couldn't hide her smile or disbelief. "Why would anyone have to blackmail a person so poor she sleeps on the floor of a train station?"

Karma leaned forward. "Because I was never supposed to survive the Exchange. Let me explain that I knew nothing about Mr. Tolbert's relationships or his job at the Exchange. But I was either going to replace Mayva Heath, or I was going to prison for stealing a necklace he had planted on me."

Karma shook her head. "Truthfully, he didn't even need to plant the necklace on me. All he had to do was call the police and say that I'd stolen from him, and I would have been cooling my heels in prison like so many other women in my position. Prison is filled with poor people who know the government runs the world and that govern- ment is run by white men like Mr. Tolbert."

Emily's smile fell away.

Karma continued. "I got to the Exchange ignorant of Galatians and their ways. I knew only what I read in papers or overheard in the news. Most were bad rumors about scary, emotionless aliens. I knew nothing about consort school or their years of training to learn to please Galatians. I knew nothing about the mutilation they are forced to undergo to become a sexual match to a Galatian. I believed the rumors that despite Galatians being the forefathers of the human race, they were unable to breed. After all, their own race is dying out because of it—and it's the reason they initially crossed the universe searching for a means to continue their kind."

"Are you saying that this isn't true?" Emily asked with interest.

"What I'm saying is that I believed it was true. I signed the contract agreeing to the terms of the Exchange. But when I consummated my relationship, I truly became Rafe's wife. He was placed in charge of the Exchange in order to investigate my part in the fraud—and to be clear, I did commit fraud. But I was protected because of the contract and because the marriage had been consummated—"

"And because he was attracted to you?" Emily asked.

Karma smiled softly. "I will say he was intrigued by me—by why I didn't do things the way the other consorts did them—the way he had been taught that humans generally reacted to situations."

"You fell in love with Lt. Sigur?"

"Not then, but I did see there was a lot of misinformation out there. Galatians aren't all that different from humans. They are loyal —specifically to their Queens. They love hard and are tireless when it comes to defending those under their protection."

"How...how were you able to become pregnant without the surgery to allow intercourse between humans and Galatians?" Emily's cheeks were slightly pink in embarrassment at the invasive question.

Karma gave a half laugh that seemed part amusement, part indulgence at the stupidity of the question. "The same way Galatians have been impregnating humans for generations prior to the Queens decreeing it illegal for Galatians to breed with other species." Emily blinked. Karma continued. "All I need is the tip, dear. And the tip is quite adequate—for both parties."

Emily's face went bright red. "Thank you for that—"

"Emily, before we move on, let me clarify. For generations, consorts have been sexually mutilated—irreversibly sterilized for the sole purpose of allowing a Galatian penis to fit fully into their bodies. But sexual pleasure is not just derived in that way. Galatians don't split human women into two. Galatians don't force themselves on a partner who doesn't freely offer themselves. And Galatians find pleasure in touch or the simple proximity of their mates.

"It was never necessary to mutilate human women for the pleasure of Galatian men. It was just a rule created by the Galatian Queens, just like the rule that said we could not have children with each other, and just like the many other rules that say Galatian men aren't allowed to govern themselves. The very same Galatian men who have protected the galaxy from Tybernees, Oxilians, Trinchians, and countless other alien predators. Those are the men who have to petition The Interplanetary Collective to no longer be controlled by the laws and rules of the Galatian Queens."

Emily's brow gathered as she quietly listened. She quickly looked at some notes before continuing.

"Karma, it has long since been the stance of The Interplanetary Collective to not involve themselves with the inner workings of other species. They themselves are made up of many different species—"

"Intelligent species," Karma interrupted. "They even have Tybernees delegates. And there are two Galatian Queens who sit on the council."

"But they have recused themselves from the proceedings," Emily interjected.

"What they don't have are human delegates, nor are the Galatian males represented. I mean, they are represented by their oppressors. And humans did not make the cut to be considered higher life forms —even though we were created by a race that is considered more evolved.

"You asked if I was the new face of the Rebellion. The Rebels ask these important questions but stop when they cloud the issue with racist ideologies and talks of separatism. In that way, they're no different from the Loyalists, who want a pure human society. It's just the Loyalists want a white society run by the government, while the Rebellion wants a human society free of alien influences.

"That's the issue with following someone else's calling."

"Some might say that those words could distance you from the rebellion—the very same people that will support your cause."

Karma sighed and then crossed one leg over the other and laced her fingers across her knee. Her smart, black suit gave her a sophistication rarely showcased with the consorts. No matter what part of the world they were located in, the consorts always showed themselves provocatively dressed, amplifying their beauty with lots of makeup and expensive jewelry.

Karma wore silver studded earrings, lip gloss, and possibly liner to amplify her rich, dark eyelashes. Her hair was a short, curly Afro that defied the long, blond locks that every other consort donned.

"The rebellion would have wanted my baby just as dead as the Loyalist."

Emily seemed surprised by that response. "But you do want supporters? Mayva Heath has more than doubled the support for the Loyalists' cause. More than ever, they are speaking out against alien rule and a call to a return of government control."

"Not everyone has taken those two sides. I didn't before I became a consort and then a wife. What about those people who don't have time to worry about what a bunch of rich white people do?

"I was worried about surviving with the measly handouts doled out by the very same government officials crying about what some aliens do in a lottery that I can never hope to afford. And as for the Rebellion, who had time to fight for a separation of species and hatred of aliens when I see men, women, and children getting their heads smashed in by human security? When I have to pick maggots and rot out of the food supplemented by the very same government that is worried about how aliens live."

"Karma, the Loyalist would say that everyone has the ability to work hard to do better for themselves. And if the poor dislike the free accommodations, then they are free to work hard to provide better for themselves and their families."

"Then I'd say the only way to get ahead in this society is with the help of the government. If you don't work for them, then you will never succeed. You will never get ahead. You will never get a job that will pay you more than the most minimal of wages—unless you choose to become a sex worker. Which is a career choice that not everyone is able or willing to join.

"Only in very rare occasions are government jobs given to people of color. When I graduated from school, I registered with Job Services just like every other white, Black, and Brown person. I never got offered a job other than on a cleaning crew or in hospitality.

"I never had the ability to go to school to become a doctor—or a lawyer like you."

Emily's eyes flashed indignantly. "I worked hard for my accomplishments. I wasn't wealthy, and my family lived in some of the poorest areas of London. My parents didn't have the money to help me further my education, and I had to put in long hours working to support myself *while* studying to keep up with the wealthy 1% that got the free rides."

Karma continued to look non-plussed. "How many of your classmates had brown skin?"

Emily opened and then closed her mouth.

~Karma's Interview pt. 2~

"Karma, you remain a mystery and a subject of interest since your inclusion in The Galatian Exchange. Soon after your arrival, several controversial actions took place."

The screen suddenly showed a video of Karma, flanked by Galatian and human security, handing out food to the homeless in a train station.

"You are responsible for many humanitarian activities, from providing food to the homeless at this inner-city train station. It is said that you even had food provided to a housing project where you were raised and gave handouts to news reporters camped outside of your building. There were even reports of Lt. Rafe Sigur's Galatian Guards providing presents to underprivileged children at an orphanage where you were raised."

"People find that curious," Karma said. "But what I find strange is that people who have great wealth don't do more to help those that are in need. But while it's easy to judge me for my actions, good or bad, I found it just as easy to judge the Galatians. Luckily for me, it didn't take long for me to think for myself instead of listening to the rumors.

"We all have heard about the Galatian's ruthless pursuit of their enemies. We hear about the lengths they've taken to keep humans in their place and the hand they've played in ending the free will of humans.

"But what we don't hear about are the lengths that the Galatian Guards have taken in order to protect mankind. Before our inclusion in the Collective, we were the target of many alien predators who have plundered countless planets. I don't need to remind you how they nearly destroyed the Earth until the Galatians made themselves known. It was only then that we learned that Earth had long since been a restricted planet, off-limits to other alien races. The Tybernees broke that restriction, and it was the Galatians that petitioned for us to fall under the protection of The Collective."

"All humans know this. It's taught in grade school," Emily interjected.

"But what if we were no longer under the control of the Collective?" Karma continued.

"Many say that we'd once again face plunder and possibly the complete destruction of the Earth."

Karma's brow quirked upward. "The Galatians aren't going to relinquish their protection of us, and they have vowed to defend us. And unlike what the Loyalists and the Rebels preach, the Galatians did not ever try to rule Earth—not in the billions of years that it existed. Just like they've never tried to rule the many other planets where they have created life."

"Okay..." Emily replied in interest.

"So, what makes you think we need the Collective to protect us from alien life forms?"

"Well, your own father was kidnapped by the Tybernees—"

"And they sit on the Collective. So, you tell me why the Collective didn't control the Tybernees?"

Emily paused. "There are outlaws in every species."

Karma shrugged. Emily waited for her to continue, but Karma didn't. "Are you suggesting that The Collective allowed the pillage of Earth?"

"*Allows*," Karma corrected. "There are still Tybernees attacks occurring—while the Galatian Guards are out there protecting the *higher* life forms. Let me ask you, Emily, do you feel as if you are a lesser life form?"

Emily looked down and consulted her notes. "Uh... what do you hope to gain from the emancipation of the Galatian men?"

"Nothing different than what any enslaved people hope to gain."

Emily swallowed at the blunt response. Karma's brow rose. "For clarification, the Galatian men would like to have the freedom to lead their lives under the same rules that any man or woman leads theirs. They don't want to be forced to be bound to a Queen who might be as old as their mother or as young as their child. Like any other person, the males want the right to guide the course of their own lives, their own careers, and when or if they want to retire. They want the freedom to live and love whomever they wish.

"Oh... and for myself, I hope to gain the right to live my life with the man I love. I hope to see others do the same without worrying about their babies being murdered or their friends and families being cut down by a hoard of Black Masked Queens whose true objection is fear of being replaced by human women!" Karma's voice shook for the first time as she glared sternly into the camera.

Emily's voice was as soft as a whisper when she finally continued. "Let me give my condolences for the losses that you and your family have suffered. We saw the security footage of the attack just yesterday. It has played continuously ever since, despite numerous attempts to have it pulled and claims that the footage was doctored. Experts have provided testimony that it was not. Many have reached out to Mayva Heath for a statement since it appears she was aiding one of the Queens in that attack. As of yet, there has been none received."

Karma inhaled a shaky breath. "Mayva Heath worked with the Galatian Queens to kill me and my unborn child. My friends and the other Guards on Rafe's team stood up for me, and many lost their lives because of it.

"But it wasn't just us. That day, more than five hundred Black Masks infiltrated The Washington where we lived. Many human soldiers lost their lives that day. Also, news reporters who got too close to the story disappeared, never to be seen again. People who witnessed the battle also mysteriously disappeared, and the news of that day was buried in lies."

"How many Queens lost their lives?" Emily asked.

"A handful and only because they were neutralized at great cost by the human military, many of whom lost organs and are permanently disabled. But they were able to stop the Queens and to get help to me, which saved my life. I will tell you now—our human soldiers are top-notch. The Galatian Guards have long been honored, but not many understand there is a difference between our Military and those government workers who call themselves soldiers and security guards who exist only to degrade others. Through fear, they control the poor—the poor they helped to create, and the poor that way outnumber the 1%."

Emily quickly changed the subject. "You spent a great deal of time in a coma after your injuries."

Karma nodded. "I very nearly died."

"Do you think Mayva should answer for her crimes instead of being held as a hero by the Loyalists?"

"She cold-bloodedly mowed down Japoxillian warriors. But it wasn't just her. Rafe's bound mate was behind the attack. During our assault, she was unmasked and identified by the Galatian Guards present."

"Why do you think Mayva Heath did this? She turned on friends she went through training with at the consort school—two of which were ultimately killed."

"She did it because the Queens gave her the right to do so.

They've called us lower life forms for so long that they think it's okay to treat us as such. It's okay to demand human females be mutilated so they can assure the consorts never have Galatian babies. To them, it is perfectly okay to kill another woman's baby just because they can't have their own.

"That's why it happened. And worse, it happened because of human complicity, and it will continue to happen as long as we turn a blind eye to injustices that occur at the highest human level.

"If I can't be a brown person free to walk through a train station and hold my head up high without being beaten down by human guards who make bets on how many people they can knock unconscious, then how can I ever hope the Queens will respect my rights?"

"Karma, my final question. What do you think humans should do about any of this?"

"We can start by opening our eyes and using common sense. Not everybody is going to do that because common sense for some is based on the amount of money they stand to make or being a part of the power elite.

"For others, hatred and racism will outweigh any good sense. They'll want the destruction of those that don't look like them in the same way that genocides and wars took place in our history by people who need to prove their superiority.

"Those are the people who don't want to see the truth, and I am not speaking to them in this interview. Tomorrow, they will make fun of me, create cartoon images of me or of hybrid children—possibly my deceased baby, with crude remarks about the nature of my relationship with Galatians. I'll be mocked, I'll be called a liar, an extremist, and accused of every type of perversion imaginable. You will see.

"But that is not all that's out there in the world. There are more of us who just need a seed to grow in our minds to think independently. We include people who remembered that when they were hungry, it wasn't a Galatian who passed them rotting food but a human. It is the Galatians who have been vilified but who have never turned their backs on us, even when it would be an easy thing to do.

My interview today is for those people who thought they were too poor, too tired, and too beat down to worry about anything but surviving the next day. Because those are the trailblazers that created a planet of intelligent, resilient humans that are no specie's lower life form, it's your support that I want because no one else is speaking up for you."

Emily remained quiet before suddenly clearing her throat. "I greatly appreciate your time today, Karma. You have made many very good points." Emily bit her lower lip, her eyes softening. She opened her mouth to say something—perhaps to confess her own mind had been changed. But Karma interrupted.

"I appreciate you giving me a voice. Not many people would out of fear of *retaliation...*" Emily blinked. She got the message. Her expression changed, and she plastered on a smile.

"I have no plans to go anywhere. So, if I disappear..." Karma nodded. Emily addressed the audience. That concludes our interview with Karma Chambers-Sigur. I am getting reports that... " Emily looked off-camera. "Our servers have crashed. We have received millions of comments! If this interview has been blacked out in any area of the world, please know that our technicians are working to restore the feed, and this broadcast will play continuously for the next several days. Thank you from News Across the World. I'm Emily Chase signing off."

Karma took off her microphone, stood, and stretched. Rafe, who was standing beside the recording device, moved forward and embraced her. She could hear his heart thudding in his chest. His vibrant scales were tinted purple in either anger or, more than likely, annoyance.

Kendrick was eyeing the room along with his team of soldiers. They were on one of the satellite stations used by the Guard when out on intergalactic missions.

Rafe knew there was no way that their location could be

traced, but broadcasting the interview with the human still made him feel vulnerable, not something he easily admitted, even to himself.

"How did I do?" Karma asked while lifting her head to look at him.

"You did very well. Better than I could have. I would have gone red with rage at some of the questions. How you can be so calm is beyond me."

Karma hugged him again. "I got practice. Being married to you takes patience."

"Is that human sarcasm?"

Karma grinned. "Not if you have to ask. Let's go home. I'm tired, and my breasts are full. I swear I thought I was going to leak on camera."

"That would have been disastrous," Kendrick replied from across the room.

"That was not intended for your ears," Karma replied.

"Oh."

Karma and Rafe left the room hand in hand. Kendrick took up the rear, his laser drawn and at the ready. Karma felt like a dignitary... well, back when they used to have them. She remembered when there was a president of the United States who had a secret service. And then there were Kings and Queens in England who had escorts to prevent them from being assassinated.

Now, the only people who needed armed escorts were movie stars and consorts.

Rafe reached over and cupped one of her breasts.

She nudged him in the side with her elbow before looking behind her at the soldiers that flanked them. "What in the world are you doing?"

"Determining if I will need to get us into private quarters during the transport back to Earth." She scowled at him. "Just to ease the swelling in your breasts, I will gladly relieve some of the pressure," he said innocently.

"Rafe Sigur, you are not drinking all of Runnar's milk!" she hissed.

"I can share."

Karma gave him a squinty-eyed look because that was not always the case. He normally rejected sweet things but was obsessed with her breast milk—especially when he could have it from the source.

And just like that, she felt an ache in her breasts, and her milk began to spill.

"Mmm..." he groaned softly. He could already smell it.

"Damnit Rafe. You did that on purpose." But she wasn't truly annoyed. Her body reacted to him just as he reacted to hers. But she didn't bring a change of clothes, and she would be soaked by the time they returned home... so might as well give it to him.

"The target is preparing to board the transport," a voice rang through the communicator.

The man narrowed his eyes. "Copy. Do not mess this up. There is no room for error and no opportunity for another extraction."

"Yes, sir!"

The man began to pace as he stared angrily through the portal window. The emptiness of outer space made him feel small—it always had and always would, but he would rather spend the rest of his days in this vast empty space than ever set foot on Earth again. He despised everything it represented: his trauma, his losses...

He swiftly turned away from the portal and powered on the television screen again. The broadcast interview was replaying. He ignored the white lady and focused on the brown-skinned woman who stared into the camera with eyes that would always be familiar to him no matter how much older she had grown.

He reached out to touch the screen as if he could touch her skin before quickly allowing his hand to fall back to his side.

She was so brainwashed by those fucking alien monsters who

pretended to be human. He'd seen them for what they really were—when impressionable humans weren't around to spread the truth. They ran like creatures able to climb walls and ceilings, with long serpent tongues and razor-sharp claws. Their unnatural anatomy was more akin to a reptile than to a human's—and yet they considered themselves the creator of man.

His poor, deluded daughter had been seduced by their wealth and their lies. But he could not ever hold her at fault. After all, he hadn't been fit to raise her. After what the monstrous Tybernees had done to him and other human prisoners, he would never be fit to be around other humans, especially not to raise an impressionable child.

His life was devoted to the destruction of aliens—all aliens. As a leader of one of the largest terrorist cells in the North American province, James Chambers was no one to take lightly.

He was going to get his daughter back on track and kill the alien bastards responsible for corrupting her!

Chapter Nineteen

Ragna had long ago removed her communicator. As of sunrise, she had gone rogue. She was still on the dreadful planet Earth in one of the safehouses she'd secretly set up years before.

No one knew of its existence, not even her human assistants. As long as she didn't utilize her tech, then she would remain undetectable. She sat huddled on one of the under-sized human sofas.

Everything was ruined. It was over. Amalia had been calling her relentlessly before she had finally discarded the communicator. And then they'd sent out an envoy to fetch her as if she was nothing more than a commoner instead of the Lieutenant of the Queen's War Council. She was an official! But that bitch Amalia couldn't stand the idea of anyone being more successful than her.

That fucking human whore was responsible for this, and this time she wasn't referring to Karma but Mayva Heath. She had snuck away like a thief in the night with that traitorous glob of flesh.

Was there something magical about human pussy? It was too soft and wet and not anything like a strong, tough Galatian pussy. Males sickened her. Even her soldiers were acting odd, as if they didn't understand the importance of locating the traitor!

She jumped up from the couch and began to pace. She had destroyed the television set after watching half of Karma's interview. She was what they had needed Mayva to be: smart but sympathetic. At first, it seemed Mayva handled things correctly by boldly claiming superiority. Wasn't it natural that all beings felt their superiority to others?

So why hadn't Karma taken the opportunities available to slam Mayva, the Queens, as well as her in particular? It soon became clear.

More than a need to be the best, humans needed martyrs. And Karma had slipped right into the role.

Ragna cursed and looked around. She needed a way to view the remainder of that interview. If there was a way to salvage any of this, it was by analyzing Karma.

Why wasn't she dead? None of this would be happening if she had died the night of the attack. Ragna paused, admitting the truth to herself. She had underestimated her opponent. The entire mission had been filled with disaster, from the bound-mates making secret arrangements with the Black Masks not to hurt their mates.

She hadn't even known about that little tidbit until later. And then Caeda had gone so far as to kidnap Haru Bano during the mission!

And then there was the little human girl—the little warrior. Underestimating that one had left her maimed and exposed. Her identity was no longer a secret. That is when she had destroyed the television set. Her identity had been revealed to everyone.

She went to the underground garage for her vehicle. There was another nearby safehouse-

She heard the scurry of footsteps. Her instincts prepared her to launch upward but was slowed without the aid of her tail. And that is when an electrical net encased her.

She felt the sharp stabs of electricity piercing through her scales only to slam her internal organs like blows from a strong fist. Wherever the electrical net touched her, it seared her, crisscrossing the softer scales of her face and torso.

She screamed with rage and pain as she slashed with claws and teeth. Damn her human boots! She needed the added slicing power of her tail and the claws on her feet—things she no longer had access to.

Completely unfamiliar with this particular trap, Ragna was surprised that something seemingly so weak was unbreakable. She fleetingly wondered if this technology was known by the Galatian Guards and if they had something in their harnesses that would at least neutralize the electrical shocks. It was said they could over-power or outwit any weapon forged against them—which is why they were warriors, and she'd nearly been beaten by a child...

The pain had a way of bringing clarity to Ragna, but the pain quickly became too much to bear. The relentless shocks of electricity quickly caused her bladder to fail as piss ran down her legs, only to fry when it contacted with the hot, electric metal.

As screams pealed from her throat, Ragna collapsed to the concrete floor. But before her vision went dark, she saw she was surrounded by nearly fifty of her own human military. The look of hatred in their eyes was unmistakable as each aimed lasers at her.

Ragna had time to realize she truly had underestimated these creatures.

Rafe and Karma had just settled into the small pod.

Karma especially liked the smaller pods as it was what they used on Earth to fly quickly from city to city. The big spaceships still made her nervous, although space itself was beautiful and serene. He had asked her if she wanted to learn to fly it, and then maybe it wouldn't be as scary. But she didn't even know how to drive a car. Rafe was amused when he replied that there wasn't much to crash into in space.

She had just given him a solemn look while replying she wasn't likely to suffocate while learning to fly on Earth.

Rafe was setting the navigation to return to Earth and thinking about how well the interview had gone when his communicator sounded.

His brow dipped in the human way he'd often observed when they were surprised. He was surprised. Haru was contacting him.

"Haru. Brother, why are you calling?" They had agreed that contact would only occur through a network of trusted allies and never person to person. To say he was surprised was an understatement. His entire being told him that his brother was in danger and needed rescuing.

"Rafe. Is it safe to speak freely?" Haru's voice did not indicate his state of mind, but what he could see of his brother's scales showed vibrant green. He was either excited or had just molted.

Karma had turned in her seat next to Rafe, her ears perking at hearing Haru's name. Haru was someone she missed and had wanted to return to the compound.

She remembered the pride he took when showing M how to properly use a sword. M often returned home with tales about Japanese culture and folklore. She missed those days, but she also missed him and the way he lovingly handled Tam when she was at her most vulnerable. It was probably due to his calm patience that had allowed her to grow into the brave woman she was now.

But Karma understood the necessity of his mission back in Galatia. He was to be their eyes and ears.

Rafe looked at her. He didn't turn on the holograph feature as he normally would.

"Karma is here. You can speak freely."

"Caeda has been called to an emergency meeting with the Queen's Council. All of our Bound-mates have been called, and all are in attendance—except for Ragna.

"Caeda has revealed that Ragna has gone rogue."

Karma's heartbeat leaped in surprise. Her first thought is her babies were back at the compound without her. Almost everyone she loved was there because she had called them...

"What do you mean she has gone rogue?" Rafe demanded.

"Ragna has defied Amalia's orders to prepare Mayva to respond to Karma's interview. Both are officially missing. Ragna's military team described her as being hostile. They sent footage of her destroying the penthouse where she kept Mayva."

"Running scared," Rafe replied.

"Yes," Haru agreed. "And it is said she has made an enemy of the Most-Exalted. Caeda says there are whispers that Ragna has her sights on her position, and Amalia intends to put her out of commission. Now, it looks like Ragna did it to herself."

"Hmmm...and do we know her last known location?"

"Yes. She was on Earth as of two days ago."

"Shit. So close." Rafe growled.

"Yes, but you know my thoughts on that. We can do nothing to break the truce."

Rafe sighed. "Have you learned anything new?"

"Probably nothing much different than what you've already put together."

"We suspect that the Collective is backing the Queens."

"Mmm. I will keep my ears open for anything of that nature. I have to leave before I raise suspicion. Caeda has just begun to trust me."

"Of course. She's no fool. I'm sure she has used you for information, as well."

"And I have been sure to feed her nice bits about you and Karma...uh...my apologies, Karma. I-uh—"

"I have no issues with you telling them any lies about me. It's just going to make your presence more authentic."

"Well... they aren't lies that I reveal. As you no doubt know, Galatians do not lie... at least not outright. But it is no lie to describe my brother's infatuation with you and that it confuses me. Because I, too, am confused as to why I love Tam as I do. Luckily, it's no stretch of the imagination for her to believe that your influence has gone only as far as brainwashing us into wanting our independence. She knows I am not attracted to you or that I would never believe I'd prefer my consort over her."

"In the spirit of full disclosure, it is possible for us to be less than truthful," Rafe explained. "There is an art to deceit."

"I recall," she smirked. "And Haru, no problems if you reveal anything about me. You just be careful. Men always think they understand women, and we rely on that."

Rafe tilted his head but decided to follow up on that at a later time. He was anxious to get home to his family. He didn't think Ragna had the ability to locate him, but when it came to his family, he would never again take chances.

Haru quickly continued. "I will have our liaison contact you once I know what occurred in the meeting, but I must go before Caeda's spies learn of my actions."

"We'll talk soon, brother."

When the connection ended, Karma leaned towards her husband. "Do you think my interview caused Ragna to run?"

"I can think of no other reason she would choose this time to go into hiding. And there is the matter of The Most-Exalted. Amalia holds the highest position in Galatia, and Ragna has always been hungry for power. I can see her turning Amalia into an enemy. She has a way of doing that to others without realizing it."

"Is that what she did to you—you and your relationship with her?"

"That is only part of the issue. But yes, she did manage to push me away." Karma looked out at the Earth as she thought about his words. "Another matter is that I've never loved her," he continued. "Which makes it easy to be pushed away." He reached for Karma's hand, and she smiled as she allowed her hand to be gently swallowed by his.

"The target has been apprehended without incident."

James turned from the portal window to the holographic image of a soldier. "And what is the ETA?"

"She should arrive within the hour, sir."

"Good." James left his office and went into his dressing room. He changed his clothes and then checked himself in the full-length mirror. He looked smart in black slacks, a shirt, and a jacket. He wore black, just like his daughter had in the interview.

He pulled on gloves and then headed to his pod. He'd have to make a trip to Earth. But this time, he wasn't filled with disgust. He would see his daughter and give her something to make up for all the wrong that had been done to her. Not that anything could replace the years that had been stolen from them. But perhaps this would make up for his part in not returning sooner to save her.

James had to push down his shame for not protecting his own child. But once he made amends with his tribute, he could show her the truth. And then perhaps she would find her place by his side, fighting for the rebels instead of for the Galatians.

Justina quickly completed the dinner dishes. Despite having a dishwasher, she enjoyed washing her dishes by hand. These days, she found joy in doing many things she never thought she would.

When she was at the consort school, she thought she would lead a dream life filled with riches. But the reality is that who cared about riches when you were a prisoner? She had been groomed as a sex slave, something she hadn't quite understood until receiving a taste of freedom.

Her eyes were opened in ways she had never considered. Now, when she rose in the morning, she dressed in pants and comfortable shirts that didn't reveal her breast or the hint of her pussy. Her shoes were comfortable, and her hair fell down her back in a braid instead of curls that took an hour to perfect.

She didn't wear an ounce of make-up, and when she looked in the mirror, she saw a young girl/woman instead of a whore.

Paris had given her a gift far greater than he could ever understand. It was the gift of freedom. He allowed her to live her life as she pleased without sending her away as they had done to Jayne...

Justina's heart still ached a little for her lost love, but when she looked at Rafe and Karma, Drago and Maddie, and even Paris and Daya, she knew she had never experienced true love. And as wonderful and fulfilling as her life was, she still longed to share it with someone special.

For now, though, she was happy just being able to be her authentic self and not just a caricature of a sex slave. She dried her hands on a dish towel and hung it neatly on the towel rack, grabbed an apple, and then headed out the door to watch the emergence of the golden hour.

It was best to catch the sunset on the hilltop behind her house. Justina grinned as she thought about this house being hers with no one to share it with, no one to dictate how things were expected to be done. And while it was no high-priced apartment in The Washington, it felt more like home than any place she'd ever lived.

As she headed up the hill, she heard M call out.

Hi Aunt Justina

She turned and waved at the little girl and boy that were playing under the watchful eye of Kemistry and Maddie. After waving, she turned quickly to continue on her course before they could invite her to join them.

She liked them well enough but enjoyed her own company better. Maybe she would always be a loner. If so, she still wanted to keep her family and friends close—maybe just not too close.

She bit into her apple as she hiked through a sparse grove of trees. It was quiet, with just the twitter of bird song and the occasional rustle of critters that sought to hide in the bushes.

But solitude was an illusion. They were in a compound heavily monitored and guarded by a team of Special Ops soldiers who were taught to guard without being seen.

She was soon to the core of the apple and tossed it a few feet away.

"Good throw."

Justina's head whipped around.

Her body was tensed when she didn't recognize the voice and only relaxed when she saw the familiar military uniform.

"Sorry if I surprised you," the soldier said good-naturedly.

"You didn't." She shrugged. "I'm not out of the limits..." she looked around. The Galatians had told them all how far they could move about the compound. They had more than enough space, and the hill where she was headed was far but still within the limits.

"No, ma'am."

Justina's head tilted. She looked closer at the soldier, who was only a medium height with a hard, lanky form. That voice wasn't a male's voice... not quite. And it was difficult to see the face of the soldier with a hat pulled low, nearly concealing the eyes. However, their easy smile was plain to see. That smile belonged on the face of someone who was still in their twenties.

"Are you a...man or a woman?" Justina asked boldly.

The soldier's smile only broadened. "Does it matter?"

Justina's mouth opened but then closed. "I guess not."

The soldier took off their hat, and a flop of midnight black bangs flopped forward, nearly falling into vibrant green eyes. The sides of the soldier's hair was shaved short in an obvious military cut, but those bangs spoke of a personality of independence, maybe even rebellion.

"I'm Sgt. Adrian Kelly, ma'am."

Justina realized that Adrian Kelly was a woman. Although not the most feminine one.

Adrian seemed to be reading her mind. "I'm non-binary. So...I'm both or neither."

Intrigued, Justina forgot her normal reserve. "How does that work being a soldier?"

Adrian shrugged. "It doesn't factor—well, except for a few stupid people. But I don't pay attention to stupid talk." Justina could have sworn that the soldier's eyes twinkled.

She knew many people—probably soldiers included, looked down their noses at consorts and their decision to mate with an alien, not to mention living a wealthy lifestyle in a world where the majority of people were struggling just to survive.

"Yeah," Justina said grimly. "I don't care what others think."

Adrian nodded once and then looked toward the distance. "Were you heading for the hill again?" Justina's brow perked up curiously. "I saw you there the other day. The monitors. I watch the circumference."

A shadow passed over Justina's face. "You spy on us?"

"I guess," Adrian replied. "It's the nature of being a guard. But we don't look in places we shouldn't."

"What does that mean?" Justina demanded.

Adrian's smile faded. "It is against our rules to invade your privacy, Miss. We are here to confirm that nothing ever hurts you again." Adrian returned the hat to their head. "I better get back. Have a good evening, ma'am."

"Thank you!" Justina said quickly, causing Adrian to pause. Justina scrubbed her hands across her face and sighed. Memories of death and violence filled her mind.

"Miss? Are you okay?" Justina looked up. She nodded and then looked around. "I think I'm missing the golden hour."

"Golden hour."

"Yes. That's the hour—"

"-before sundown. Or the hour after sunrise."

"Yes." Justina smiled and gave Adrian a surprised look.

"Well, it's not too late to catch it."

Justina nodded and turned. She stopped and turned back around. "Hey...would you...?" Adrian's smile had returned. It was a beautiful smile.

"I'd enjoy that." Adrian took off their hat again and joined Justina. They walked up the hill together, and if Justina thought they would walk in comfortable silence, she was surprised that Adrian spoke easily and even managed to engage her in conversation."

"Aren't you supposed to be working or something," Justina laughed She was surprised she felt so comfortable with someone that was a stranger. It took a lot for her to open up, but when she did, it was only to someone she considered a friend.

They were sitting on the warm grass of the hill, and while many young adults experienced a sense of independence by going out drinking and dating—consorts never did that. This moment was akin to adulting.

"They give us off-duty time." Adrian plucked a blade of grass and fidgeted with it.

"And why are you spending your off-duty time in the woods?" Justina said playfully.

Adrian's cheeks reddened, and Justina's mouth parted.

"Oh..." she said. The soldier had come out specifically to meet her. Justina's heart swelled a bit. Adrian was attractive, but...Wait, why was there a but? Because she'd only ever been attracted to a very feminine woman? Was she attracted to Adrian? There was something androgynous about the soldier, although they also exuded masculinity. It wasn't unlike the way the Galatians were graceful but hard, softspoken while still stern. That was Adrian Kelly in a nutshell.

There was suddenly the call of a monitor, and Adrian quickly looked down. "We have to go!" A second later, Adrian was on their feet, offering their hand to Justina.

By the look on the soldier's face, Justina didn't hesitate to give her hand and was pulled swiftly to her feet. Adrian didn't release her hand and pulled her down the hill back to the compound at a full-out run.

"What is it?" Justina called, fighting to keep up and not trip and fall.

"There's been a breach."

"A breach?"

Adrian never stopped running but managed to look behind them at Justina, and the look in Adrian's eyes shook Justina to her core.

"Is it Ragna?" Justina's voice was less than a whisper.

"Yes. But I'll protect you! Stay with me!"

As Karma and Rafe traveled back to the compound, they listened to reports concerning her interview. She felt optimistic one moment and then had her hopes dashed the next. It had only been a few hours, and depending on which news channel they watched, the response was incredibly positive or filled with suspicion and hostility. Some called her a liar, while others applauded her strength.

Rafe had told her not to put too much stock in what the news reported. He didn't trust the human sources as he considered them too easily swayed by fear or self-preservation.

His monitor sounded, and he looked down at its face, he went red with anger. One moment, he was a deep, beautiful green, and the next, he was red.

"What's wrong?" Karma asked.

"My Commander."

"You're retired. You don't have a Commander. Plus, they fired you when they hired Mayva as head of The Galatian Exchange. Hey! Do you think he's calling to offer you your new job back?"

"It does not work that way. Einar will always be my Commander."

Karma stifled an urge to make a rude sound. The Commander had been nothing but a disappointment to Rafe and his men.

While she was fighting for her life in the hospital and Rafe was at his lowest moment, Commander Einar had disassociated himself from his very own team, even going as far as to approach The Collective to renounce their actions and disavow himself from their fight.

That had been the end of Rafe's respect for his Commander. While he and his men still technically worked for their local government, Einar no longer took their reports or communicated with them. In many ways, it was as if Rafe's team was nothing more than collateral damage that wouldn't be around too much longer and wasn't worth the bother.

Rafe answered the call. "Commander."

"Rafe. I watched the interview that your consort gave."

"I have no consort, sir. Karma is my wife."

Einar's release of air sounded tired. "Yes. As you say. But there is some concern among the Galatians about your wife."

"Sir. When you say concern among the Galatians, are you referring to the Queens?"

There was a slight hesitation. "Yes, Rafe. I've been contacted by Amalia, and she believes that we all should parley."

Karma's annoyance was nearly as strong as Rafe's red tint. So now they wanted to talk? After all those months that they had Mayva Heath spreading lies about her.

"We?" Rafe asked. "When did you ever have anything to do with this?"

"Rafe, I respect you, and I respect your team. You're the best that I've ever commanded and perhaps the best that has ever served The Collective. But I'm no politician. I am a warrior, and my pursuits aren't the same as yours."

How long did it take him to think of that sorry excuse? Karma wondered. He'd turned on his own men. Sold them out to the Queens, and now he wanted to act as an emissary? To hell with him!

"I will speak to my men about it, sir."

"Rafe, I think you fail to see how important this could be—"

"With all due respect, I know what is important."

"Your wife should cease giving interviews."

"She's not a soldier, and neither of us is her commander. She will do as she pleases." Silence stretched out as if Einar was surprised he wasn't getting what he wanted. "Now, if you'll excuse me, sir. I'm getting another call."

"Well, will you think about Amalia's request?"

"Probably not. Goodbye, sir."

Rafe disconnected, and Karma nearly laughed. He touched the communicator answering the new call. "Yes, Drago?"

"What's your ETA?"

Rafe stiffened, drawing Karma's attention. "Approximately forty-five minutes. What?"

"A human male has just arrived in a space pod."

"What do you mean *arrived?*"

"Don't worry, he's been secured, and his pod is nowhere near the compound. He showed up at the compound's military base. Almost like he knew exactly where to go, not to be instantly vaporized. But that's not the important thing. This human did not come alone." Karma's nails were digging into the armrest of her chair as she listened.

"The man arrived with Ragna."

"Oh my Guardian." It was her worst nightmare.

Rafe began pushing buttons on the ship's interface, and a split second later, she was being pressed into her seat as the ship moved in an accelerated speed.

"Rafe, it's not what you think. Ragna is half dead and trapped in an electrical net that is still giving her continuous electric shocks. When we asked the man to turn off the electricity long enough for us to unwrap and then secure her, he refused. The man says he wants to talk to Karma."

"Me?" Karma exclaimed.

"Hell no!" Rafe said.

"Look, there's another wrinkle."

Rafe cursed. "What?"

"A doctor came to treat Daya before her surgery. He's been fully vetted. Paris knows him. But, if he finds out about Ragna being here..."

"Then we can't let him leave."

This time, when Rafe cursed, it was a long string of harsh words spoken in Galatian.

Dr. Brookstone examined the culture in the small glass vile. Daya watched closely, her eyes never left the skin that the doctor had surgically removed and placed in a solution within the glass. It was that piece of skin that would grow and then be precisely sliced and applied to her body—once her old skin was removed, that is.

Paris was beside her, more concerned with the small bandage on the top of her foot. Daya had explained that it didn't hurt. The topical Dr. Brookstone had given her to numb the area hurt much more than the actual biopsy.

One thing that Daya considered fortunate is that the injection had been painful, but by comparison, her burned flesh didn't have nearly as much sensation. Yes, there were times when she felt shooting, stabbing, or even burning pain across her body or face, but that just meant her nerve endings were still alive and letting her know they weren't going anywhere.

"If this survives," Dr. Brookstone said, still staring at the glass vile, "then this will be what covers your entire body."

"I guess foot skin is better than butt skin," Daya joked.

"Much better," Dr. Brookstone agreed. "Butt skin has a different texture. Foot skin is great. I'm just happy that we have enough to biopsy." He gave her a steady look, his pinkish eyes still moved as was characteristic with people stricken with albinism. "If this accepts, then we'll have to harvest more. You might not be able to walk for a while."

"We've already ordered a hovercraft to act as a wheelchair," Daya explained.

"I don't want you in a sitting position for too long. It's not conducive for circulation."

"But I can do it for a little while, can't I?" she was worried she wouldn't be able to stay lying down for two or more months.

"Yes, but don't over tax yourself."

Paris's head suddenly turned toward the window as if he heard something that human ears couldn't detect. A moment later, his communicator sounded. When he answered, the only thing Dr. Brookstone and Daya could hear was the clicking and chirps of the Galatian language.

Suddenly, a loud alarm trilled out across the compound. And while Daya had never been instructed about what to do if an alarm rang, she knew that this was serious.

"What in the hell is that?" Dr. Brookstone asked while looking around.

"Follow me!" Paris shouted. "We've been breached." He grabbed Daya and swiftly lifted her into his arms, knowing her foot was more sore than she wanted to admit.

"Paris," Dr. Brookstone's face went stony. "What have you gotten me into?" But Paris was too busy running out of the room with his woman to answer, and Dr. Brookstone had no choice but to follow.

James Chambers sat in a small, solitary room. There was nothing but one chair and a table. He knew he was being monitored, although none of the equipment was visible. All he would say is he wanted to see Karma Chambers, so the soldiers eventually left him alone.

Of course, no one knew how to take him. He'd shown up in a pod with an unconscious Galatian Queen who was secured in electrical chains. He had left his military crew behind—they knew the deal. He didn't want anyone questioning or torturing his soldiers. They were too valuable to the movement. He could be replaced. They could not.

James sat quietly with one ankle crossed over his knee. He could have been at a lounge listening to jazz for as chill as he looked. But deep down, he was afraid.

Over the years, he had killed and tortured and, in turn, had been tortured and nearly killed. He'd been enslaved, violated and had witnessed the murder of his wife before his eyes. He had jumped into battle with nothing but his bare hands and teeth, not fearing for his life because its only worth was to destroy as many of his enemies as he could before dying.

But sitting here in this room, waiting to see his daughter, was the scariest thing he had experienced since being dragged from her life by the vile aliens. Because saving her was more important than his vow to destroy every alien that dared to set foot on Earth.

Chapter Twenty-One

Drago and Dorf entered the interrogation room. Drago stared at the human who sat so casually in a metal chair. He moved to the table opposite the man, expecting to intimidate him with his size and quiet force—not that it was his intent, it was just what always happened in these situations, especially when dealing with humans. But while this man's eyes followed him, Drago could not sense his emotions.

Well, that was what Dorf was here for.

"Do you know what I am?" Dorf spoke.

"You are a Japoxillian," the man replied. Dorf wasn't altogether surprised. He drove a military pod. He would, of course, know of their existence as well as their abilities because he was far from an average human. He had brown skin, and Dorf immediately detected a mid-western American accent. There were several scars on his face, faded but still prominent. One was at his temple, another across his chin that ran up to his lower lip, and finally, several pit marks on the right side of his jaw.

Therefore, he wasn't military. They would have repaired those scars. Then how did he get the pod, and more importantly, how did he come to possess an unconscious and barely alive Ragna?

"You wouldn't speak to the others. If you don't speak to me, I will take the information from you—with the help of this Galatian." Dorf only gestured to Drago.

The human's eyes moved from Dorf's back to Drago before returning to him.

"You can try."

Sgt. Kelly continued to grip the beautiful woman's hand as they fled through the wooded hillside. It did occur to Adrian that they'd picked the most inopportune time to shoot their shot.

Adrian had first caught sight of the lone consort just a few days before when she had been added to the household. Instead of griping about the addition of more Protectees like the rest of their crewmates, Adrian had volunteered for the tedious assignment of watching the field cameras. Adrian's wasn't as stoic as those actions might infer, it was just that they'd caught sight of the pretty consort at arrival and wanted a closer look.

The consort was little more than a girl with a fresh, make-up-free face. At first, she appeared to be paired with Kendrick. Everyone knew Kendrick, who went a long way in teaching the soldiers that Galatians weren't all freaking scary. He often times used the computer room on the base to handle his duties, but it seemed to Adrian that the Guard really just enjoyed vibing with the humans and learning their ways.

Adrian liked Kendrick, which provided yet another layer of acceptance for a lifestyle that Adrian had at one time frowned upon. It wasn't so much about sex with aliens but the corruption that had made the Galatian Exchange a game for only the wealthy. In Adrian's opinion, the lottery should have only been offered to the poor because who would appreciate the opportunity more? But yet again, the rich had found a way to control the human trafficking of their own daughters.

Mrs. Sigur was the other factor that changed the minds of Adrian as well as many of the other soldiers. The way Lt. and Mrs. Sigur interacted reminded Adrian of the way Mom and Dad acted. They talked, listened, touched, and even laughed with each other, just like any other couple. It didn't take long to see the same went for Lt. Drago and his consort as well as the other paired couples. It wasn't a master-slave lifestyle that everyone speculated about.

But the pretty girl, Justina, was not a part of a pairing. And there was a stoic strength that seemed to exude from her as she went about her day, mostly in solitude.

So, after watching Mrs. Sigur's interview, Adrian had gathered enough courage to finally speak.

And now this had to happen...

The compound had been invaded, and they were going into full lockdown mode. They had to get the pretty woman to safety. There was no way she was going to be injured under their watch!

"Adrian!" Justina gasped. "I can't keep up!" Her heart was pounding in exhaustion but also fear. She had nearly tripped, and only the sheer momentum of Adrian's speed and the hard grip on her wrist had kept her from falling to her knees!

Adrian came to a quick halt, remembering their training of running and marching would have made them far superior in endurance. Looking back at the frightened, wilting girl, Adrian crouched on the ground before them. "Climb on my back."

"What? No—"

"HURRY! We've been compromised!"

Justina jumped into action, wasting no time climbing onto the soldier's back. She was surprised at the hard plains of their body that had been hidden beneath the camo uniform. There was not an ounce of the softness she would have expected from a woman.

It didn't take long for Justina to stop worrying about slowing the soldier down with her added weight. Adrian continued their fast-paced run. It wasn't a jog, but a run!

It seemed that within a minute or two, they were back in the compound heading for Rafe and Karma's house. But the entire clearing was crowded with soldiers in battle gear and holding lasers at the ready. They were in a tight formation, surrounding the entire house. Nearly every single eye was focused on them.

Ignoring them, Adrian lowered her to her feet only once they were outside the door. Justina took a moment to look at Adrian, who barely panted. She wanted to say...something.

"Go inside, Miss." And then Adrian took their place beside another soldier, withdrew their weapon from a back holster, and went into formation.

Justina hurried inside the house. It, too, was filled with soldiers who stood in formation around the perimeter of the interior. She was relieved when she saw Maddie, Kemistry, the children and babies, as well as Runnar's nurse, Daya Porter, and a man that had hair and skin as white as snow. All were standing in a group in the middle of the room.

She hurried to Maddie, who quickly gripped her hand. A look of terror was on her face. She propped her baby up on the opposite hip while the baby watched everything with interest.

"What's happening?" Justina asked, looking around for Paris and noting that Drago was also nowhere in sight.

"Drago said that Ragna was back at the base, and then he told me to stay, and he left." Her face was nearly as pale as the albino man standing nearby, looking perplexed. "I can't do this again, Justina." She was trembling and shaking her head. "I can't—"

"Shh, honey. It won't be like before." She gave her hand one last squeeze but looked around for a weapon and then spotted M a few steps away holding a laser gun. She hurried over to the little girl. "Where is your father's weapons room?"

Instead of answering, M took her through the crowded living room. Soldiers were everywhere, and although they watched, no one stopped their movements. Justina supposed it would have been different if they were heading out the door, but they weren't.

"M!" The nanny called after them, but the little girl ignored her, and the nanny, who was holding Runnar, seemed unsure if she should stay put under the watchful eye of the soldiers or if she should go running after the little girl. With an anguished sigh, she stayed put and snuggled Runnar close.

Kelsie gripped Kemistry's paw with one hand and Bain's with her other while their mother stared at the closed door as if trying to pick up thoughts or emotions from the other side. She had donned a small weapons belt that fit perfectly around her body. Beyond containing a few essentials, two lasers were holstered at her waist.

Dorf had gone with Drago, calling back for her to protect the kids. And Kemistry had almost told him he should stay back and watch the kids himself while she went to defend the compound. After all, she had both wings and both eyes...but she didn't. And not just because she wanted to preserve Dorf's newfound sense of self, but because *she* needed to be the one to watch her children, to confirm that Bain wasn't going into shock or that Kelsie's breathing wouldn't deteriorate, causing her to need a breathing treatment. In a sense, taking care of her children had become her bigger priority.

Once in the weapons room, Justina took stock of what was available before grabbing a pistol. She was surprised when Daya Porter reached past her to grab a long sword. Justina met her eyes.

"There are no more lasers," Daya explained. "Let's get back to the others." Justina nodded, and she and M followed.

Rafe and Karma landed a scant twenty minutes later, and soon after, the pods of his security team, which included Kendrick, also landed. Rafe was in the lead, then Karma, and finally Paris, who had joined the party, and Kendrick walked side by side at her back, reminding

Karma of the protective stance that Galatians took when in guard mode.

"The family is gathered and protected at your house," Paris announced.

"I want to see my kids," Karma said.

"Aye," Rafe agreed, walking fast. Karma was nearly jogging to keep up with him. "I want you nowhere near the base. Stay with the family." He made a quick clicking sound, and then Paris was beside him, leaving Kendrick to take up the rear. "Paris will take you there."

"Wait, where are you going?"

Rafe didn't turn, but his tail bobbed as he continued walking away with big, rapid steps. "I'm going to find out who brought that bitch here, and then I'm going to deal with her."

"Come, we should go," Paris said and then led the way to a transport vehicle that would take her to the compound.

When Rafe entered the observation room, he merely saw the human sitting in a chair, patiently waiting.

Rafe turned to Drago and Dorf. "Who is he?"

"We have no idea," Drago replied. "Facial recognition software hasn't identified him."

"And he knows how to block my reading," Dorf replied.

To this, he turned bodily to Dorf. "What?" But Dorf was already shaking his head. "I connected with him, but all I detected was an irritating humming...the blocking technique that the *Kasperians* use."

"*Kasperians*... How in the hell would he learn that?" Their planet was light years away from Earth, and so small and obscure that one basically would need an invitation to locate it.

Dorf turned back to look at the observation window. "At some point, he would have been trained by one of them. It's no easy feat to block a Japoxillian so completely."

"The only thing the man would say is he wanted to speak to Karma—but he called her Chambers, not Sigur."

"A rebel, then?" Rafe asked while staring at the man through the security cameras.

"Presumably, except why help us?" Drago asked.

"He's not helping us," Rafe replied. "He's helping Karma."

Rafe stormed out of the room. A moment later, he was in the observation room. This time, the man came to his feet. It was as if he recognized the aggression that came from the Galatians and had no intention of being in a vulnerable position. Yet he didn't take a defensive stance, not even when Rafe got so close to his face that they were practically nose-to-nose.

"Who the fuck are you!"

"If you really want to know, then ask Karma Chambers."

Rafe growled. "No. You will tell me!"

The brown-skinned man's eyes didn't flinch. "Do you see these scars around my head? They were made when an Oxilian put his claws on my face and ripped it from my skull. Fuck you, Rafe Sigur. Fuck you all the way to Galatia and the depths of hell! I am far from afraid of you and your kind."

Rafe straightened, his eyes boring into the humans. He spoke the truth. There was no fear, only...disgust.

Rafe inhaled, calming some. "You brought Ragna, trussed like hunted game. And you left her with us—"

"Not you," James interrupted. "I left her for Karma."

Rafe continued to stare into the eyes of the human. He frowned as he suddenly recognized that those eyes were ones he had looked into many times before. Rafe inhaled deeply, scenting the man at his deepest level.

No one knew his mate's scent the way he would. They were one. She was marked as his, but he was marked as hers, and her essence that made her who she was not only a part of Karma but also their son...as well as this man.

Rafe took a step back. "You..."

James's brow lifted. "Me." His eyes narrowed in his first show of hostility. "You fucked my daughter up. But I'm home now." He turned his back and walked to his chair, where he took his seat again.

He gave Rafe a look so chilly that it reminded him of a Galatian Queen who had lost favor with a subject. "Now go fetch my daughter."

Chapter Twenty-Two

The moment Karma entered the house, she ran to M and then scooped her son up into one arm. "Are you alright?!" She asked M, running her hand over her face and making sure that nothing had hurt her.

M simply hugged her. Her arms going around her body. And Karma knew that while she wasn't injured, she had been hurting with worry.

She knelt beside her daughter and hugged her close. "Oh, baby girl. It's going to be okay." Karma stood and looked at her worried friends and family.

"Do you know what's going on?" Maddie asked. "Drago didn't tell me much before he ran off."

"Look. What I know is that a man landed on the compound's military base. That man had Ragna's unconscious body still wrapped in some type of electrified mesh. He dumped her here and then was taken into custody."

"Is it some type of trap?" Maddie asked.

Karma just shook her head. "I don't know."

Paris had moved to Daya, and she was now in his arms, her

courage slipping so she was near tears. He rubbed her back but addressed the room full of people, including the soldiers who listened expectantly.

"We don't know who this man is, but at the moment, he only seems interested in talking to Karma."

No, Mama! M exclaimed, her eyes desperately wide. Runnar, who had been fairly quiet, began to cry at the sight of M's fear. He might have only been just three months old, but in human terms, he was more like a six-month-old and recognized his sister's and mother's anguish and fear. He clung to Karma as if he thought she would put him down and leave again.

Karma hugged her daughter. "Shhh, I'm here, and we're alright. Ragna can't hurt us." M gave her a dubious look, and Karma cupped her face. "Do you see all these soldiers? They won't let anything hurt us. Do you understand?" M nodded. But Karma's face was etched in concern.

Rafe was back in the observation room.

"What?" Drago asked, seeing his brother's deep concern. "How does he know Karma? You know who he is, don't you?"

"Yes. He is Karma's father."

Drago looked at the security screen. "Her father. The reports say he was taken by the Tybernees in one of their last Earth attacks. We saw nothing indicating he had been rescued."

"I don't understand myself. He will only speak to Karma, but there is no way I'll leave him alone with her!"

"Well, if we intend to keep Ragna alive, we're going to need him to turn off the electricity. She won't survive much longer."

Rafe's color darkened. He wanted Ragna dead but by his own hands. The idea of saving her life went against everything he valued. He pulled out his communicator and contacted his wife.

"Karma. There has been a...development."

"Rafe, don't beat around the bush. Tell me!"

"I'm going to send you a picture of this man from the security cameras. I want you to tell me if you know who he is."

"Okay," Everyone was watching Karma quietly, understanding she was the key to this standoff. Karma waited, and in seconds, an image of a black man filled her small monitor.

Karma gasped. It didn't matter how tiny the communicator screen was. She knew this man. She would know him in the dark, and she would know his walk, maybe even the span of his shoulders if she saw him from behind.

"Daddy..." she whispered. "That's my daddy! Rafe...?"

All she heard was a soft growl. Finally, he spoke. "He claims to have brought Ragna for you."

"What?! Where's he been all this time? Show me the picture again!" He did, and she studied the image of her father, finally turning it into a hologram the entire room could see.

Runnar's interest was now on the image, and he was no longer crying but preoccupied with trying to reach for the phantom image.

"Where your father has been all this time is a big mystery."

"Well, I want to see him—"

Rafe's image suddenly filled the screen. "I don't want you anywhere near him. I think it's too convenient. I don't trust anything about it."

"Rafe, I have to talk to him. He's my father!"

"And your father managed to capture a Galatian Queen, a Black Mask. He brought her to the base where you have been hidden—unknown to anyone but our military team. He has proven to be a... unique challenge." Rafe's color lightened with concern. "But yes. You must speak with him. But not here. I need you to go someplace private, and then we will set up a holographic feed.

"Yes." Karma nodded enthusiastically.

"Not in our house. I don't want him to see our kids or to determine anything about us from our surroundings."

"Okay, but I'm sure my father means us no harm."

"We can't know that for sure. Because if his intentions are good, then where has he been all this time."

"You can use our home," Paris interjected. "We haven't done much to it. The man won't find any story within our possessions."

Karma nodded enthusiastically. "Let's go. Please set it up, Rafe. I need to speak to my father and understand all of this."

"Yes. I will set it up."

He was gone, and Karma passed her son to his nanny. Runnar instantly began to cry for his mommy, rejecting even M when she attempted to soothe him. Karma's breasts suddenly began to ache. She had to feed her son. That came before anything else. She took him back, and his cries instantly abated as he clutched her and hiccupped. She moved to sit on the couch and quickly began to nurse him, ignoring everyone else in the room. She just watched her baby, her thoughts calming as she went through this age-old ritual of bonding with her child.

Runnar drank gustily and soon fell into a contented sleep. She kissed the inky black curls on the top of his head and carefully passed him back to his nanny.

By now, everyone in the room had relaxed. Even the soldiers were standing at ease with their weapons holstered. M, Bain, and Kelsie were huddled together, talking very seriously for three children.

Karma's brow furrowed as she told herself that children didn't deserve to live like this. But if not this, then an orphanage or the streets. The only question is, was this type of fear worse?

Paris led Karma to his and Daya's home. It was true that it was as nondescript as a home could get. The furnishings were sparse, with just a love seat and a simple upholstered chair. There was no place to sit that would accommodate Paris's size or tail. But she didn't see him spending time in this room. He would be spending it wherever Daya would be healing.

"This will be perfect," she said. Paris stood by, refusing to leave her alone even though several guards had followed them and were stationed outside the door. She wished they would call back some of the guards. This was her father. There was no way he meant her any harm.

She sat in the loveseat and called Rafe. "I'm ready." She enlarged the image until it was a life-size hologram projecting into the room as if they were right there together.

"Where are the children? I don't want him to know about our family," Rafe spoke.

"They are back at the house. Runnar's been fed and is sleeping, and M is with her friends. And I understand. I won't mention anything about our family."

He nodded, and then she watched as he walked into the security room. She focused on the man sitting in the chair, dressed all in black.

Rafe activated the full-size holographic screen, and she saw her father's eyes light up as her seated image came to him.

James Chambers came to his feet and walked closer to the hologram, ignoring Rafe despite him being the biggest thing in the room. No. In size, he was, but for James Chambers, the biggest thing in that room was the beautiful woman sitting before him.

"Baby Girl..."

Karma instantly broke into sobs. "Daddy. Is it really you?"

He nodded. "It's really me." James's voice was filled with emotion. "You are so beautiful. You look so much like Nina. Oh, baby girl, I am so sorry you had to see what was done to your Mama and then me being taken away." His eyes glistened with emotion. Karma longed to reach out, to hug him, but more importantly, to be hugged by him."

Her father had obviously aged in the time since she had last seen him, but he still looked remarkably good. There were visible scars on his face that made her wonder, but they didn't detract from his good looks. He was tall and stood just as straight and proud as ever. Somehow, that made her proud, he was a prisoner but still looked as if he was in control.

His very short hair was shaved close around the back and sides with finger dreds along the top. That was new. He'd had a neat Afro the last time she'd seen him and had never been partial to having a shaved head. But it looked good on him.

What hadn't changed was the mustache and trimmed beard. Her father looked good, actually better than expected.

"How is this possible?" she asked.

"I was kidnapped and sold into slavery by the Tybernees. From there..." his mouth formed a grim line, "It's a very long story. A story that I will tell *you*," He looked at Rafe for the first time. "And you alone."

Rafe ignored the comment. He was being courteous due to the man being his wife's father. But there was only one boss here, and it wasn't James Chambers.

Karma searched her mind for relevant questions, but it all centered around how he'd managed to return to Earth. After a moment, she just gazed at a man who had basically returned from the dead.

"You look good, daddy," she sniffed back her tears.

"You do, too, Karma. You are a beautiful woman."

"Are you okay?"

"I am now. Seeing you."

She nodded. "It's a miracle."

"You remembered your church lessons."

"Of course. We went to church as often as we could."

"Sometimes we couldn't go when it was freezing out."

Karma laughed a bit and wiped the tears that streamed from her eyes. "That time Mama slipped on the ice, and she turned right around—"

"And she said, 'No, man. No!'" he finished with a chuckle.

"We couldn't afford a computer to watch services online."

James shook his head, once again sad. "Our church was so poor they couldn't have set up a video feed. Most of their money went to helping the poor not freeze to death during the winter months."

"We were basically rich, having a regular place to live."

He looked stricken. "We were far from rich."

"I've been out on those streets, Daddy." She kept the accusation from her voice but was unable to keep it from her eyes. "I know the difference."

James Chambers's eyes closed, and he sighed. "I know. I couldn't do anything about that then. But... I hope to do that for you now."

"Is that why you brought Ragna?" she shook her head with another frown. "But how did you even find her?" She didn't say it—had never even said it to Rafe, but she knew he still had others out searching for her. "How did you do it?" How did a human do what Black Ops Galatians hadn't been able to do?

"That's easy. I'm part of the Resistance."

Karma was smart. She knew whoever brought Ragna here would have to be connected in some way with a powerful organization. What wasn't quite so easy was connecting her father—her sweet, protective, family-oriented father with a group that bombed, murdered, and tortured anyone who got in the way of ridding the planet of aliens—*all* aliens.

"When you say the Resistance, you are referring to the ones who want to kill the Galatians and end The Galatian Exchange."

James Chambers looked at his daughter unapologetically. "Yes. That is the Resistance that we are both referring to, daughter."

Chapter Twenty-Three

Karma let her father's words sink in. *I'm part of the Resistance...*She eventually nodded. Her father's eyes took in her expression.

"Look, Karma. There is a lot that we have to discuss, a lot that I want to tell you." His eyes flitted to where Rafe stood nearby, projecting the image of his daughter to him instead of allowing her in the room as if he were the monster. James returned his attention to his daughter. "And I understand your...circumstances and how my situation might affect you.

"But I brought that creature to you as a first step in reconnecting. It's up to you what you choose to do with it. Keep it, give it to *him*." James gestured with his head to Rafe. "But that's my gift to you."

Karma just shook her head. "I can understand you can't reveal a lot. But, Daddy, you've been gone for over a decade. Alive, but not *here*—not with me. Why?"

James looked down.

After nearly a minute, Karma stood. "Thank you. I accept your gift." She moved to turn off her communicator when he eventually looked up.

"Do you know what PTSD is?"

A shadow fell across Karma's face. She nodded slowly. "Yes."

"By the time I returned to Earth, I had been gone for four years. Most of that time was me being broken down so my humanity no longer existed. My mind was shattered. I am shattered. I am not the same man you knew, the man that was married to your mother, the man that was your Daddy." His voice began to tremble, although his eyes remained dry.

"I was consumed with locating my baby girl. I fought to get back to Earth just so I could find you and to hell with anything and anyone else! And when I got here, I was able to find that you were in an orphanage—a real orphanage and not some corner whorehouse. And as much as I despise government-run facilities—anything run by this fucking government, I knew you were at least safe... safer than if you were being raised by a man that wakes up screaming and fighting off invisible creatures." James sighed and ran a hand over his face.

"I-uh. I'm sorry. I'm sorry I wasn't there for you, that I didn't tell you I was alive. I felt then that it was better not to be a constant question about why. Why is my father not raising me? Is triggered by... memories he gets when he sees me?"

Karma sighed softly. "But you don't feel that way any longer?"

"I'm not the same man." He met her eyes—at least the pixelated ones. "But I am still not the father you remember. You will have to trust me when I tell you that. Keeping my distance from you has been the hardest thing I've ever had to do. Never think that I don't love you." James sighed and seemed to get his emotions under control.

"There's more. A lot more. But due to the sensitive nature of my... circumstances—that is an explanation I will have to save for another time. And I hope that there will be more conversations between us—" James glanced at Rafe. "... and just us. What you do with that information is up to you."

Karma blew out a long breath but then returned to her seat. "You want a relationship with me? Are you planning to leave the Resistance? Because before there ever was a threat from the Galatian Queens, the biggest threat I faced was from *your* group. I had to have guards in case the resistance shot me or blew up the building where I lived. Consorts have to go into hiding after their contract ends."

James continued to watch her calmly, and Karma's brow dipped in anguish. "Well? Aren't you going to deny it?"

"I would enjoy having that conversation with you. But that's a conversation between the two of us." He clasped his hands behind his back. "Now, there is the matter of the creature that I presented."

Damn, he is calm, Karma thought. She felt like she was on an emotional rollercoaster. She didn't know whether she wanted to scream at him or run up and hug him. And yet, there was one thing she absolutely understood: PTSD.

Many men and women were on the streets with untreated mental illnesses. Seeing people crying and screaming was part of a norm that you learned to ignore. Daddy had said he was shattered. Broken.

And that was what allowed her to keep her opinions to herself.

"Yes, let's talk about the murderous creature you managed to capture, injure, and drop onto a Black Ops military site."

James nodded. "Aptly put. The creature's heart should give out within approximately two more hours—give or take an hour if that should be your choice. You see, *it* is being administered enough electricity to light up the entire Washington Hotel. I can assure you the alien that hurt you is under a tremendous amount of pain. It still retains enough consciousness to feel every electrical pulse, every burn, every heart-stopping jolt."

Karma's eyes closed, and she relived that night of terror when Ragna and Mayva had tortured her and her family. Her eyes opened.

"Mayva Heath. Do you know where she is?"

"Do you mean that human who helped the lizard?"

Lizard. Creature. His dislike for the Galatians was obvious and insulting. She was happy he knew nothing about Runnar. What did he really think of her murdered baby? Would he be angry if he knew she'd named her baby after him? Surely, he was happy with the idea that there was no "lizard" creature out there that had his direct bloodline.

No. As long as he was part of the resistance, she couldn't have a relationship with James Chambers. He was no longer the daddy she had loved and respected. Maybe he did love her, but he was also a danger to her and to her family.

"Yes," she replied. "The traitor. I can't quite call her human..." In her opinion, she was as much a creature as her father considered Ragna.

James snorted. "And you want to find out what the creature knows about her whereabouts? Then we should probably turn off the electricity much sooner than later. In my pod is a lockbox." He explained the device that would turn off the electricity and finally provided the lockbox's combination.

Rafe spoke in Galatian to the security camera, sending Drago and a small team to retrieve the device from the pod. He then looked at his wife's father.

"This interview is over. Karma, do you have anything else to say to your father before we...question him?"

Karma's breath caught in her throat with a jolt. "Rafe, he's my father..."

"I haven't forgotten. I will speak to you later."

James just gave him a bored look.

The searing pain coursing through Ragna was unimaginable. Every nerve ending in her body felt as if it was being sliced with razors. She couldn't even manage a scream, only soft whimpers.

She lay seizing on the cold cement floor of a small cell. Blood had streamed from her nose and lips, and on some level, Ragna knew she was going to die. She prayed to the Great Guardian for death. She'd never felt such pain in her entire life.

Please...mercy, she prayed. But there was no mercy. Just the smell of hot piss and the feel of razors cutting through her. And it never ended.

Mercy...

Karma turned off the communicator and stood. She looked at Paris with fear etched across her face.

"Paris, I think Tam might be compromised. We exposed Ragna and Mayva, but in doing so, we also showed Tam—"

"And she is training with the Rebels," Paris completed. His color faded in concern.

"My father is in the Resistance, and he knows too much."

"I will send her a message."

"Then I want you to take me to where you have Ragna locked up."

"Rafe won't like that. He wants you nowhere near her."

"You'll be there to protect me."

Paris managed a semi-humanlike scowl. "And who will protect me from Rafe..."

He led Karma to a truck as he spoke in Galatian through his communicator, leaving instructions for the message to be delivered to Tam. Haru would be devastated if something happened to his human. And honestly, it would be devastating to each of them.

Chapter Twenty-Four

Rafe walked into the cell. Two Galatian Guards had accompanied him in order to deactivate the electric net encasing Ragna. But for the moment, he had them wait outside. He wanted to see her alone.

She lay convulsing on the wet floor. His nose told him it was wet with piss and blood. His nose also told him she probably wouldn't be alive much longer.

And still, she managed to mutter words. He wasn't sure if she was even conscious, but she uttered the same word repeatedly in Galatian.

Mercy.

Did she even know he was present, that she was actually asking for mercy from him?

He knelt but at a distance of a few feet. He knew not to be trapped in an electrical loop with her. Although, if he was, his harness contained a simple device that discharged electricity safely.

In other words, Galatian Guards had known about the electric net for years and had already developed a method to make it as harmless as a child's toy. But as proficient as the Black Masks were—and he could admit that they were dangerous fighters—they had not learned the many technological advances that gave the male guards such advantages.

He gazed at her, trying to determine the depths of his hatred. He certainly had never hated anyone as much as he did this individual. He had fought the most heinous of pirates and ruthless traffickers, but true hatred was personal.

"Ragna." His voice was hard. "You should know where you are. You are here with me *and* my wife." He snorted, drew mucus from his sinuses, and then spat on her. It landed in her face.

"As long as you are in my custody, you will never know mercy."

She continued to beg for mercy, obviously no longer aware of her surroundings.

Rafe stood and called to the two Guardians. "Deactivate the net. Make sure she doesn't die." He wanted her to be aware, to hear his words as well as those of his wife. Karma's father was right about one thing: Ragna was hers to punish. What she had taken from Karma couldn't be quantified.

Karma stood outside the cell where Ragna, who was no longer being electrocuted, lay in one of the military cells cuffed to the wall. Two Galatians were stationed outside per Rafe's orders.

The door was unlocked for her, and Paris accompanied her into the small room. Ragna lay curled on the ground. A convulsion periodically caused her body to jerk. Her harness was missing, and strips of scalded scales could be seen crisscrossing her body, an indication that the harness had probably been destroyed by the electricity.

Karma's eyes scanned every inch of the woman. No emotion showed on her face as she took in the Galatian's horrific condition. Her eyes were closed and appeared swollen. Blood had seeped from them, which had darkened to near black. Her leather-like skirt was still intact, but the pleats revealed the sorry condition of her lower body. Her misshapen tail was hideous.

Where M had cut most of it off with the tingsha had left an uneven stub. But a new tail was growing from that stub—or had been until the electricity had killed it. It was a disgusting deformity now.

Her boots were in shreds, and Karma could see her repaired foot —also courtesy of M and her tingsha was bent at an unnatural angle as if it no longer merged with the old flesh. She was going to lose that foot—among other things.

Karma continued to stare, remembering her first sight of the tall, arrogant Galatian and how she had been unmasked to reveal brown scales that had none of the beautiful colors and intricate designs of their male counterparts. Galatian Queens weren't special to look at. Without the beautiful scales and designs, there was probably not much individuality to allow them to stand out.

Is that why they hated humans so much? Because human females came in different hues and shapes and with countless levels of beauty?

Even at her best, Ragna was nothing much to look at, and Karma now had a keen eye for Galatians. Each Galatian male she knew was beautiful in different ways; Paris was tall and lean with as much grace as a dancer, Kendrick carried himself with a cocky swagger and could mimic human expressions to such a degree that it was alarming —as well as charming. Drago was thick and muscular, but as scary as that was, he was just as sweet and caring. And then there was Rafe, with chiseled features and wiry muscles that allowed him speed and agility.

But what did this female have to offer in light of such beauty?

"I hope you can hear me," Karma finally spoke. "You've been brought here and placed at my very feet. You tried to run and hide from Rafe and his team—from Galatian Guards worldwide. And you're still lying here at my feet.

"I can tell you that your injuries are more than likely permanent. You wanted your tailback, but that's gone. So is your foot. And I doubt if you can see." Karma saw her mouth move slightly but could hear nothing. Karma didn't dare go closer, though. Even chained and unconscious, Karma didn't trust that the Galatian couldn't still strike out.

"What are you saying?" Karma asked, not expecting clarification to come from the Galatian. It was Paris who responded.

"She is asking for mercy."

Karma's eyes widened in surprise. "Mercy? Ha!" She chuckled mirthlessly. She suddenly stopped laughing to glare at the fallen creature. "You're pathetic. I had the lives of my family, my children, and *myself* to think about, and I still maintained my pride! How dare you ask for mercy for *yourself*! Not an unborn child. But for yourself. You had not an ounce of mercy for me when you pointed that laser at my pregnant belly and slaughtered my baby!" Karma's voice finally cracked, and she sensed Paris move forward toward her. Karma turned her head and held up her hand to keep him at bay, all without looking at him.

"I'm okay. We can go now." She turned to look at Ragna again. "But don't worry. I will be back, and you'll have plenty more opportunities to beg."

Paris was quiet as they left the cell and headed back to the transport. "Karma," he finally spoke.

She looked at him quickly, a hard expression on her face. "What? You don't approve?"

"I just wonder. Does this help? Seeing her like that, does it help?"

Karma didn't answer.

When they returned to the compound, the soldiers had already dispersed, leaving the family with a shadow crew. M ran from the yard where she was sitting with Bain and Kelsie and slammed into Karma, her arms wrapping tightly around her.

"It's okay, honey. Everything is okay. That bad lady cannot hurt anyone. She is a prisoner, and she has strong Galatians keeping her right where she is."

M was content to be held by her mother. She was happy to hear those words, but it wouldn't stop her from keeping a laser hidden in her bedroom.

Later, Karma held a meeting in her living room with the other members of the family, and at the moment, that included Dr. Garry Brookstone. Rafe and Drago weren't there as they were occupied with questioning James Chambers. That stayed at the back of Karma's mind, but as much as it bothered her to think this way, James wasn't part of the family she needed to safeguard. He'd been safeguarding himself for years, as had she, and she was certain that both would continue to do so. Separately.

"Ragna is here. I've been to see her, and it is no trick. She is a prisoner." Karma explained the Galatian's condition. M's head lifted in pride at the description of the tail and foot. Karma hadn't excluded the children from the meeting. In this circumstance, age shouldn't be a factor in keeping a person in the dark. In the dark, fears just had a way of multiplying.

"What are your plans with this woman?" Garry asked. "Her injuries seem to be substantial, and if you haven't killed her yet—the matter of her life might be moot."

"No one has said anything about killing her," Karma replied.

"And even if someone did," Maddie glared at the doctor, "it would be within our right to do so. In this world, it's an eye for an eye."

Garry nodded, raising both hands. "I met no offense, and I'm in no position to pass judgment. However, I am a physician who has specialized in combat medical skills. I'm also proficient with the treatment of Galatian physiology. I would like to offer my services."

Paris was standing beside Daya, his hand on her shoulder. She was still trembling. He could only imagine she had not ever thought to have to face something like this again. He wanted to gather her in his arms and hold her—but that would be later when they were alone.

He turned his attention from Garry Brookstone to the others. "I trust Garry emphatically. He repaired my injuries during a battle several years ago, and I have witnessed the work he does. I would not have him treat my mate if it was not so."

Everyone stared at Daya. It was the first time Paris had openly referred to her as his mate. Next, eyes moved to Justina, who met them with defiance.

Paris continued. "I would appreciate any assistance you can provide on keeping our prisoner alive—at least for now."

A shadow crossed Garry's face. He didn't like those words. He was a doctor even though he was also, at times, a soldier. He'd taken lives—many of them. But one thing for certain is once he put on his physician's cap, he took the saving of lives seriously.

"It is out of respect for my mate that you haven't been chained right along with Ragna," Rafe stated. He saw the subtle clenching of the human's jaw. He was certain it was the reference to Karma being his mate. The man's hatred for Galatians was obvious.

It didn't bother Rafe. He was used to the dislike of the Rebels. What concerned him was that this man was Karma's father, and for that reason, he had to tread carefully.

That didn't mean he intended to allow him to just get away with infiltrating their Black Site—especially since he was part of the Rebellion. If this man expected to walk away from this situation, then he was going to have to reveal how he'd gotten the information about their location.

"I've accomplished what I've come here for."

"You seem unconcerned," Drago spoke from where he stood by the doorway. "Rafe may be more understanding of his relationship with Karma. But I am not."

"Is this good cop, bad cop?" James asked.

"You've picked a poor time for sarcasm," Rafe said. "I am not the good cop." Rafe gestured back to Drago with a slight gesture of his head. "He is."

Drago came forward, past Rafe, until he was standing a foot from James. James, who was also standing despite the chair behind him, had to crane his head to meet the Galatian's eyes.

"I'm not afraid—"

Drago gripped his shoulder and pushed him until he was sitting. James struggled, but it was fruitless. He went sprawling into the chair, and still, he glared at the Galatians in hatred. Drago kept hold of his shoulder while turning to look at Rafe. He spoke in Galatian, turning orange in amusement.

"I wouldn't take his actions so lightly," Rafe replied in Galatian to Drago's comments that the human apparently had a set of big balls.

"Don't worry about my fucking balls!" James snapped. He jerked hard enough that Drago released his grip—although the fact that Drago released him was mostly due to his surprise. This man had understood Galatian.

Rafe moved to stand next to Drago.

"I see that you are a unique individual. I don't want to hurt you, James Chambers, and it's not because you are my wife's father. I also don't care if that fact angers you. Your daughter and I are mated out of an act of love and not due to a contract or the fulfillment of some family agreement."

James watched the alien without comment. Strangely, his demeanor calmed, although his dislike hadn't. Rafe continued.

"The reason I don't want to hurt you is I think you have a lot to tell. And I believe your story doesn't have to end here. But you should also understand that my biggest priority is to my family—and that includes your daughter. And to protect that family, I will end anyone who puts them at risk. Right now, this includes you.

"You found our site, and only my most valued soldiers know about this place. Not even my Commander can find me. So, when I ask you how you were able to find your daughter, you should think carefully before using your sarcasm skills. Because once I take off your head, one of two things will happen. One, you're dead, and I get no answers. Two, your crew comes for us, and if that happens, it means you've put your daughter in danger. *You*, not me."

James sighed. "I'm not afraid of death. I paid a huge price to gain that condition. It cost me my daughter. As long as I have something near and dear to me, then I'm compromised." James stared into Rafe's eyes with a hard but sad glint in them. "My daughter won't understand that. But maybe you do."

Rafe did. But he didn't respond. If he didn't have Karma, Runnar, and M to think about, he would have never put an end to his search for Ragna. Loving and being loved was a joy he couldn't describe. But having them hurt was more pain than he could imagine.

"Your assessment might be right," James said almost reluctantly. "Others would come for me, and there would be a deadly battle. So, I will tell you what you want to know. I will tell you how I came to possess the she-bitch, and how I knew where my daughter was located."

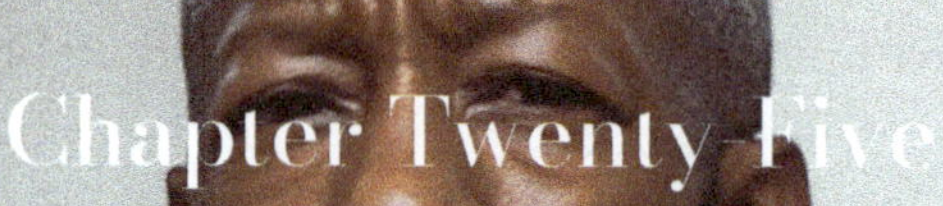

"**A**s I told my daughter, I am a member of the Rebellion. Although, that's your word for what we are. We go by another title. In this organization, I am more than just a soldier—just as you are more than just a Guardian."

"So, you hold rank?" Rafe asked.

"Yes," James replied simply. "I assume that you think there is a mole in your organization. If there is, they did not assist me or my organization. It's much simpler. The majority of my soldiers are ex-military—many of which were Black Ops. Once they became disenchanted with being treated like the alien's custodial staff instead of the warriors they were trained to be, many came to us.

"They knew we had the talent and the strength to rid our Earth of your presence. It was just a matter of finding like-minded people."

Rafe was tiring of his not-so-passive-aggression. He used to being hated—by most beings in the universe, so James wasn't exactly hitting home with the verbal attacks. The butcher didn't care what the cow thought. However, the best-case scenario was not to have to threaten the father of the woman he loved.

Rafe did find it very interesting that James had begun his story by stating that there were no traitors on his team. Nothing the man said could ever convince him of anything different—not when it came to the human Guardians—or what was also known as his personal Black Ops team.

The Galatian Guards were proud of their soldiers, but their human Guardians were the most elite of any soldier on Earth or outside of it.

James was still talking, almost boasting. "We value *all* members of our organization, unlike you. And that is from the best-trained killers to the mildest mannered school teacher." He paused to let that sink in. He didn't mind letting the aliens know how far their reach went. They were everywhere, and it would be impossible for the lizards to weed out their members.

James had made it his business to understand the Galatians, which is why he didn't lie about any of these facts, why he relished letting the head lizard in charge understand their importance. He had come here knowing they would detect deception. But that didn't mean he had to be completely transparent.

"But you wanted to know how I got her here. Getting the she-bitch here was a simple matter. We are friends with the team that guarded her and that wench who sided with her."

Rafe suppressed his surprise at those words. Many of the Queen's guards were those favored humans that had been taken into the family as babies but who were generally discarded when they grew and no longer interested the Queens. Yes, at times, Queens took on humans as if they were pets. It was another thing best left unknown by the human population. When a Queen was unable to fulfill her maternal instincts the natural way, they sometimes resorted to doing it by other means.

The point is these human offspring were generally very loyal as they had been given the best education, government jobs, and top military training. But being ultimately discarded by an emotionless

Galatian family who took you from your own kind could also backfire —which evidently had happened with Ragna.

Rafe studied James but felt as if he spoke the truth. Still, he wanted to test him by baiting him a bit. "Then the very same military that you and your team have attacked are also in your pockets? Humans that you have killed and maimed have reached out to help you? That makes no sense," he scoffed.

James appeared mildly annoyed. "I never said they are in our pockets. I said we are friends. Or better put, some of them are interested in converting to our side. Your kind hasn't figured out what it means to treat others with common courtesy. Simply put, the lizard that I captured forced her team of guards to go against their human nature." James shrugged but was far from ambivalent. "It was her oversight to misjudge our ability to be compassionate."

James Chambers was very misguided. Just because a being didn't show emotion did not mean they didn't experience it. But his words did sound accurate in reference to Ragna. She always took things too far—pushing him to be what he had no desire to be, as well as her ruthlessness when it came to attaining status. He could only imagine what she had forced her human soldiers to do in order for them to turn her into their own enemies.

When Rafe replied, it was with the knowledge that his words would not matter. "You should know that no two Galatians are the same. Just like I can't judge all humans because there was once a serial killer called Jack the Ripper, or a Hitler, or a Thomas Dorst." James didn't comment. "Is that how you found us?" Rafe continued.

Him locating Ragna was one thing, but delivering her to his front door was quite another. How had he found them? Was he going to say their military was so mistreated that they had turned on his team?

He would refuse to believe that, even if James spoke those words and he didn't detect a lie. His Black Ops teams weren't mere soldiers but had been recruited not only for their ability but also due to their special circumstances...

When a child's family was destroyed by a rebel's bombs, a Guardian team swept in and offered them not just a home but a means for revenge. No one trained harder or fought with more tenacity than a person who hated their enemy with every ounce of their being.

It was the difference between how the males did things and the way the Queens did. The Galatian men offered their soldiers the ability to become highly trained human Guardians—a prestigious title impossible to attain unless hand-picked by a Galatian Guard.

He waited for the human to lie.

"Like I said. No one on your team gave you up. We didn't need them to. You can never be completely safe or stealth as long as there are those who know where you order your equipment, who monitor the physicians who specialize in trauma, who know when a shipment of building supplies has been distributed but the delivery site never recorded—and most importantly, when over a hundred Special Forces soldiers are suddenly removed from duty, and their whereabouts left undisclosed." James smiled mirthlessly while Rafe's breath stopped in his throat.

"And when you have a number of soldiers that gave their lives at a battle at The Washington Hotel where hundreds of Black Masks massacred them just so they could target one lone woman..." James's lips pursed, and he paused before his eyes glinted with accusation. "Well, you have the recipe for a whole lot of deserters. And those deserters became our forensic spies. They no longer work for you, but they know how you operate. And *that* is how I found you."

Rafe caught himself before he grew pale, but he was sure that James had seen his scales lighten before he corrected his mood back to a vibrant green. What the man said made sense. He, nor anyone on his team had been tracked, but eyes had been watching for any suspicious activities.

He cursed to himself. Of course, he would only reach out to the best physicians—ones he knew by reputation based on their experience out on the field. And where did they acquire the supplies to fortify the compound—not to mention the hundreds of humans he'd taken from other missions? Fuck. He had trusted his men to be discreet, and they had been, but he had not realized how, even with stealth, he had still left footprints.

"And what are your intentions? Now that you have found us?"

James's jaw clenched almost imperceptibly. "I want a relationship with my child. I want to rebuild all that we lost."

"You're our enemy!" Rafe snapped in outrage. "Do you really think we'd just open the door and let you in?"

"I'm your enemy—not my daughter's."

Rafe leaned forward as an inkling of an idea came to him. "You never intended to be released. You intended to stay here with us."

"With my daughter," he glowered.

Rafe laughed. "Your daughter is with me. That is how relationships work. You can't be with her without being with me as well."

"Bullshit!" James snapped, losing control of the slight reign he had on his emotions. "If my daughter doesn't choose to come away with me, it's because you've held her as a prisoner! It's because a lizard alien has no idea that family will always outweigh your over-extended ego!"

Rafe smirked once and then turned his back on the human as he walked out the door. He had one thing right: Karma would choose family over anything else.

"My First Lieutenant will show you to your cell."

"I want to speak to my daughter! Face to face!" James shouted after him.

Rafe addressed Drago in Galatian as he left the interrogation room. The human might be able to understand his words, but it didn't matter.

"Make sure he has a cot and food."

"Aye," Drago nodded before storming towards James with zip ties, ready to cuff the prisoner.

Garry Brookstone was in the truck, seated next to a soldier who was driving him to the headquarters where the female Galatian was locked up. Garry resisted looking around, but he was calculating.

He did not think about the injured Galatian—he didn't care much about her after what he'd seen earlier in the interview Karma Sigur had given. That Galatian had aimed a laser at a pregnant woman's stomach with every intention of killing both her and her baby—succeeding in the latter.

His ploy was just to get away from the others long enough to make his escape. He was a soldier and knew the deal even though no one had yet to say it.

None of them had contacted the Collective or the Queen's Council to report that Ragna was injured and in their custody. They were going to break the truce The Collective had put into place, meaning he was in the middle of a great big shit storm.

They were not going to allow him to leave here with the information he knew. Even though Paris had a fondness for him—it wouldn't outweigh his loyalty to his Commander and team. If Garry knew anything about Paris Frenchman, he knew this. The man was a devoted soldier more than a good friend.

That meant Garry had to get out of there while he had an opening.

The problem is he had been escorted here by soldiers and didn't have his own vehicle. As a military-trained physician, he knew he would need an aircraft versus a truck. He could be on a deserted island for all he knew.

For the first time in a long time, he doubted his intelligence. Why had he gotten involved with Paris, knowing he served under Rafe Sigur? While Rafe wasn't a wanted criminal, he was the catalyst of a possible civil war.

He should have steered clear but was so curious when Paris had actually asked him for his help. And once he'd seen Daya Porter, he knew he could improve her quality of life. It still sickened him that she had been left to live with those injuries.

At the heart of everything, Garry knew he was a softie. How could he not be with the childhood he'd had? Treated as a leper, bullied, and overlooked by his family, he had worked on his body and then his mind.

Now, at six foot five, the man with albinism was as sculpted and strong as any "normal" man, and despite his strange white skin, white hair, and pink eyes, he was better than average-looking. More importantly, Garry was smart. He had always been at the top of his classes and was now a celebrated specialist in his field. But he was also a fighter who used his skills to help those who couldn't help themselves.

He considered himself to be a brave man. But he was also smart enough to know when it was time to get out of dodge.

He had a plan. Once he determined the location of the pods, he would then visit the prisoner, pretend he'd left important equipment back at the compound, and pretend to need to return. What he had in his favor was he was considered an ally—a protectee as well as a protector. As a doctor, he was always given license to move freely because who would want the responsibility for a person's injuries going untreated... or worse, just in order to question a doctor's actions. Hell, he could make up anything, and what soldier would question him?

Yes, he had no doubt he would be able to break away from his escorts long enough to hijack a pod.

A short time later, when Garry finally arrived at the cell that housed the Galatian Queen, he felt confident. He had spotted the pods, ingratiated himself with the two guards that had escorted him, and had determined an excuse for why he would need to leave the prisoner.

But then everything changed when he saw the broken, half-dead Galatian Queen. She was unconscious, half nude, and sprawled out on a dirty cement floor, secured by a heavy chain attached to the wall.

She had swollen as her organs began to shut down. Her breathing was shallow and periodically stopped. The most horrific thing was her scales no longer looked like scales but like food.

She had been cooked alive.

That is all he could think. She had to be in excruciating pain. When he knelt before her, he could smell cooked flesh.

At that moment, his training had kicked in as he barked out orders for this piece of equipment or that gadget. Her heart stopped beating, and he got it going again with more electricity and well-placed pounding to her chest.

When her breathing evened out, he set up a blood transfusion with himself as a donor, as well as three other soldiers.

Garry worked on his patient for most of the night before the first signs of a chrysalis began to form.

"Unchain her now! I need to get her to the nearest pool."

"I—doctor, we can't—" A soldier sputtered. A Galatian guard stood nearby, never speaking, never moving, only watching.

"Which one of you want to answer to Rafe Sigur when his prisoner dies because you wouldn't do what I say?"

The Galatian wordlessly unlocked the chains. They fell heavily to the floor, and Garry quickly lifted the half-dead woman who was showing the very first spark of life since his arrival.

Even with the woman in his arms, Garry had no problems following the parade of Guards that led him to the barracks where the pool for the Galatians was located. Garry didn't take off his shoes but deftly climbed the rocks and stepped into the pool. Luckily for him, he had stepped into cool waters instead of the hot spring. A moment later, he released Ragna, watching as she sank beneath the water's depth. But within seconds, she floated to the top. As he watched, more chrysalis began to form, spreading across her limbs like white tendrils.

It was fascinating, but he had watched this more times than he could count. Still, he couldn't take his eyes off the broken creature. Garry backed away until his back hit the rocks, and he was helped out of the pool by two soldiers. He saw several guards were now surrounding the pool, and before long, the barracks were filled with humans and Galatians who guarded the prisoner.

It wasn't necessary. The chrysalis would be a far better prison than any chains ever could.

Chapter Twenty-Six

Dorf pulled the blanket up securely around Kelsie. She was sound asleep, but the apparatus beneath her nose that allowed her to breathe easier didn't seem to be helping much anymore. With every breath, she seemed to have to forcibly pull oxygen into her little chest. He sighed and then walked into Bain's room. He was also sound asleep with his covers kicked off one foot.

Dorf pulled the covers up, and his son stirred and then settled back to sleep. He was happy the children hadn't been so adversely affected by the day's events that it disturbed their sleep. But he still worried. He worried about Kelsie's surgery and, of course, her declining quality of life. He knew the surgeons were the best and needed to prepare her new lungs, but she was suffering—both of his children had suffered so much. How would this event affect Bain with his deep-seated trauma at not only witnessing his mother's murder but also being nearly killed by his own father? He was trying to acclimate to this new life, but anything could set him back, could even crack his fragile psyche.

Dorf padded quietly out of the room and to his bedroom. He

couldn't stand the thought of his children feeling the deep depression he experienced almost every single day. With Ragna being at the compound, it had opened up a wound that was barely closed.

He closed his eyes and tried to get control of his emotions before entering his bedroom. It took a remarkably long time before he could convince himself that everything was alright.

When he finally walked into the room, Kemistry was preening her feathers, and there was a soft layer of down on the floor surrounding her. He had to pause momentarily just to absorb her beauty. He was so lucky someone so pure and unaffected by the ugliness of the world had chosen him—a man who had a hard time shaking the trauma of the past few months.

Kemistry flapped her wings, sending the feathers fanning out around her, and Dorf moaned softly. Their room was layered in fluffy clouds of white and blue. Together, they made a beautiful living canvas with their feathers and down. Soon, they would gather it, and Kemistry would make another nest—hopefully for M this time.

Her expression froze, and her pleasant smile slowly melted away. "Are you okay, Dorf?"

He walked forward and spread his one wing and then enclosed her against him. He rested his head against her shoulder but said nothing.

Kemistry rubbed her cheek against him. "Dorf, it will be okay. Ragna can't hurt us."

He shuddered. "I have too much to lose..."

"Oh, honey."

"She has to die. It can go no other way. She must die, or we are all in jeopardy."

"I'm sure Rafe will do the right thing. No one wants her dead more than him."

He looked up and met her eyes. "He wants her dead, but he fears The Collective. With M, Runnar, and Karma, as well as all of us to look after, he is second-guessing himself."

Kemistry looked surprised. "Did he tell you this, or are you reading it from him?"

"He hasn't said anything. I don't think he even wants to admit it. He could give in to his urge to kill Ragna, but The Collective would sentence him to death, and there are too many people to keep this a secret."

"No one from Rafe's team would ever speak of this outside of the compound—"

Dorf shook his head. "There is no team more loyal, but there is an old human saying that there is no such thing as a secret if more than one person knows it. It only takes one wrong word..."

"Oh no," Kemistry shook her head. "What do we do? We can't let that monster loose after the way she slaughtered our friends-!"

He pulled her tighter against him. "I won't let that happen. I'll never allow her to get away with what she did to us. But with Rafe being conflicted, I don't know what he intends to do."

She took his paw and led him to their nest and then stroked each of his scars before lifting her tail feathers and offering herself to him. When she sang her beautiful mating song, Dorf settled into her warmth, singing his part as they made love. He counted his blessings and reminded himself he was lucky despite the dark cloud that would never completely dispense.

When Rafe returned to the house, Karma was curled on the sofa, holding a sleeping Runnar in her arms. He crept over to her and reached for their son to place him in his crib, but she jerked awake and snatched the baby against her as if a kidnapper had tried to whisk him away.

Rafe felt instantly sorry for his actions when he saw her large, frightened eyes a moment before she realized that Runnar was safe, and so was she. She offered Rafe a crooked, apologetic smile but didn't relinquish her baby, who barely budged. He was exhausted from all of the activity of the day.

Rafe sat down next to her and placed an arm around them both, drawing them close. "I am sorry I woke you. Shall I carry you to bed?"

"No. I've been waiting up for you to come home."

"Yes. Let's put the baby to bed. Is nurse asleep?"

"Probably. If anyone can sleep after the day we had."

"None has been longer than yours," Rafe said as he stood and guided Karma to Runnar's nursery. The nurse was in her adjoining room with the lights out, and Rafe could clearly hear her quiet breathing as she slumbered.

Karma closed her eyes as she gently buried her face into the top of her son's curls. She inhaled him and, after a moment, was content to pass him to Rafe, who watched her carefully. She gave him another smile but knew he was worried about her. There was a lot they needed to talk about.

Rafe cradled the baby in his hands and looked him over before placing him in his crib. There was no kiss or cuddling of the babe, but his optical as well as tail scans had made sure that his son was well fed, that there was not a scratch or bruise on his perfect brown skin, nor a scale out of place where the vibrant green scales had formed. His son was safe and comfortable. He and Karma left the room and then went to check on M.

She lay sprawled on her bed, deeply asleep, even with her hand concealed beneath her pillow.

He and Karma went to the bed, and while she pulled the little girl's covers up over her, Rafe retrieved the laser gun hidden under her pillow. Karma's brow shot up.

"Wh-?"

He placed a finger over her lips, and they left the room—him with the laser in his harness.

"What in the world?" Karma asked once the door to M's room was closed.

"She probably has another weapon hidden somewhere. I will have to go through my weapons to determine what else is missing."

Karma ran her fingers through her short, unruly Afro. "Poor little thing. She doesn't feel safe, Rafe."

"No. But we will rectify that."

"How?" Karma took his hand and led him to the kitchen. "There's not anyone here that feels safe tonight. Not as long as that-that-*bitch* is here!" She spat the last and then blew out a long breath before opening the refrigerator for a bowl of broth.

He stopped her, taking both of her hands until she faced him. "Karma, Ragna can't hurt anyone, not in the condition she's in. Dr. Brookstone has seen her placed in ecdysis and—"

"Wait, what?!" Karma snapped. "Are you telling me that we're facilitating her improvements?"

He blinked, surprised at her outrage. "No. We're preventing her from dying, at least until *we* can kill her. I'm not going to allow Ragna to die by any means than my own!"

Karma calmed down and then hugged Rafe. "I'm sorry, honey. This day has been..." she shook her head. First, the interview and having to anticipate questions *and* responses so the interviewer wouldn't intentionally trip her up. Then, finding out that Ragna was at the compound, and finally, her father. Damn, this was some day.

Rafe swayed, carrying her with his gentle movements. "No apologies. Not between us. I just want to absorb what you feel, Karma. I want to anticipate what harms you and prevent it before it can take root."

She smiled. "You always do that. But Ragna is a wild card. And the fact that my dad delivered her here doesn't exactly make it better."

Rafe pulled back to look at her. "What do you mean?" he asked carefully.

She gathered her thoughts as she moved to continue retrieving items from the refrigerator for Rafe's dinner. "Daddy is filled with so much hatred. I don't even recognize him." She warmed the entire bowl of broth in the microwave, shielding her expression from him as she did so.

"When he said he was part of the Resistance, I had to wonder about ulterior motives." She turned and met Rafe's eyes. "Is that crazy? He's my father. He wouldn't..."

"There is no way you would, or should try to understand James Chambers. He's been out of your life for nearly as long as he had been in it. Even he admits he's not the same person he once was."

The microwave sounded, and Karma retrieved the broth, and after setting it on the counter, she retrieved a spoon to stir it. She had a number of thoughts swirling through her mind, but Rafe was right. James Chambers was a different man.

The daddy she knew used to work hard doing low-paying jobs and working long hours just so she and Mama could live in a place that wasn't the streets—so they had regular food even if that food was just the garbage that the government couldn't do anything else with but throw it away. He worked so that every blue moon mama could buy a piece of music, and they could sing and dance as if they lived in a different world.

Her daddy rarely complained about anything other than sore feet or the blisters on his hands because he had always counted his blessings that they had a tiny bit more than what most people had.

But this man took potshots at the man she loved, and the hatred exuding from him was tangible regardless of the fact that it hadn't been directed at her.

He had said he had PTSD and was too shattered to care for a little girl. But she wasn't too shattered to care for him. Together, they could have taken care of each other.

Instead of eating, Rafe was watching her.

"It hurts you knowing he lives." He really could change that for her...

Karma shook her head. "It hurts me knowing he didn't care enough about me to come and get me. He left me." She shook her head. "I just don't know how to reconcile that. And until I can, I don't know how to take my father."

Rafe considered her words. "For now, your father is secured in a comfortable cell." Although it wasn't too comfortable. The man had referred to him as a lizard one time too many in order for him to receive better accommodations. "He wants to talk to you again. But that is up to you."

Karma sat at the counter on a stool, and Rafe sat next to her, still not touching the food. His focus was on his woman and not on the fact he hadn't eaten since early morning.

She fiddled with a covered container where quiet sounds of tiny, spidery legs could be heard scurrying over each other. "What did he say?"

Rafe skipped all of the snide comments he'd made and explained how he had come to be in possession of Ragna and how his group had managed to piece together their location.

"Oh my Guardian...So they can attack us at any time."

"Which is why Drago and I have been gone for so long. We're not staying here. Your father—and I take no joy giving him such a title—doesn't appear to want you hurt, but he doesn't give a damn about the rest of us. There is no way we can stay here with his rebel group knowing our location."

Karma nodded. "Yes. How soon can we leave?"

"Considering how his team located us this time, we would need to be much more careful. There can be nothing on grid. At least not on Earth's grid."

"Wait..." she blinked. "Are you saying that we leave Earth?"

"That is what I am saying."

She thought about it. Of course, all little kids thought about what it would be like to live on a mysterious planet with strange aliens, but the reality is that other worlds were hard to acclimate to.

She had been in outer space twice with Rafe since awakening from her coma. She'd gone to a satellite site that had to have an artificial atmosphere piped in just so she could breathe. There was no going outside; there was no real air or grass, or even crumbling old buildings abandoned and sealed off by the government so they couldn't be used by people too poor to pay taxes.

What would it be like to leave Earth for an alien world with... well, aliens?

Rafe reached for her hand and gently clutched it. "Trust me, my love. The place Drago and I have in mind will be safe. No one can track us there. We can leave tomorrow, and I promise you it will be okay."

Karma nodded. "I'm just worried we'll lose our traction with the media. The wave is turning in our favor—especially with Mayva not responding to me telling her true nature."

"Hmph," Rafe snorted. He had finally lifted the bowl of cooling broth and drank most of it in two big gulps. He set it down and wiped his mouth with the back of his hand, grunting in appreciation. He finally looked at her. "Commander Einar has called me twice more. He's even offered me a return to my prior position as head of the North American Province's Galatian Exchange."

Karma made a face. "So, they don't like the job that Mayva's doing."

He shrugged. "I was too busy to return the call. Besides, he has washed his hands of me and my team, and I am retired. I don't need him even though he suddenly needs me."

Karma nodded in agreement while studying her hands. "I would like to speak to my father before we leave."

"Of course." He eyed her. "And we are in agreement he knows nothing of our family or our plans?"

"I would never put my real family in jeopardy," she said while tilting her chin up as if she backed those words wholeheartedly. "And with that said, we need to kill Ragna before we leave."

Rafe paused. "Her chrysalis protects her."

Karma's jaw clenched subtly. "You honestly can't get her out of it?"

"It can be done. "His eyes narrowed. "How would you get your vindication if you don't have a hand in her death?"

Karma's hand moved to her chin. Her eyes stared off into the distance. "I want her to suffer. I don't want her to just die. She needs to suffer. And it's not just by my hands that the suffering should be delivered. When I look at Dorf and his poor missing parts... I will never unsee those Japoxillians. I can never forget watching Titus die and the look of surprise on his face..." Karma drew in a shuddering breath, and Rafe's tail moved to wrap lovingly around her.

"I, too, see those things and more. I hear your screams, and I'm unable to move to get to you." Rafe's body darkened before a red tint began to creep up his torso. "Ragna left me alive because she had no time to dispose of me. She knew I would hunt her down, which is the reason she went into hiding." She asked for mercy, but it wasn't mercy that prevented her death. It was just a lack of time.

Rafe stared at her. "So, a long, slow death?"

"Yes. I think she deserves that."

"Then, we will need to take her with us." A shadow crossed Karma's face. "Ragna is a weak individual," Rafe continued. "She sacrificed many of her Black Masks just for a spiteful attack. And in the process, my child took her body parts and very nearly killed her. A little human girl. Do not make Ragna into a superior force. She had luck, not skill, on her side."

Karma stared deeply into his eyes and saw he believed those words. In her mind, Ragna had always been so large. She was the monster in her nightmares. She was the fear she had lived with when initially hiding her pregnancy. Rafe was right. The broken alien she had seen chained and lying half dead in her own piss was nothing like her imagination had envisioned.

She stood, taking his hand. "Let's swim. Let's make love and be alive and happy and live like we've never lived before."

Rafe's mouth opened, but he had no words. She'd said it all. He followed her to his—*their* den.

Chapter Twenty-Seven

Karma closed her eyes and allowed the Galatian waters to swirl around her body. With Rafe's help, she had located the perfect area of the pool. The waters here bubbled with a warmth reminiscent of a soothing bath, neither too hot nor too cool.

Beneath her, she felt Rafe swim, his body rolling and forming somersaults. Periodically, he brushed her back with either his tail or hands, and she giggled. It still amazed her he could stay beneath the surface of the water so long.

He surprised her when he emerged right by her head with barely a splash. He deposited a kiss on the top of her head. Karma turned and put her arms around his neck for a real kiss. Rafe held her close, his hands supporting her rounded ass. He could never get enough of her curves. By Galatian standards, she was voluptuous—but most humans were. However, he was familiar enough with her to know she hadn't regained her pre-pregnancy weight.

In time, she would be healthy again. It was his purpose in life to care for her—and not just her but his entire family.

Karma pulled back enough to gaze into Rafe's topaz eyes. Once upon a time, those eyes were alien and foreign but strangely not scary. She didn't remember ever being afraid of Rafe's looks. Cut from the same cloth, humans and Galatians were still the same species, only taking a different route through evolution. In the end, both races were very similar.

Karma gazed at the man she loved and saw none of the differences, just everything that made him special.

"I love you, Rafe. More than I know how to express."

He pulled her close again, his hands cupping the areas he loved so much. Rafe kissed her deeply, reveling in the feel of her full lips against his. He couldn't help but to open his mouth and to take possession of her lips. He was rewarded with the feel of her tongue seeking his.

Rafe moaned and then forced himself to pull back long enough to look into her big, pretty brown eyes. They still looked soft and innocent—but that didn't mean she was always soft or innocent. Many times, Karma Sigur was fierce, and yet her eyes still had the power to break him.

He could never do wrong by this woman as long as she had the power to bend his will with those eyes, those lips, that ass—but more importantly, his love for her.

"I am under your power. I have never known this level of desire for anyone or anything. I will always be yours." He cupped her face. "We will prevail over our enemies—"

She quickly placed her index finger against his mouth. "No. This is our time."

He nodded in agreement. He swam her to the edge of the pool where the waters were cooler, but she could hold on to the rocks while he entered her. When he urged her to face away, she locked her feet around his waist.

"No. I want to face you."

He grunted in agreement. Any way he could enjoy his woman was fine by him. He would just have to be easier. He still worried that his prick would be too much for her after all of her injuries despite receiving the sex surgery.

Rafe easily supported her body in the water as he moved forward to stoke her desire. Knowing what he liked, Rafe's lizard tongue flicked Karma's hardened nipple. She sucked in a hard breath.

He looked up. "Too sensitive."

She shook her head, her eyes hooded in desire. "Feels good... "

He quickly moved to her other breast and flicked that nipple. Karma rolled her hips against his hard torso. She had never considered herself to be overly sexualized, but Rafe brought something out in her. It was the hard lines of his body and, of course, his massive prick became rock hard when in her vicinity. But it wasn't just the physical; it was the way he handled Runnar and the care he took with M. It was also in the way he watched her as if she represented everything a man could desire—her, Karma from the urban streets.

"You are my man..." she groaned as she rolled her hips wantonly against him. She reached down for his prick and gripped it hard. He loved it when she remembered he could withstand rough handling. He was actually comfortable with it. Making love, making gentle love with a human took more care than fucking a Galatian. But it was oh so much better. He just had to remember to never completely lose himself in the act. Rafe swore he would never hurt Karma again.

She pulled him close so her breast was smashed against his chest —forcing his attention away from the erotic torture he was delivering to her nipples.

"Kiss me... "

He kissed her the way he had learned from humans—from this human. They explored the other's mouth, gliding along each other's tongues while Rafe suckled and flicked her lips.

His prick pulsed in her grip as she held him between them. His prickhead was just at her breast, and she played with it, squeezing and stroking the glands there.

His breathing tensed as he controlled the spiraling desire. It didn't stop him from squeezing the globes of her ass, rolling her pelvis against him so the petals of her lower lips spread to expose her jewel.

I must lick her there...

Rafe could not stop himself from lifting her bodily from the water. Dutifully, Karma's legs went around his head, locking him into place as he smashed his face against her pussy. His tongue probed and slid along the swelling bud, causing Karma to whimper.

She gripped his head in place and called out her impending orgasm as if it were a warning instead of an aspiration.

It was so good, the way the heat moved across her body like small electrical shocks, locking in on her nipples while her essence streamed from her, feeding the hungry pool of Galatian water with their desire.

"Please, Rafe..." she begged. It was too soon to cum. She needed more of him before her desire exploded around them. "Please..."

He pulled back reluctantly, his hands trembling as he lowered her so that once again, she was pressed against his torso. This time, he positioned his prick between her thighs. His hips rolled erotically, forcing his shaft to fuck the canal created by the V of her thighs and pelvis.

"Yes..." he growled. In this way, he was able to fuck her hard. Rapidly, he rocked his pelvis against her, and Karma squeezed tight, creating a delicious friction that also grazed her sensitized parts.

It was everything he wanted, to fuck her hard, to hold her, to hear her whimpers of desire. He cried out his need to cum but refused to waste his seed in the water when he could spill them into her depths.

He pushed her back rougher than he had intended and then quickly aimed his prick at her opening. She was looking down, watching his massiveness as it quickly disappeared into her depths.

The waters, her desire, and their mutual love made the forceful entry more pleasurable than painful. Rafe drove into the sleek, delicate folds of Karma's vagina, thrust past the opening where her cervix had once been, and into the belly that had grown their child.

Groaning, he stayed buried deep inside of her. Karma's body

vibrated as her orgasm gained force. He felt her tighten convulsively against the base of his prick, where his balls were now jammed against her sweet ass.

To the Great Guardians! He wanted to move! He wanted to slam into her again and again, but he might have already done irrevocable injury. She was human, delicate.

"Fuck me, Rafe! Fuck me now!" she cried.

In surprise, Rafe pulled out of her spasming canal several inches and then quickly slammed home again.

Karma cried out in pleasure. Her head fell back, and her hips rolled with wild abandon.

She liked it... He did it again, and she squealed a sound that was a mixture of words and groans. *Fuck me*, she was crying. *Fuck me...*

Rafe reached out and gripped the rocks along the ledge of the pool He gripped so hard the stones formed grooves, but he held on, and Rafe thoroughly fucked his woman.

Rafe and Karma lay in each other's arms in the comfort of their bed.

"Are you sure you are not injured?"

"Will you relax? I am okay," Karma replied. "I liked it."

"But are you injured?" Rafe asked seriously. She chuckled, but he was looking down at her humorlessly.

She sighed. "A little. I'm still healing. But...sometimes it feels good to hurt." Rafe darkened, although he knew her words were true. Ragna would bite him, and her teeth were strong enough to actually penetrate his scales. He had enjoyed it despite the discomfort. He was revolted by thoughts of her. "Don't overthink it, honey," Karma continued.

Rafe felt guilty that his thoughts had veered from their conversation to that vile creature hopefully still suffering in pain.

He pulled her tightly against him. "You must promise to always warn me if my passion gets out of control."

"You'll know," she said seriously. She glanced down to where his prick lay semi-erect against one leg. "Not that we talk much about *it*," Karma said—with the exception of Auras and Polat, who incessantly talked about sex, "But it's my understanding that the Galatians are very considerate of their sizable...attributes."

Rafe's brow dipped. "What do you say about our attributes?"

Her cheeks warmed. She didn't like talking about things like size or length. But invariably, someone would mention the size of their mate, which didn't necessarily match another male's size. They were all different, just like human men. But in the end, it didn't matter who was thicker or longer when there was no way that even the smallest Galatian prick could completely penetrate a human woman.

"I don't care about other pricks," Karma wisely replied. "I have enough to contend with right here."

Rafe just grunted but dropped the subject.

Rafe only slept a few hours and was up and preparing for a long day. When he called his team, all were already awake and ready to join him, and that included Dorf. They met in Rafe's den, as his house was the central location within the compound.

"What are the updates?" Rafe asked.

Drago pulled up data from his monitor. "The human physician has indicated that the asset is stable but still in critical condition. The foot will be lost and is being absorbed by the chrysalis—"

"Why is she still alive?" Dorf shot out.

"There is much to consider before we determine her fate," Rafe replied tiredly.

Dorf frowned. "Why should there be a need to consider anything? She's been dropped right into our laps! Kill that bitch now and be done with it!"

Rafe stared at his friend and comrade. Dorf was so angry he

shook. Paris, who had been standing quietly, stirred. "I stand with Dorf."

Rafe turned to look at him. "You do not agree she should have been kept alive while we determine our next move?"

"I think she should die, and then we should shit and piss on her dead body!" Paris's scales burned red in rage. Laylay should be here talking sense into him whenever he had second thoughts. She should be here to enjoy the fruits of so many years in battle. Instead, after so many years caring for him, fighting alongside him, she was cut down by a traitor's laser—all at the command of that despicable bitch they had spent months hunting for. No. He did not agree she should have been kept alive while they considered options. There was never any other option but her death.

After a moment, Drago spoke. "And what about The Collective? They won't consider the fact she was dropped into our hands as a reason for killing her. If they ever learn that we have Ragna and she dies, then they will carry out their decree to kill us—and by us, I don't mean just Rafe. They kill all of us."

Dorf looked doubtful. "Anyone should sympathize—"

"The collective doesn't sympathize," Kendrick interrupted quietly. "They didn't care about Titus or the Japoxillian that were murdered. They didn't give a damn about the humans that lost their lives or the loss of Rafe's babe." Everyone listened quietly. "What they care about is which one of us will further their power dynamic."

Rafe scrubbed his hands across his face. "For months, all I wanted was to see Ragna burn for what she did to us. She killed my son." His eyes were fierce. No one spoke, respectfully allowing him to continue. "She tried to take my woman's life, not to uphold some fucking law, but out of spite for my rejection of her!

"When my woman lay so close to death that I did not think I would ever see her eyes upon me again, and after I sent my first son to reside with my ancestors, I wanted nothing but death; my life in pursuit of revenge against Ragna." Rafe looked around and met the eyes of each of his friends. "I swore revenge to you and to our dead.

"And then Karma lived, and I could place another one of our children in her arms. At that moment, I found a reason to continue to live. I still want revenge. I still want that...that *abomination* destroyed! But I also want freedom for my son, my future children, and any other Galatians who choose to love outside of their race, bear children, and live their lives without fear of being murdered! That will never happen if we don't fight!"

Rafe was the most highly decorated Galatian Guard that had ever served. He was defiant and free-thinking. Rafe was meant to lead this war. And he would be damned if he ran thoughtlessly into revenge, no matter how much his hatred for Ragna burned.

When no one spoke, Rafe continued. "We need to leave here. With James Chambers as a high-ranking member of the Resistance, we cannot trust that his people are not waiting to wage an attack. We have him as our prisoner, and I have all but confirmed that if he doesn't return to them, at some point, they will fall down upon us."

Everyone's interest was piqued. Drago continued. "Rafe and I have determined several locations that have a comparable atmosphere to Earth—"

"Comparable to Earth?" Dorf interrupted. "Are you proposing we move to another planet?"

"Just while the Resistance has a bead on us," Rafe replied. "If we can trust the human's words, then they can track our usage of supplies. But there are several abandoned outposts that are already settled and have a shadow crew."

"Rafe, I have a sick daughter. Kelsie needs more than a shadow crew. She is about to receive a lung transplant in a matter of days."

"We can bring a physician—"

Dorf shook his head. "I cannot take my family off Earth. Not now."

Rafe stared at his best friend in disbelief. "But Dorf... you have always fought by my side."

"And I will continue to do so, but I will not join you until my child is safe."

Rafe nodded in reluctant acceptance. He looked at Drago. "You have a child as well. What say you?"

"I won't make a final decision without Maddie's input, but I will be your right hand even if it means that I have to separate from my woman and son while we fight. If Haru and Tam can make the sacrifice... "

Rafe nodded and looked at Paris. "Paris, your woman is due to have a serious surgery. You do not have to stand with me—"

Paris burned even redder at the insinuation behind those words.

"Rafe, I stand with you whether I move off-world or not. This battle must be won." He looked off into the distance as he thought about a future where he and Daya could have their own children. He inhaled deeply. "Daya will determine her best interest, but mine hasn't wavered. I fight by your side."

Rafe nodded and then looked at Kendrick. Strangely, he was the one to hesitate despite not having a family of his own.

"Someone will need protect those that are left behind."

"Perhaps it is time to bring Haru back," Rafe said.

"Karma suggested that Tam's cover might be blown since the video was released showing her fighting for our side," Paris added. "Facial recognition software can easily compare the image with Tamsyn."

"We need to get her back." Paris left the office to comply with the directive. "And call Haru back."

"Aye," Paris replied.

Rafe darkened. As much as he had wanted Ragna's life in his hands, he certainly hadn't wanted this type of upheaval. And he still hadn't revealed he intended to bring her off-world with them.

Chapter Twenty-Eight

It was fruitless to have a meeting the way they used to back in the days when the only consideration was Rafe and his men. Now, there were too many others who would be affected by the decisions made, so Rafe had his men retrieve their spouses. This is the way all meetings would need to be held going forward: with everyone providing their input.

With the exception of the children, nanny, and Dr. Brookstone, everyone sat around the large dining room table with steaming cups of coffee, tea, and Galatian broth in mugs. It was very early, and the sun had yet to rise, so the children slept while the spouses had barely managed any sleep at all. There was too much to worry about for sleep to come easy.

Daya was thinking about how complicated her life had become, and she longed for the days of waking up each day to care for the little ones at the orphanage. She missed her perfect life—well, perfect for her. Her old life also addressed the complication of the asset in the basement of the facility...

Justina had automatically migrated to sit next to Kendrick since he was the one who had fetched her to the meeting. She had already resolved to fight. She had no children or spouse of her own to protect, but this family was more important to her than her own blood family. For them, she would risk all she had—because without them, she had nothing.

Kemistry looked around the room in worry. Dorf had only told her that they needed to have a meeting, and she had jumped up, ruffled her feathers, and hurried here.

"Is something wrong?" she asked.

Maddie was looking only at Drago. He reached for her hand and held it, his expression and scales an even tone. She was very familiar with how he operated, though. It could be the end of the world, and he would maintain his cool.

"There is a lot that needs to be discussed," Dorf said while pacing. "Rafe wants to go off-world since the Resistance knows about our location."

Kemistry's mouth parted, but Maddie spoke first.

"We are talking about leaving Earth? For how long?"

Rafe replied. "That we don't know. But James Chambers is in the Resistance, and he revealed how he was able to locate us. We went dark when we came here, and he was still able to locate us. But there are places that are already developed, outposts that are managed by shadow crews."

"Outposts? On a different *planet?*" Daya asked. She was familiar with humans visiting out-of-space satellite facilities where manufactured air was piped into the huge warehouses. Planets were a different matter, and it seemed Rafe might be speaking of something more long-term.

She generally didn't interject as the last person to join the family; she had always felt as if she was the least important. But now, her life was irrevocably intertwined with Paris, and everything he did affected her.

Rafe nodded. "Yes, it would be on a world that is completely off-grid. It has an atmosphere comparable to Earth, and no breathing apparatus would be necessary. Unfortunately, I cannot say how long that would be."

She and Paris exchanged looks. They were thinking the same thing. They would have to make a decision about their prisoner. For now, he was existing week by week on whatever food and water Paris found fit to leave for him. He wanted the man dead and didn't care if he ran short on food or water.

Daya, on the other hand, didn't want the man tortured, but she also wasn't ready to actually end his life. He deserved it. He deserved to suffer and to die, but she just hadn't been able to give those final orders.

Karma remained quiet. She felt guilty. So much of this fell back on her—all beginning with her trickery. Yes, Mr. Tolbert had orchestrated it all, and she had been just a pawn. But there was a point when she had kept the lie going—meaning becoming pregnant.

Now, there wasn't just the matter of emancipating the Galatian males to live and love freely, but there was her father and his connections. Just being a part of the consorts had upset so many lives.

"Our daughter is to have a life-saving surgery, and the team of surgeons who specialize in this procedure are Earthlings..." Kemistry was shaking her head. She looked at Dorf, who came to her and nudged the side of her face with his. The act was a form of comfort but also a sharing of information. Kemistry nodded and looked at Rafe.

"We won't be able to join you."

Rafe nodded in acceptance. "I understand, Kemistry. You and Dorf are invaluable as the only Japoxillian trained to read the members of this team. But the main reason for any of this is to preserve our families."

Dorf looked at his fellow teammates with sadness. "I will rejoin you when my daughter is safe."

"Thank you," Drago said.

Karma understood, but she had always been with Dorf, and not having him to dance, laugh, and sing with would be hard. But all of this was hard.

"We all came together not simply for the sake of safety but also community. We are the group that stands against a history of injustice." Rafe looked around at those who he counted on the most. "But I don't expect you to follow me. In this, I am not your commander. I am just a soldier who is committed to making a change for the future of my family and all families."

"As I told you earlier, Rafe," Drago said. "I will be by your side." He looked at Maddie. "You and Rex should stay—"

Maddie was already shaking her head. "Rex and I will go where you go."

Drago colored in relief. He squeezed her hand again.

Paris was sitting next to Daya. He didn't look at her as he spoke. "I want a future that allows me to choose who I want to love. It should be that way for everyone in this room." Justina straightened as she gave him a meaningful look. "I will always serve by your side as your brother." He finally looked at Daya as he continued speaking to Rafe. "But we have other issues that have to be settled before I can join you."

Assuming Paris was talking about Daya's surgery, Rafe nodded in understanding. However, before he could continue, Daya spoke.

"I don't want to be a factor in the decisions that are made. I've decided to put my surgery aside—" Paris's head swiveled quickly to look at her. "It's okay; it's something I've been thinking about since we arrived." They were involved in something more important than her physical aesthetics. There was no way she was going to allow herself to be left completely helpless in light of everything happening. And there was no way she would be a burden to Paris when he was fighting for their future.

Karma gave Daya an appreciative look. These people were sacrificing so much.

"I don't know how I can be of help," Justina spoke, "Other than not to be a burden. So put me where you best see fit." Karma and

Maddie both smiled at her in relief. Facing the future with her core group of friends, as well as the new addition of Daya, would help her face what was going to happen moving forward.

Kendrick simply nodded. "I stand with you all."

"Then it is settled," Rafe said in relief. "There are other matters. Drago has spoken with both Tamsyn and Haru, and both have agreed to return home." Maddie, Justina, and Karma looked at each other happily. They will join us at our new location. But that brings us to another issue: Dr. Brookstone and James Chambers."

Daya frowned. "What about Dr. Brookstone?"

"He's not a part of our crew, and he knows we have Ragna in our possession," Rafe replied. "We can't allow him to leave."

Daya's eyes widened as she looked at Paris. "But you trust him, don't you?"

Paris's head inclined. "I do in matters of medical care. But this is politics. Garry has more liberal ideas than even we propose." He met Rafe's eyes defiantly because although he apparently sided with him in most matters, there was one he most definitely didn't. "He is obviously important to our mission for reasons other than assisting Daya." Daya looked from one to the other in curiosity.

Rafe hid his annoyance. Although he loved Paris dearly, he was the most contrary individual he'd ever met. But this was an important topic, so he looked at them all seriously.

"As you all know, the doctor has been tasked with preventing Ragna from dying from her injuries. And there hasn't been a decision made to have the doctor... stop those efforts."

Maddie frowned and looked from Rafe to Karma, knowing her best friend couldn't want that dangerous bitch to continue to live.

"You're not thinking about keeping her alive, are you?"

It was Karma that responded. "This may be hard to understand, but neither Rafe nor I want Ragna alive." Karma leaned forward, and there was a glint of something hard—maybe even sinister in her eyes. "But when she dies, we want her to know who brought that death to her." No one spoke, but what she said sank into each and every one of them.

Karma looked at Daya apologetically. "I'm sorry, Daya. You've been dragged into so much of this. And now you have to see this insidious side of Rafe and me. But we're not letting that bitch go—not into the hands of the Queens or The Collective, who never punished her for what she did." Karma looked around the room.

"We are going to kill Ragna. We. Us. And not that cage she was brought to us in!"

"You're not proposing keeping Ragna as a prisoner, are you?" Maddie asked in surprise.

Rafe shrugged. "Yes. That is exactly what we are saying."

No one spoke for a moment. Finally, Daya inhaled deeply. "Then there is something that I have to tell you all."

Karma looked at her with a hint of sadness. Daya must be disgusted by her. Now, they were going to lose her. She was probably going to run back to the orphanage and take Paris with her. It wasn't so much the idea of not having their support but the loss of a new friend.

"It's probably old news about how I got my injuries," Daya said.

"I don't know how you got them," Justina piped up.

"It happened during a sexual assault," Daya explained.

Justina looked appalled. She had thought it was an accident but not that someone had intentionally done this to her. Guardian, that was horrendous! She looked down in embarrassment that her blunt attitude might have hashed up bad memories for the poor woman.

"The man who assaulted me was a college counselor. Evidently, he had been targeting women he felt fell under the radar, meaning poor women who didn't have government positions.

"When I told the authorities who had done this to me, they sided with him and said I was lying." Karma made a fist, and Maddie frowned deeply. They knew this, having read her file when hiring her for the orphanage, but having her voice this aloud brought it all slamming back.

Justina met Daya's eyes in sympathy and surprise. But after all, she'd seen, surprise was the last thing she should ever feel concerning the actions of the government.

"You all knew about the hidden basement prison of the orphanage. I didn't until I stumbled upon it and found that Paris had placed my attacker there."

Everyone but Paris was surprised at those words, and that included Rafe.

"He had been in that dungeon for months with Paris supplying him with food and water and basically nothing else. When I found him, I had a choice." Daya looked directly at Karma. "I guess it's the same choice that you have. Paris left the decision up to me, and I decided that this monster had to pay for his crime. Death is no punishment. Death is just a release."

Rafe's teeth clenched. *Mercy,* Ragna had said. She hadn't been asking for help but for death.

Maddie cleared her throat. "Are you saying there is a serial rapist in the basement of the school that I am the administrator of?"

Daya nibbled her lip. "Yes. There is."

"What the fuck...?" Rafe looked at Paris, whose tone took on one of chagrin. Rafe let out a string of Galatian curse words.

"It was the only way I could monitor him without others knowing. No one but me is culpable. None of the guards or soldiers have anything to do with keeping that thing in the basement a prisoner."

"But there are children in the facility!" Maddie exclaimed.

"It's a dungeon," Daya interjected. "It has nothing to do with the children because there is no way for him to escape. And if it was possible, the more than one hundred soldiers and Guardian that protect the facility would capture him before he got within a foot of leaving that prison.

"Look, I do understand your concern. I have worked with those children on a daily basis, and no one has their best interest more than me. I love those kids, and I'd never do anything to put them at risk.

Locking that man in the dungeon could never affect the children because they are in two different worlds."

Karma was torn. She had seen the dungeon through the broadcast that the men had fed the consorts at the time they had discovered M and the other children... children and babies. It was solid with cement and iron bars. There weren't even any windows. Soundproof, fireproof, and close enough for Paris and Daya to monitor, she understood on some levels.

But M had been there while she was in a coma. Her daughter had been living above the prison of a murdering rapist.

But how was that any different than them housing a dangerous Galatian murderer in the compound where their families lived?

Chapter Twenty-Nine

"Okay!" Justina exclaimed. "I understand, but we have more important things to think about—not to say those orphans aren't important, but right now, we need to focus on the present danger."

Maddie's mouth formed a hard line, and she looked away silently. Karma looked from Daya to Paris, but when neither responded she cleared her throat and spoke tentatively.

"Let's table that discussion for now." Maddie gave her a swift look, but Karma continued, "And we will come back to it. But Rafe thinks we are sitting ducks, and I tend to agree. I think we should get out of here sooner than later." She looked at Dorf and Kemistry. "Do you know where you will go?"

Dorf and Kemistry exchanged looks, coming to some quiet consensus. "Yes," he said. "We are going to stay at the military base where the medical facility is located."

Karma nodded solemnly. She inhaled and then looked at Rafe, who was happy to allow her to take the helm. She had simply said what he would have.

Karma stood almost reluctantly. "I need to speak to my father. For now, the answers are with him."

Rafe stood and looked at the other members of his family. "Gather your things. I want to be out of here by the break of dawn."

Everyone began filing out, but Karma placed her hand on Rafe's chest. She didn't speak until the room was empty. "If we're leaving that soon, then you need to gather our belongings. You have your weapons, both children and mine, to deal with."

"I can have one of the soldiers..." Her eyes widened in disbelief at what he was getting ready to suggest. Leaving this important task to a stranger? Rafe sighed.

His plate was definitely full. He gave her a stern look. "Fine. But I don't want you in the same room with him—"

"I'll be in there with guards, Rafe. Galatian Guards."

He didn't speak for a beat. James Chambers was simply a human with no weapons, and he was her father who had risked his very life to do this idiotic thing.

"Fine," he sighed. "But keep your monitor on the broadcast. I want to see and hear everything."

"Okay," she agreed.

Rafe called for two of his trusted Galatian Guards to escort Karma and then hurried to gather their belongings. He'd done this before, and uprooting his family like this bothered him a great deal. He longed for a day when none of this was necessary...

James had refused the bed. The room was small and comfortable, but not too comfortable. He was sure that was the intent of the alien. But he was accustomed to worse. Besides, he had no need for comfort. He hadn't slept since his arrival and had only drank a few swallows of water. He had ignored the wild game stew that had been left for him despite how enticing it smelled and the fact he hadn't eaten in nearly twenty hours.

He had swallowed a slow-release nutrient pellet before arriving that gave him a feeling of fullness as long as it was activated with water. But James didn't even truly need that. Many times, he had existed on barely enough to keep a grown man alive. Unfortunately, that hadn't only happened once he was captured by the filthy aliens. He'd often go without food so that his wife and child had something to fill their bellies.

James closed his eyes and made a fist. It took some time before he could control his emotions again. He simply sat quietly in the hard wooden chair and waited for what was to come next.

When the door finally opened, he wasn't surprised to see his daughter, obviously flanked by two large Galatians. He felt sad she sought protection from them against him. He hoped to change that kind of thinking.

"Hi, Daddy."

He stood. "Hi, Baby girl." Some emotion crossed her face, only for her to quickly shield it. James looked down because that stabbed at him. He had never been able to handle seeing pain on the faces of either his wife or child. The image of his wife being cut down by an alien laser filled his mind, and it nearly dropped him like a gut punch. Memories like this had been pushed to the recesses of his mind for a reason.

Karma was looking around the small room. "I'm sorry you were locked up. It's just... well, you're with the Resistance, and obviously, you know they aren't exactly fans of ours."

"I wouldn't say that's true."

"What?"

James sighed. "First, there isn't just one Resistance. As I told the one who appears to be in charge, I am an officer with what he would call a Rebel force. We consider ourselves Patriots."

Karma's brows lifted. In truth, Rafe would consider them traitors, but that might not come out so good to a self-proclaimed patriot.

James continued. "And in addition, my team doesn't put you in the same category as the *rest* of them."

"Rest of them?" Karma asked.

He waved his hand to the door. "Those consorts that were trained to be used by the aliens."

Karma shook her head. "Dad, those consorts had no idea what lay ahead of them. They were children when they were sent to that school. And those *aliens* have been kinder to those women than some of the humans here on Earth. That has certainly been the case for me."

James listened without responding.

"Daddy..." Karma was shaking her head. "Why have you come back in my life? You've evidently been back on Earth for some time. Why are you here now?"

"Karma, I discovered you were a consort, the first Black consort ever. I wanted to rescue you then, but it was too dangerous." Her mouth parted at the word "rescue", but she allowed him to continue. "That hotel where you were housed is basically its own military base. And while I wanted to pull you out of there and destroy everyone in my wake—my comrades would not risk me or our team." His face took on a look of anger. "I explained that you are my team—that everything I want and everything I do..."

When he didn't finish, Karma shook her head in anger. "I am your *team*? All of a sudden, I am your *team*? When you got back, I wasn't your *team*? When I slept in bus stations in the winter and scraped by with no food day in and day out, I wasn't your team? But suddenly, when I'm comfortable and cared for, I need rescuing?"

James watched her. "No, Karma. It's not like that. You were in a government-run orphanage, being fed every day and getting an education. You were living better than I could have provided for you at that time—"

"I was living better?" she exclaimed. "I was in a facility where those monsters—those *human* monsters were caging and then incinerating the children they didn't think they could place—the hard-to-deal-with children, the ones with disabilities and trauma...the ones like me. I was nearly one of those children tossed like garbage into the fire because after watching my mother killed before my eyes and my dad ripped away from me by aliens, I stopped talking. That is *my* PTSD! And *my* shattered psyche!"

She saw her father pale and took more satisfaction than she probably should. "It wasn't until Rafe and his team showed up and discovered what was happening that those children were freed and given a real home. *Aliens* saved babies and children from humans. And it was the Galatians that have been rescuing the kidnapped men from the Tybernees! The Galatians are the aliens that are protecting man from the rest of the galaxy!"

"There is a lot that you need to understand," he said softly. "I was hoping to tell you the truth, Baby girl; the truth that the aliens don't want us humans to know."

"Back to blaming the aliens. It's the same rhetoric despite everything I just told you." She shook her head in disappointment. "You all just want a reason to hate."

"That's not true, Karma. There used to be another Earth, another world than what we know!" The Galatian guards that were on either side of her moved subtly when he raised his voice. He ignored them. One of the many things he had lost over the years was fear of aliens. They had taken nearly everything, and the only thing of value he had left to lose might have already been lost to him by his own words. But if only she understood.

"We have been led like sheep to the slaughter. And look where we are now! Our Earth is managed by the so-called Collective so that we can be saved. But when you look around, does it appear that we're saved? We are just slaves, but this time to a nest of vipers that call themselves the Interplanetary Collective. And all the Galatians do is their bidding!"

"Dad—"

"Baby girl, the Galatians sold us out to The Collective, sold our daughters to be maimed and then screwed by them! And our own government facilitated it for a little bit of money and power! And this time, instead of countries warring with each other to protect their interests, the rich don't have to war with anyone to stay in the top 1% because the aliens handed them power over the rest of us! And if you don't think the Galatians didn't have a hand in it, then Baby girl, you are blinded and brainwashed!"

"DADDY!" James quieted at Karma's raised voice. "You and I aren't on opposite sides in this matter! I know that The Collective is our enemy and not our friends." She quickly closed her mouth, and James also quieted. After a few breaths, Karma continued, a bit less agitated. "Daddy, we might not agree about everything, but we can agree that we both want freedom and that government rule needs to be given back to the people."

James sighed. "We can agree on that much. And Karma, I didn't leave you because I didn't want you. I'm sorry that your life was terrible and that bad things happened to you." James sighed and then reached up to touch his temple. He dug his fingers into the flesh of his face, and Karma started, her hands flying to her mouth.

Blood began to pour down the side of James's face. But that didn't stop him from tearing away the flesh. The guards quickly formed a circle around her using their arms and tails, urging her back out of the room. But Karma was frozen, unable to unsee the horrible thing her father was doing.

James dropped the flesh to the floor, and Karma realized that instead of bone, her father's skull was made of some type of strange, black metal.

"But bad things happened to me, too." His voice was as soft as a whisper. "It's true the Tybernees kidnapped humans to sell them as slaves, and those slaves didn't make it for much longer than two or so years.

"But some of us were sold to be experimented on. The aliens that purchased us wanted to make humans that could withstand more pain, less oxygen, and less nourishment so that we could work harder and longer for the aliens that enslaved us. But, you see, something else happened. In trying to create a better slave, they created better warriors.

"The few hundred of us that went through the experiments overwhelmed our captives and killed those mutha fuckers." The good side of his face broke into an angry grimace. The other half just continued to drip blood, soaking his suit and pooling at his feet.

"We got back to Earth thinking we'd be celebrated. And you know what happened? We were handed over to The Interplanetary Collective, who happened to know all along what had been happening to us. The fucking Collective had sold us! And guess who knew about this? The Galatians. Those Galatians that you love so much!" Karma shook her head emphatically.

"No. They wouldn't do that."

"The Galatians want you to think they are better, more evolved. But they can't even think for themselves! They need others to guide them. And Karma. You are doing just that right now. It's obvious by the way they followed you when you handed out food to the poor at that bus station. They have never done anything like that before you, even though they had to see how poor the world is around them! And I know you went back and helped the people at our old building. Karma, you can't deny that *you* are the influence of change!"

Karma heard Rafe's voice coming from her communicator. "Karma. Get out of there. We need to get medics in there before your father bleeds out."

And that was all the time the guards gave her. She was bodily removed from the cell, and the doors clanked close behind her.

They need others to guide them...

Chapter Thirty

"Wake up, Little One." Kelsie's eyes opened, and she saw Mom standing next to her. Relief filled her. Sometimes, when she slept, she wasn't always sure what she would see when she opened her eyes. Her dreams were so vivid. Maybe the things she saw would creep into her new life.

She struggled to sit up, preparing herself for a breathing treatment. Mom or Dad sometimes woke her up to give her a treatment, but why was Bain standing on the other side of the bed with a strange look on his face? Dad was pacing again.

"What's wrong?" She sat up with her first thoughts being about that scary lady who had come to the compound. Mom and Dad said she was locked up and had been hurt really badly, so she couldn't do anything to hurt them, but Dad was afraid, and that was easy for anyone to see—even a human that didn't have the abilities that the Japoxillian had.

"Nothing is wrong," Mom said while placing a soft paw on her hand. "But your uncle Rafe thinks it is best if we leave the compound. And he wants us to do it quickly."

"Okay," she moved to get out of the bed, but Mom gently pressed her back down. "No, I don't want you straining yourself. Dad and I aren't very good movers," she looked at her paws while wiggling the claws on her feet, "But Bain is going to pack the things that you want to take now. We'll have the rest of your things sent later."

She nodded, and Bain went to her closet. "Tell me what clothes you want," he called while Dad dragged a suitcase behind him.

She had no idea. The residue of sleep still lingered, along with a trace of fear. "Some underwear, I guess," Bain looked over his shoulder at her, and his cheeks were turning red, but he nodded dutifully. "And my dark jeans and my Bobbly Boop shirt. Let me just do it," she said while sitting up and looking at Kemistry, who was gathering her breathing apparatus. "Can I, Mom?"

"Well, as long as you do it from your chair. And have Bain and Dad do the lifting."

As she got her things together, Kelsie noted that Bain's expression remained strained. She wanted to ask him what was wrong, but what if it wasn't something he wanted to mention in front of their new parents? She could fully understand that. It was hard not to be any trouble.

As if on cue, Dorf looked at her as he zipped one of her bags. "We explained to Bain that we would be going to the medical facility to stay. They have housing units, and we'll be able to stay close to you while you're having surgery.

"In the meantime, everyone else will be going to a new planet until we all feel it's safe to return to Earth."

She was surprised. "We won't be going with M?"

"No, dear," Kemistry replied. "M has to go with her own mom and dad."

"But don't worry," Dorf added quickly. "We'll join them when things settle down."

"After my surgery?" she asked.

"No...not right away. A lot is going on, and for now, you are our biggest concern."

Kelsie's expression dropped. They couldn't go with everyone else because of her—because of her sickness, because she was a trou-blemaker.

"When I get better, I'll be able to help out more," she explained. "I'll get strong, and I'll be able to use my hands to move things for you. I can cook, too—"

"Kelsie." Dorf moved to her.

"Please don't send me away! I swear I won't be a burden! I promise I'll be good! Please, I want to stay with you!" Tears sprouted in her eyes, and she swiped them away and forced herself to smile. *See? I'm not a crybaby. I'm strong. I'm good.*

"Little one!" Kemistry flapped her wings with a gentle movement and was beside Kelsie a moment later. She and Dorf held her. "We are not sending you away."

"We will be with you," Dorf said while hugging her. "We're not letting you go through this alone."

Kelsie gave in to her tears. "Okay," she agreed. "Okay."

Baine looked on in surprise. He didn't understand why she would say such things. He knew she wouldn't want to leave M because he didn't. But it wasn't her fault. It was the fault of that bad lady who had attacked M and their family. He didn't necessarily want to leave, but he definitely didn't want to stay with that bad lady, and Dad had said the bad lady was going with the others.

Yeah, he didn't care how sick that woman was because just like in the game *Galactic Firefight*, the enemy put trackers and even bombs on the dispensable people and then slipped them in over enemy lines.

He tried to tell this to his dad, but he said they already knew all of that and had taken safeguards. Maybe they had, but keeping your enemies too close could be a disaster. He was worried about that lady going with the others but especially worried M would want to be their Protector, just like the Galatian Guards. He wanted M to stay with them and not go with her family.

It was selfish, but they were supposed to be together to take care of each other. M thought she could do it all by herself, but sometimes, when she saw things that were right in front of her, she needed someone to watch what was on the side and behind her, and that is where he and Kelsie came in.

Kemistry was speaking to her softly, using her most soothing tone. "We will never give you up, Kelsie. We're not like your other mother and father."

Kelsie looked up from Dorf to Kemistry and then back again. "But...my real mother and father didn't want me."

Dorf placed his wing around her and Kemistry.

"But we chose you. We chose you, the Kelsie with the sick lungs, the sweet smile, and the wonderful personality. We know what happened with your birth parents, and we knew about your illness all before we ever met you. But Little-one, I don't consider those other people your *real* parents. We are."

"You never have to be afraid to open up to us," Kemistry continued. "We would love to share our feelings with you without mouths that can sometimes be deceptive. But that is ultimately up to you. If you ever truly let us in, you will know without a doubt that you are ours completely and totally."

Kelsie looked at them doubtfully. They knew about how she'd come to be at the orphanage, probably even about the fire in the old building her family squatted in and how the poisonous smoke from the burning drugs after they had exploded had slowly begun to corrode her lungs.

She had kept it a secret from the other children for so long she had almost forgotten that grownups had access to her file. However, those files only gave a small amount of information about her life. Only she knew the entire story about them seeing her as a burden until, eventually, they just up and left her behind, moving off without even telling her.

We don't have money for medicine for that girl. She should have just died in that fire...

But, when Kelsie looked from Kemistry to Dorf, she finally began to embrace an idea that Baine had come to days before—that these people might really want her...

She lifted her arm slowly and then offered it to Kemistry, her mother. "I want to connect," she whispered. And she meant it.

Kemistry nipped her wrist while Dorf embraced them using his one wing and strong body. He looked at Baine.

"Come, son."

Baine slid into his mother and father's embrace. He fit just perfectly.

"Why did you have them drag me out of there!" Karma demanded the moment she stepped into the house.

Rafe had just placed a large bin of clothing in the living room to join the others he had packed.

M came out of the kitchen where she had been having a quick meal. Nanny and Runnar were out of sight as she fed the toddler his bottle. But even her ears perked at the anger in the voice of the normally mild-tempered woman.

Rafe straightened. "Why do you ask me this? I told you the medics needed to treat your father. You don't want him dead, do you?" In Rafe's opinion, it had been a ridiculous show to rip half of his face off in front of his own daughter. She wouldn't see it for the manipulation intended.

Based on that artificial skull, what he ripped off and threw to the floor was probably also artificially grown skin that either didn't have pain receptors or just a very few. He felt less respect for the human after that obvious show of sympathy.

Karma lowered her voice when she saw M watching, although her face betrayed her annoyance and disappointment. "I wasn't done talking to him, and you made me leave."

"I am sure there will be more opportunities for you to speak to the man. But only if he is still alive to do so." Rafe turned to M. "Little one. If you have completed your meal, then finish collecting your belongings so they can be loaded onto the ship."

The little girl went to her room. She stayed and listened by the door, certain her enhanced hearing would allow her to hear what they were saying. She quickly checked the ankle harness as her parents argued in low voices. She had fashioned it from an old hair ribbon and felt comfortable that her knife was nicely secured against her leg.

She didn't need any of the other 'stuff' in her room. The knife and maybe her old Galatian suit was all she wanted. She no longer wanted to be a Galatian, but she was pretty certain that putting the Galatian cloth around her Mama's belly had done something to save her life, even though it hadn't helped her baby brother. If only she'd had time to put the scales onto the cloth. Then maybe her brother would still be alive.

Baby Runnar couldn't save himself, so she would have to be there to do it. She quickly shed her clothes and pulled on the old Galatian scales suit. It was tighter but still fit comfortably. She put on her other clothes over it, hoping the scales wouldn't cut through them so quickly. As long as she got on the spaceship before it happened, then there wouldn't be anything anyone could do about it because she wasn't going to bring any more clothes! Later, when the suit became stinky, she would just borrow something fresh to wear from Kelsie or Bain.

Being in outer space with her best friends would be an adventure for sure, but they would have to remember to keep a watch out for that Black Mask first and foremost since Papa said they were taking her with them. M knew better than most that grown-ups didn't always make the right choices. If her life was a graphic novel like <u>The Dark Death Trader</u>, then the bad lady would only pretend to be sick so she could get up in the middle of the night and try to take them all out.

Her knife might not do much against scale, but she could take out her eye and make sure she was dead before it ever had a chance to grow back.

"Karma, please calm yourself," Rafe spoke. "I know this is upsetting—"

"Did you hear what my Dad said?" she stared at him pointedly.

"I did." He placed his hands on his hips.

"Is it true? Were the Tybernees selling the humans they kidnapped to be experimented on? And did The Collective know about this? Did you Galatians know about this?"

He shook his head. "I can't believe you are asking me this... "

He was being evasive, and she knew what that meant. "You can't lie—not directly. And the reason you can't lie is because other Galatians can sense it, smell it, even see it in the color of your scales. But not humans with our hindered senses! But I also know you, Rafe Sigur. I know you won't lie to me because of our promise. On the life and death of our baby, you swore never to lie to me—"

Rafe grabbed her arms. It was firm but not enough to cause pain. "Do not use my dead son to influence my response!" She looked at him in shock, and he instantly released her, his anger and hurt fading. "I am not going to lie to you because I keep no secrets from you. Ever."

She rubbed her arms even though she wasn't injured. It just took her back to when they had first met, before there was trust when there was fear and intimidation.

She was calm when she spoke. There was no room for anything else. "Don't ever touch me like that again."

Rafe looked at the floor and nodded. "I am sorry. I will not do that again." He met her eyes then.

He had taught his woman that in Galatia, there was no word for thank you. There were also no words of apology. But there should be because just like it was important to be appreciated, it was just as important to voice your remorse, as well as to accept it.

When Karma allowed her arms to fall, he continued. "There have always been rumors of corruption within the Interplanetary Collective. But the level of corruption that your father speaks of is not known to me or my men. And if I don't know about him and other humans being sold for experimentation, then none of us know this.

"Humans have to understand that our initial purpose in bringing them under the power of The Collective was to protect you from the destruction of the Earth. Before your time, this world was fertile and safe. And then man ignored the warning signs and continued to strip it until it was virtually a polluted husk. When we stepped in, it was to save man but also this planet.

"Your father is right. We took away your democracy, but it wasn't so we could sell it to the wealthy officials. It was our naivete that prevented us from seeing that power creates corruption. There aren't enough Galatians to rule you. We needed your governments to continue to enforce and regulate your laws. And in truth, Karma, there are some of us who don't want to be on this planet as the human's villains! There are those that want to leave Earth to its own devices.

"But you are *us!* It is because of us that humans even exist! What those few Galatians want won't just result in leaving you alone to fight it out amongst yourselves, but it's the unfair disadvantage of having humans become the targets of every other alien lifeform. Should we ever turn our backs on you, what happened to your father will happen to every man, woman, and child."

Karma released a long breath. "The Patriots aren't opposing you and other aliens because they think they will lose." Rafe wondered if she even realized she had gone from considering her father as a Rebel to now being a Patriot.

"I truly believe they will fight to the death for their cause." Karma continued. "As will we." Rafe's relief she still sided with the Galatian was short-lived when she continued.

"You did not know about the Interplanetary Collective allowing the Tybernees to steal our men, but did you know about the experimentations?" Karma watched him closely. He had indicated there were rumors, but it didn't actually answer whether he knew that the almighty savors to the galaxy, The Interplanetary Collective co-signed on the experimentation of humans by other life forms.

Without even the smallest hesitation, Rafe nodded. "We knew there were humans captured and then sold to others for various experiments. But," he stared unflinchingly into her eyes. "I never knew The Collective was behind it, and I still do not know that. I won't accept anything as fact that comes from that man's mouth."

Karma nodded tiredly and then took a tentative step forward. She took another and another until she was standing against the tall, hard form of her man. She placed her arms around his torso and clung to him. She didn't feel any sense of relief until his arms moved to close around her body, holding her against him.

"I'm sorry, Rafe. This is so hard, but I know and trust you. I don't know my father anymore." She looked up at him as they still embraced. His topaz, lizard-like eyes held no emotion, but his scales colored with love and tenderness. "I just want to get off this compound before my father pulls something else from up his sleeve."

"Good." He kissed the curls on top of her head. "I don't want anyone from his team that might be watching to know we are leaving. Once we move our belongings to the ship, I want the take-off to occur within ten minutes. It can be done, but it will be work. From this point on, we don't use our communicators until further notice.

"And, you should check our bedroom for any belongings that you may want to take."

Karma shook her head. "There's nothing I need more than what I already have. Let's get going."

Chapter Thirty-One

There was a knock at the door, and both Rafe and Karma looked at it before Rafe moved to open it.

Dorf, Baine, and Kelsie in her hoverchair were at the door. "We wanted to say goodbye," Dorf said.

Rafe gestured with his head for them to enter, and Dorf looked around and shook his head at the clutter of bins and items stacked by the door for the move.

"This looks like our house. Kemistry is back home packing everything but the kitchen sink."

Karma sighed. "Dorf. I don't know what I'm going to do without seeing you or hearing your voice."

Dorf cleared his throat and then turned to his kids, who looked equally as downcast. "Kids, why don't you say goodbye to M." The children barely whispered their hellos to Rafe and Karma before heading to M's room.

Rafe's eyes grew large.

"What?" Karma asked.

"I forgot to tell M that Dorf's family won't be joining us."

"Rafe..." Karma's mouth fell.

"I was so preoccupied that it completely slipped my mind." Everyone turned to look at M's bedroom, where her friends had disappeared.

"What are you doing?" Baine asked when he saw M standing at her door. Her communicator was turned to a whisper when she spoke.

Mama and Papa are arguing about her father. The man that brought that Black Mask is my…Grandpa, I guess.

Baine frowned. "If he's your Grandpa, then why do you have to leave?"

M shrugged. **That's why I was listening.** She looked at her friends curiously. **What are you two doing here?**

"Saying goodbye, silly," Kelsie said. She was looking around her friend's bedroom. "Aren't you taking your gaming system? And what about your posters?"

Saying goodbye? M asked. Bain stared at her.

"You know we aren't going to the other planet, don't you, M?" Kelsie continued, still feeling a bit guilty. "I have to have my surgery, so we're going to live at the hospital—"

M walked out of the room, and all of the adults were already staring at her when she did. It didn't take much to see that the little girl had discovered the bad news.

"M," Karma went to her. "I am so sorry, honey. I guess Kelsie and Baine explained that they won't be going with us—"

Why do we have to go? M demanded, stopping Karma before she could touch her. **I heard you tell Papa that your father captured the Black Mask. And you said she's hurt and can't hurt us!**

Dorf looked surprised at the little girl's outburst. "Uh…we better go. Kelsie. Baine. Let's go. Talk to you later."

M ignored them as she shook her head adamantly. **I don't want to go—not without my friends.**

Dorf got his family quickly away from the impending battle. He knew M to be nothing but accommodating and sweet, but things had been hard for them all as of late, and he didn't want to witness this transformation. He was just happy that the emotional showdown in his own family had been dealt with.

Rafe went down on one knee. "Little one, if there was any other way, I wouldn't take you away from your friends."

Karma spoke. "M, you know I won't treat you like a child, so I'm going to be straight with you." The little girl looked at her, distress evident on her face. "That man who brought the woman that hurt us is my father. But he is also part of the Resistance. I know that you know who they are. Those are the people who want to hurt the Galatians, and they want to hurt us, too, because we want to be with Galatians. Your aunt Tam has been training with them to get invaluable information."

M wiped her wet eyes and stared at her mother. The look in her eyes broke Karma's heart, but she had to make sure that M was safe, and for now, that was more important than her disappointment.

"I have spoken to my father, and his hatred of aliens and particularly his disrespect of your father and the other Guards makes him dangerous to us. He found us when we were in hiding, which means that our enemies can find us. So, you see why we have to leave."

M's expression became doubtful, but she listened quietly.

Rafe continued speaking. "M, there are places in the world where people will sacrifice their family members for their own beliefs. You happen to know someone that this happened to. Bain. His father did something despicable by trying to kill him because, in his mind, he thought he would be better off dead than without him. Kelsie's mom and dad just abandoned her when she got too sick for them.

"We can't trust that just because he is your mother's parent, he will not hurt her or us. He could hurt your brother because he's part Galatian. We can't take a chance."

M looked over to the closed door of the nursery. Her resolve began to deteriorate. She was going to put her foot down and demand to be allowed to stay with Kelsie and Bain. But she had a little brother to protect, and as much as she wanted to be with her friends, Runnar had to come first.

"They will join us as soon as they are able."

M looked at her father again and then finally nodded.

I have to finish packing. She turned and went back to her room, closing the door behind her.

Rafe rose to his feet. His heart ached for her. He would find a way to make her happy again as soon as he got his family to safety. Karma came over and hugged him, and it made him feel better.

Daya was already packed and pacing anxiously. Paris had left immediately after their earlier meeting. She wasn't going to complain because she understood that there were a lot of things going on. But she did want to talk to him about what Madeline thought about them holding Mr. Conrad in the dungeon beneath the school. But he had simply gripped her hand and explained he'd be back as quickly as possible.

After returning to their home, she had not immediately packed. It was because she wasn't sure if she wanted to go with them. Why should she? She knew Maddie was pissed at her, and Rafe wasn't happy about their decision either. Karma was the one person she couldn't quite figure out.

She could just return to the school, and now she had put her surgery on the back burner, she could slip back into her old life, taking care of the kids while she kept watch over her prisoner.

But to be truthful, Maddie was probably going to fire her. The idea of losing her dream job was just another boulder on her mountain of worries. One of them was what to do with Mr. Conrad. If she was banned from the school, then she would have to put him to death because what else could be done with him?

Daya had finally begun to pack her few belongings as she considered that being without Paris was something she was simply unwilling to do. She would follow her man to the ends of the Earth— or to another planet, as the case may be. But Mr. Conrad still nagged her mind. He deserved to die—and yet, not by her hand. Paris had offered to do the deed, but him doing it was no different than her doing it—not if she was the one who gave him permission.

She slumped down in the living room that she hadn't even had an opportunity to familiarize herself with. There was no choice, really. Mr. Conrad would need to be put to death. And she would have to live with that. At least it was more humane than what she knew Paris intended—just leaving him to die from hunger and thirst. Mr. Conrad was indeed a monster—but she wasn't.

Whenever Paris returned, she would tell him that they would need to make a detour to the school, and she decided that if she was woman enough to determine the end of another's life, then she was woman enough to carry out the deed herself.

With that decided, she felt something close to relief.

Instead of contacting Paris on the communicator, she decided there was something else she needed to do that was long overdue.

She left her house. There was a soldier stationed outside her door. She wasn't surprised. Rafe had ordered a guard outside of everyone's house. The soldier nodded at her.

"Ma'am. Is there anything I can help you with?"

"No. I'm just visiting." For a moment, she wondered if he would tell her to go back into her house. That was from years of conditioning of being treated poorly by the city's guards. But this guard simply nodded dutifully.

"Would you like me to escort you, ma'am?"

Daya shook her head and pointed to the house visible in the distance. "I'm just going there."

"Yes, ma'am."

Daya walked quickly, not because it was still pitch dark outside because she'd walked in the pitch dark for years—but because she didn't want to back out of this task.

When she finally reached the house, she was surprised there wasn't a guard stationed outside. She knocked, and a second later, the door swung open. A soldier with a stern expression answered the door.

"Uh..." Daya began. "I'm here to see Justina."

Recognizing her, Sgt. Adrian Kelly's posture and demeanor changed. They were expecting one of their teammates to give them shit for coming inside. Everyone always turned things dirty when Adrian just wanted to assure the mistress that they would be stationed to accompany the starship. Of course, maybe Adrian had given them a reason to talk when they had traded favors in order to get this assignment as a guard to the mistress.

But it was the right move. The beautiful woman looked relieved and even smiled when Adrian knocked on the door. After being invited in for coffee, the two resumed their talk, which had been interrupted earlier.

Justina was looking from over Adrian's shoulder. "Come in, Daya."

Daya stepped in, not sure if she was interrupting. But Adrian stepped out the door.

"I will be out here if you ladies need anything."

"Thanks for checking in on me, Sgt. Kelly." Justina's eyes lingered on the soldier, and Daya's brow arched imperceptibly.

"Of course," Sgt. Kelly closed the door after them. Justina looked at Daya.

"I hope I'm not interrupting... "

Justina smiled. "No. I was just having coffee. Have a cup?"

"Yes, thank you." Justina led her into the kitchen. The home was nice but in disarray. She liked the way Justina had decorated her home. It wasn't extravagant but seemed very comfortable with throw blankets and oversized pillows. There was even a fire burning in the fireplace.

"I like your home."

"I had just gotten it the way I like… " Justina shrugged. "But oh well." She poured Daya's coffee and then automatically added sugar, and then went to the fridge for the sweet cream. She peeked at the other woman.

"I would ask how you take your coffee," Justina said. "But I think I know."

"What?" Daya asked in confusion as she accepted the hot beverage.

"Who do you think made that thermos of coffee Paris brought you each morning?" Justina looked amused. "I knew something was up when he asked for sugar and sweet cream in it. You know Galatians don't really like sweets. They prefer savory things—salt would be their treat."

Daya's face flamed. "I didn't realize—"

Justina waved her hand dismissively. "You probably enjoyed it more than he ever could."

Daya inhaled anxiously. "I just wanted to thank you for what you said back at the meeting. Paris cares a great deal for the children, and I hate that anyone would think he would do anything to put them at risk."

"He is a good person. Please take care of him."

"I will. I have. I'm trying…" Daya felt like face-palming herself at her stuttering response. She hated being so nervous. Justina had been nothing but nice to her. But it still felt like facing the other woman.

Justina chuckled. "It's not easy. There is a huge learning curve being with a Galatian."

"Being with a man, period," Daya added.

Justina just smirked. "I agree with that."

Daya blushed again. "I just mean that I've never had a boyfriend or anything like that. Well, except for when I was a kid and I had a little neighborhood boyfriend."

"When I was a kid, I had the equivalent—only mine was a girl-friend." Justina sipped her coffee and then got up to warm it in the microwave while Daya watched her. Justina continued. "Paris was kind enough to recognize my predicament and to not insist that I perform my... *wifely* duties."

"Oh," Daya said in dawning understanding.

"He didn't send me back as defective and insist on another consort. Somehow, he understood, and to show my appreciation, I became his friend." Justina smiled more to herself than to Daya. "Best of all, he became mine."

The bell rang on the microwave, and she retrieved her coffee and returned to the table. "So, as he has protected me, I'm here to protect him."

"I can tell you I love Paris—probably more than I've ever loved anyone. But you are right about the learning curve. But we are committed, and as long as we have that, then we can accomplish anything."

"Good to hear. I know Paris loves you. I think his life is better with you in it. After his Japoxillian died, you are the only thing that brings happiness to his scales." They both laughed.

Daya held her mug of coffee with a broad grin. "I do have a confession."

"Do tell?"

"I actually prefer my coffee black." Justina threw her head back and laughed loudly. She jumped up, got another mug, and poured Daya a fresh cup. When she placed it before her, Justina decided she was going to like this woman.

Daya didn't stay long since she knew Justina had more packing to do. When she left, the sun was beginning to rise. That meant Rafe would want to head for the planet. It was frightening to think about living on an entirely new planet. But first things first. Deal with Mr. Conrad and then follow her man.

When she stepped into the home, Paris came out of his weapon's room. He paused as he gazed at Daya. "I admit I thought you might have decided to run off, but then I saw your suitcase."

She smiled. "You did? And you didn't blow up my communicator searching for me."

He walked to her and pulled her gently into his arms. "No. You have a tracker."

"What?" she pulled back, but he made a laughing sound and pulled her to him again.

"And I didn't use it. Your guard told me you went to Justina's house." She relaxed against him. He didn't tell her he panicked before questioning the guard, nearly biting his head off—literally.

He kissed her, relishing the taste of her mouth: coffee and, of course, her own individual essence. He pulled back reluctantly. "We have a lot to talk about, but unfortunately, a transport will arrive soon to collect us. I need to finish up."

"Babe. We have to deal with our own prisoner. I know you're going to say we should leave him to starve to death—"

Paris was already heading back to his weapon's room. He stopped and looked over his shoulder. "That is one of the things I wanted to talk to you about." Although he wasn't facing her, his tail didn't move as he observed her. "I've released him."

Chapter Thirty-Two

"You WHAT?" Daya screeched.

Paris raised his hands. "I just returned from the school, and I released him—"

"But I thought we didn't want to risk him telling what we did!" Of all the indecisions that Daya had, there was never one concerning turning the man loose!

"No. That is not going to happen. I doubt if he'll ever talk. My love, I have to gather my weapons. Come to the room with me, and I'll explain."

She followed him, wishing he could just tell a story straight without her having to ask follow-up questions. "Okay, Paris. Tell me what happened."

He began opening weapons cases that looked as if he was arming a militia instead of just himself. He went about his task of packing as if his words weren't the most important of their lives—or at least, of hers.

"I put him in the incinerator first. But no worries, I didn't kill him, although he screamed like he hadn't torched several women to death."

"You put him in the incinerator?" Her words were slow and measured as if she examined the meaning of each.

"Only for a minute—not even a minute. Just thirty seconds or so. Long enough, though. And then I dumped him at one of the hospitals meant for the city dwellers."

"Okay..." she said slowly.

He paused at her distress and then came over and pulled her into his arms. "Daya, we both know the horror that man inflicted, not only on you but on other women who didn't survive. They suffered a great deal before they died, but you survived. And for that reason, your suffering has been long-lasting.

"I admit I went there with every intention of killing him. But his utter sniveling angered me. I wanted him to have just a taste of the suffering he inflicted on others. And so, I gave it to him."

Daya placed her forehead against his chest. "Oh, Paris. I love you." She raised her head to look at him, concern in her eyes. "But what if he does survive and he talks to the authorities?"

He gently rubbed her arm, mindful of her fragile skin but needing the contact as much as he sensed she did. "There's very little chance that the hospital where I dumped him will have the ability to treat someone with such extensive injuries. And they will probably assume he's another in a line of homeless unfortunates who got into an accident. I hear that that particular hospital receives many patients who burn themselves up while creating illegal drugs—like what Kelsie's parents very nearly did to their daughter.

"The point is that *if* he manages to survive, and *if* he speaks about what happened to him, then he will wish he had died." Paris tilted her chin so she looked directly into his eyes. "I will take great pleasure in finishing what I began."

Daya nodded in understanding. Paris had been holding back for a very long time out of respect for her. But his instincts and training were to destroy the monster.

There was a knock on the front door. Paris craned his neck and tilted his head. "The transport has arrived. Go on and have them load your belongings while I finish up here."

"Okay."

With Daya out of the house to supervise the collection of their meager belongings, Paris checked his communicator. He hadn't wanted to involve anyone else, but he did trust the Galatian Guard that had replaced him as head of security for St. Aloysius. He would report if there was any news that the human had survived his ordeal.

While he hadn't lied to Daya, he hadn't explained everything—like the arm he'd broken in two places. And there was the matter of some internal bleeding... No, the chances he would live through the day was slim, but the Guard would let him know if he did, and then they would take final steps to end Martin Conrad.

Someone had been kind enough to bring Garry a pallet to sleep on. It wasn't much more than a sleeping bag and blanket. He'd slept on worse but had gotten very little sleep. The Galatian wasn't faring well, and whatever had possessed him to actually treat her had also driven him to make sure she survived—at least long enough for the Galatians to do whatever they intended.

It seemed strange he worked so hard to save her life with the knowledge she would be given over to be put to death—or worse.

He shouldn't care. He'd seen the video interview given by Karma Sigur and just a few moments of the horror that had been captured by the security cameras.

Obviously, this beast should be put down. As a mercenary, he had taken the lives of individuals who had done much less. But it had been in pursuit of the causes he supported, mainly the fight against human trafficking. His other passion of working with the Médecins Sans Frontières gave him the perfect cover to indulge himself.

His mind went back to the little boy that had changed everything for him...

I am evil.

You are not evil, Oskar! We have albinism, and that doesn't make us bad...

He rubbed his eyes and rose from the pallet. The prisoner was unconscious within her chrysalis. That was probably a fortunate thing for her. In just the few short hours he'd treated her, she had lost a foot, which had been previously injured and repaired. Worse was that the majority of her tail had also been lost, and due to the electrical current, it could no longer be regenerated. Her tail stump was all she would ever have. And since Galatians used their tails not only to sense objects, to "see," but also as a weapon and to assist in their jumps and balances—this was a greater loss than a mere foot.

It was probably a good thing she wouldn't be allowed to live much longer.

The door to the den opened, and two soldiers entered. "Doctor. Prepare the prisoner for transport."

He offered the man the briefest look as he continued to review the scanner. He had removed his clothing until he was down to just boxer briefs. It would be ridiculous to get his only set of clothing wet since he had to get into the pool with her in order to treat her.

"That's impossible. She can't be moved."

"Orders are she will be placed onto the transport dead or alive."

He straightened a scowl on his pale face. "I haven't worked on this woman for twelve straight hours just to have all my work go down the drain! Where are you planning to take her?" He demanded.

"Not just her, doctor. You are to come as well—whether she is dead or alive."

Garry climbed out of the pool and reached for where he had placed his clothes. Instead of dressing, he grabbed the upgraded communicator that had been recently issued to him and made a call.

"Paris. What is going on? You want me to move the prisoner to a transport when she's in the beginnings of stasis! I just got her stable—"

"Good," Paris replied. "There will be a modified Galatian pool onboard the ship for her use. Her chrysalis will have to do without water until she's onboard. How quickly that is will depend on you." Neither had bothered to place the communicator on hologram mode, so Garry had to squint at the small screen. He'd had corrective eye surgery but still struggled whenever he was tired.

"There is a big chance that we might lose her. Her organs were shutting down—"

"I don't give a fuck," he replied in Galatian and then switched back to English for Garry's benefit. "This is not my call, Brookstone. If it was, I would have gutted her the moment she arrived. You'll just have to do the best that you can. We're leaving within the hour—"

"What about my equipment? I have monitors-

"The ship will have everything you need."

"Where are we going? I'm staying behind—"

"Where we go will be revealed, but you will not stay behind, Garry. I am sorry, but this is a matter of security. You are not a prisoner."

"But I am also not free."

"Who among us is completely free?" Paris replied before disconnecting.

Garry cursed. How had a one-day excursion to see after a new patient resulted in him being held captive by the most wanted people in the galaxy?

"Okay then."

James Chambers paced. His face ached, but he'd been given a painkiller for the repair. How gracious. He certainly hadn't been given them when he'd initially been entered into the HAE.'

They'd taken the flap he'd discarded and managed to create a graft that had been used to close the wound. It wasn't pretty, but it was the least of his thoughts. He was waiting for Karma. She should have come to him by now to find out more about what he'd had to suffer at the hands of his capturers. And, at the very least, to ask questions that would benefit the Galatians and their cause. He was certain they wanted to know as much as possible about his group.

He sipped the bottled water, and after what seemed like hours, he finally rammed on the locked door.

"Hey! I want to speak to my daughter!"

A Galatian stationed outside of his door spoke from the other side. "Quiet, human! Mistress Sigur will contact you when she wants to speak to you."

"To hell with that! How long do you think I will allow you to keep me here?"

The Galatian said nothing.

"It will be in your best interest to let me speak to her now!"

His people had only given him a finite time to make contact with his daughter. If he couldn't convince her to be open to coming over to their cause, they might not ever allow him to make contact with her again and have seen her with his own eyes, talked to her, and heard her voice; there was no way he could ever allow that to happen. His life was for the cause—but the only purpose for the cause was so he could make a world worthy of his daughter.

It was an hour later that the door to his cell was opened, and two Galatians were standing at the entrance.

"Follow," one said simply.

He did. They hadn't handcuffed him. Had Karma decided that their lives were meant to continue in synch, working for the cause to eradicate the evils that had befallen their world? What a force they would make, his daughter by his side.

He was outside in the bright sun, somewhat surprised he wasn't being led to another secured room. He wished he'd washed up a bit. There was still blood on his hands. He rubbed them on his black slacks and hoped his bandaged face wasn't too jarring—she'd already had one shock seeing the prosthetics.

James's eyes narrowed as he took in his surroundings. It was quiet. Too quiet. He looked at one of the Galatians. "Where are you taking me."

"You're being released. By orders of your daughter." Now he saw that his pod had been moved and was close by. He stopped walking.

"No. Not without speaking to my daughter."

The guard reached into his harness, and for a moment, James thought he'd overplayed and was about to get blown up. Instead, he was handed a handheld projector. He looked at the Galatians curiously before accepting it. After pressing play, an image of his Karma appeared as a hologram before him. She was seated in the same room she'd first talked to him. Only this time, the room was in disarray, as if someone had quickly packed.

"Hi, Daddy. I wanted to tell you goodbye. I'm sorry we didn't have an opportunity to speak face to face this one last time—but we have left this compound, which is more your fault than ours." James looked quickly to the sky for any sign of transport vehicles. Of course, there were none to be seen. His guards had made sure of that.

Karma continued speaking. "We can't stay here, not after you were able to locate us. And you represent our enemies, and that makes you my enemy."

James frowned. How could she come to such a conclusion after all he'd done to get here, all the years of waiting and all the bargaining and promises just so he could talk to his Baby girl?

"I hate to say that as much as I think it hurts to hear it." And, in fact, her eyes brightened with unshed tears. "I appreciate you bringing that woman that hurt me. But will you bring the heads of the Resistance to me next? Because they want to hurt me just as badly."

Tears sprang to James's eyes. "It doesn't have to be goodbye, Baby girl..." he whispered.

"Dad, don't try to find me again. You won't. And even if you did, I'd just have to leave because whether you are dangerous to me or not, your people are. And I won't put my friends and family at risk again. Goodbye, Dad... and... I do love you. If you feel the same, just leave us alone."

The recording ended, and the image of his daughter disappeared. Burning tears dripped from his eyes. It hurt to lose her again, first because of the aliens and then because of his own actions. He grit his teeth and looked at the lizard people before moving towards his pod.

He did not agree that any of this was his fault. It was the aliens that had caused him so much loss, and his desire to end them had just been reinforced.

Part Three

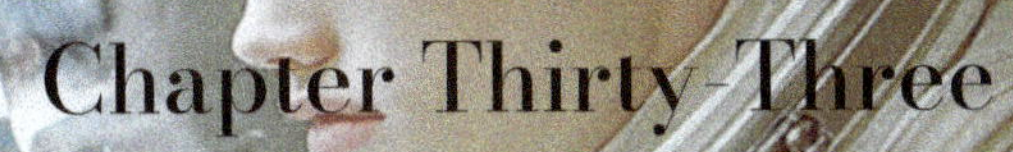

Chapter Thirty-Three

M looked around, taking in all the strange new things around her. She'd never been in a real spaceship before —not counting the space pods. She'd been in those plenty of times, but only high in the sky, never breaking out of the Earth's atmosphere.

They had to use a transport just to get to the spaceship, and that was a little scary. Aunt Maddie had closed her eyes when they left Earth, but not her. She had stared in awe at the large observation window. It was so quick! Then, the transport landed inside the large spaceship that would take them to a new planet.

Aunt Maddie stopped being scared and went right to the window, where she stared at Earth for a long time.

The first thing Papa did was hold an important meeting, and she was happy they didn't make her go somewhere while the grownups talked. Ha, but where could they send her on a spaceship?

Papa said the planet they were traveling to was called EX-112. M thought it was a cool name, but he said the names were based on the star chart, but people called it lots of things, including Eden.

He said they wouldn't need breathing apparatus because the

planet was a lot like Earth, and the terraforming, which added Earth resources, had helped normalize it for humans. But he did say it might take some time to get used to the purple atmosphere and longer days and nights. She thought that part was especially cool.

Uncle Drago went on to explain that it was very small, one of millions of planets that were too small to count and only had a land mass of North America. There was water, and it was developed for human beings who claimed not to want to live on an Earth run by aliens.

They had financed it to be similar to an exclusive retreat—only, once they lived there for a few years, nearly forty percent of the occupants had wanted to return to Earth. Papa and Uncle Drago didn't know why but thought it was that even paradise wasn't as good as being home.

M thought they wouldn't say that if they had lived on a sidewalk with cardboard and a blanket as their bed.

After the meeting, everyone had to go to the medic to get vaccinated. She was a big girl and had to have surgery on her throat and ears, so it wasn't scary—well, not very scary. Then Papa said they would go to sleep, and when they woke up, they would be on the planet.

Aunt Maddie got scared again, but Uncle Drago explained they would be asleep for three days so that they could go into warp speed. Otherwise, even with the spacecraft's atmosphere, their innards might rupture, so they would need to be placed in special chambers.

Even M didn't like the idea of that. Because the Galatians did not have to go into special chambers, their bodies couldn't be damaged by the warp speed. But that meant the Black Mask wouldn't be put to sleep either.

Papa had gone down on his knee in front of her. "Little one. Do not worry about Ragna. She is too sick to come out of her chrysalis. Dr. Brookstone says she is barely alive. Besides, even though the soldiers will be asleep, there are half a dozen Galatians that will be guarding her, and that doesn't include me and your uncles. Okay?"

She gave him a doubtful look.

I want to see her.

Papa and Mama exchanged looks. Mama frowned but said nothing.

"Will you feel better if you saw she is no threat to you?"

M nodded.

He straightened and took her hand. "Will you come?" he asked Mama, who bounced Runnar even though he wasn't crying. He was looking around as if he understood that something new and exciting was happening.

"No. I'm going to feed him before we go down," Mama said tiredly.

"No need," Papa said. "Your system will be slowed down so you won't burn any fuel while asleep."

"I understand, but... "

Papa nodded and then led M down the corridor to the Galatian pool.

"You are more concerned with the prisoner than being put to sleep for three days."

She looked up, craning her neck. **You said that even if I woke up, nothing bad would happen as long as I'm in the chamber. I'm not worried.**

He smiled, his scales brightening. "Good girl.

Maybe she was right, Rafe thought. Maybe she did need to see that Ragna was of no threat to anyone. Dr. Brookstone had explained that the damage done to her by prolonged electrocution had not only affected the loss of a foot and the majority of her tail but might also affect her heart and liver. He'd said that in time, the damage could reverse. With many more instances of—"

"Just keep her alive long enough to gain consciousness," Rafe had growled. And then he had walked away.

When he and M entered the den much later, he saw that it wasn't empty. There were three Galatians enjoying it. The ship was large enough to accommodate the needs of dozens of Galatians, and he was unsure if he liked seeing others obviously enjoying it with her in it.

"What is this?" Rafe's voice boomed through the room. The Galatians within the pool became still.

Dr. Brookstone was standing at a holographic monitor inputting figures. He barely gave Rafe a glance as he responded. "The pool needs ongoing nutrients. Her body is absorbing the minerals at an unimaginable rate! I asked them to add to it."

Rafe spoke in Galatian, and the Guards immediately got out.

"Hey!" Garry exclaimed.

"Feel free to add to the pool, but I want my guards on high alert, and that means standing guard outside of the pool."

Garry frowned and then looked down at M. "Who is this? Someone else for me to treat?"

"No. This is my child. I want her to see that our prisoner is of no danger to anyone."

M watched the entire scene silently. Once the Galatians left the room, she eyed the chrysalis that housed the scary lady.

Just like Papa's chrysalis, she could see the silhouette of a form. But it didn't move like Papa had.

The doctor's voice pulled at her attention. His voice was nicer and softer when he spoke to her.

"What's your name? I'm Dr. Garry."

M

"Hello." Garry recognized her from the video shown at Karma Sigur's interview. It seemed a million years ago, but it was just yesterday. He felt saddened by what she'd gone through, and he couldn't help but be reminded of Oskar. Try as he might, he couldn't save all of the little children.

This little girl's ordeal would have been incredibly traumatizing, seeing so much death at such a young age. He pressed some buttons on the holographic interface, and it showed a full-body scan of the female Galatian.

"Okay, M. You see here? This shows the prisoner's brain activity.

Normal would be around five hundred thirty to six hundred or so. Hers is only barely one hundred. That means this prisoner is completely unconscious and actually comatose.

"Also, you can see her image? No movement." He pointed to a shadow on the display. "I hope this doesn't get too morbid for you," he said gently. "But this shadow is her foot. You can see that it has almost disappeared. That's because her chrysalis is absorbing it and then feeding it back to her as nutrient. The same goes for her tail. It's already gone and will never regenerate—grow back."

M looked at him closely as if checking for a lie.

"Any questions?"

Can she get out early?

"I've treated many Galatians out in the field, and while it's possible for them to break free before their change is complete, I have never seen anyone do it without the claws on both feet and the power of their tail. M. I can assure you she is not going to escape this pool. And once we are on the planet, she will be secured by more electrical bars. She can't hurt you or anyone else."

M looked at the monitor again and then at the figure of the entombed Black Mask before turning back to Dr. Garry.

Okay.

It didn't appear as if she'd be able to hurt the Black Mask until after they were off the ship. And then, she would have to figure out how to open the electric cell. But once she did, she was going to end the bad lady before she could hurt anyone again.

"Isn't there any other way?" Maddie asked anxiously. She was pacing around the small room that had been assigned to them. What was the point if she was going to spend the majority of the trip in some sleeping chamber?

Drago inhaled. Maddie very seldom complained about anything. She followed him without question and not out of a sense of duty but out of love. It made it difficult for him to tell her no. In this matter, there was no other way.

"If we do not go into warp speed, then the safest speed that would not be damaging would have us arrive at our destination in one year and three months."

"What?" she exclaimed. "I...what if something goes wrong, Drago?"

"Maddie, we have traveled like this on countless missions. It is very safe."

She looked at him closely. He hadn't said that they had never lost a human, and she decided not to ask. She looked at her son, who was sitting on a blanket on the carpeted floor, playing with several toys. He pounded them against each other when he wasn't trying to eat them.

Her heart clutched in concern. He was so precious with his shock of black hair that fell into big blue eyes.

"He's just a baby. Are you sure it's safe?"

Drago nodded once. "Our son will be safe. When the humans made this journey, they also brought babies. There were even pregnant women. None were adversely affected."

"But Rex had corrective surgery for his Down's Syndrome. And what about his hearing and eyesight? What about the surgery M had? The surgeons always say it will take a full year before complete healing, and it's only—"

He hugged her, swaying with her until she calmed.

"I'd never risk my son. But if you believe leaving Earth is the wrong decision—"

She pulled back long enough to look at him quickly. "I'm not saying that! I just don't know. I don't know the right thing to do."

He kissed the top of her head. "My love, we both know we cannot trust the Rebels that are associated with James Chambers. We cannot trust The Collective, who have been incessantly trying to contact Rafe and me. The Queens have to know there is a possibility that we might have taken possession of Ragna. They are probably the biggest threat to us at the moment. If James Chambers found us, then—"

Maddie hugged him. "You're right. Of course, you're right!"

"No. I am not always right." He hadn't been right to leave Rafe behind after the attack. They should have never separated. It was just at the time he felt as if the target that Karma brought was one he didn't want to be aimed at his own family.

Later, he realized they were all the same in the eyes of their enemies. They could kidnap any of them in order to get to Rafe. And make no mistake, Rafe was the target of their enemies.

Mayva stretched out on the chaise. She spread and then lifted one leg, exposing her rosebud. She enjoyed anal sex now that it wasn't with that dead old prick she'd murdered. It wasn't something the school had ever taught them, as sexual pleasure with a Galatian would never occur within that particular orifice. But Heinrich hadn't cared.

But Pod was different. He could make his manhood slender so it perfectly fit. And then he could use a digit to titillate her clit and then another to fill her pussy.

How things had changed in less than a week! To think he had initially revolted her.

"Pod. You know what to do," she demanded. He crawled forward on all fours, but she stopped him before he could touch her. "You're slacking! You don't look enough like Rafe. Do I need to show you another picture of him?"

"No, mistress," he replied. He closed his eyes and made the adjustments.

"That's better," she sighed. "Why can't you be a different color? That gray is ugly."

"Gray is my natural color, Mayva. I can change my form. I can't change my color." He allowed himself to exhale. "You should allow me to be my own form. You may like me the way that I'm intended to be—"

"No. I can guarantee you that I will not! Now hurry and lick my asshole."

Pod moved between her legs, wondering why he had ever thought she was beautiful.

Chapter Thirty-Four

Rafe was heading for the flight deck when he saw the incoming communication from Commander Einar. The morning had already been a long one, and the last thing he wanted was to have a battle of wills with Einar.

Over half of the human crew was in a state of suspended animation within safety chambers that would protect them from the damages of warp speed. The onboard physicians were busily overseeing the other half.

Karma had insisted on being present for the first few procedures to ensure she understood the process. The physicians were happy to explain the simple steps as the first soldiers went through the procedure.

First was the injection that would place the recipient into a deep, pleasant sleep. And then, once the glass dome closed over the sleeping module, a special mixture of air would maintain that sleep. The chamber would open on its own once arriving at their destination, and they would awaken naturally with no residual sleeplessness.

Karma spoke to some of the soldiers as they were undergoing the procedure, and they assured her they'd done it before—in some cases, many times. But within seconds, they were out cold with happy smiles on their faces. And Karma was more at ease with it all.

Rafe could not have felt more-proud to have a partner like her by his side. She never shirked away from the difficult actions. She pushed him to do better by forcing him to see the reality around him. Once that happened, he had never again been able to close his eyes against the obvious injustices that surrounded them all.

Still, Karma had a vulnerability that drew him, something that his other lovers, specifically Ragna, had never possessed. He was driven to protect her and his family because of the softness that existed within her, just as he knew she was fully capable of facing the tough decisions of their predicament.

Their prisoner was a testament to that.

She and M had wanted to be present when they secured Ragna within the den. Dr. Brookside was one of only a handful of humans who would not be within a chamber. For him, there was a protective suit that would allow him to move around the den for several hours at a time before recharging within a chamber.

Karma and M both seemed satisfied when they activated an electrical cage around the den's pool.

Dr. Brookside explained that if the prisoner awoke—which was quite impossible, but *if* that happened and she touched the electrical barrier, the electrical shock magnified by the Galatian waters would kill her instantly.

Both Karma and M had seemed satisfied.

And then it had come time to place their children in stasis. It literally tore at his soul when Karma wept at the sight of Runnar's sleeping form. He understood the symbolism. It gave him an emotional jolt as well, but he assured her that their son would be okay.

By the time they placed M in her chamber, it had been easier on Karma, although M seemed suspicious of it.

What if I have to go pee?

"You won't."

What if I can't breathe?

"Your breathing will virtually stop. It won't hurt you, Little one."

But how do I get out?

"I will be there to get you out as soon as you wake up. Do you see this button? If ever there was an emergency, then this button will open the compartment. But my daughter, you will be asleep, and it will feel like mere moments. When you awake, this will all be over." She had just stared at him, and Rafe knew there were many thoughts swirling around in her complex mind.

And that was pretty much confirmed once she had been put to sleep and Karma realized she was wearing her old Galatian suit beneath her clothing. Once Karma removed her outer warm-up jacket and pants, leaving her with just the Galatian suit, Rafe discovered his hunting knife strapped to her ankle by a makeshift harness made of ribbons.

He left it where it was.

It was by silent agreement that if she was this worried, it was best to leave her with her weapons.

After all this, to say he had little patience for his Commander and his endless requests was an understatement. Rafe decided he would put down his foot and end this once and for all. He was retired and had been fired from his position with the Galatian Exchange. The two men had no need for each other.

"Commander Einar." Rafe spoke simply.

"I have been attempting to contact you for the last few hours." Einar's response was reproachful.

"Then you must know that I am busy. Sir." Rafe hadn't allowed a visual, so there was voice only, but the prolonged pause told him everything he needed to know—Einar obviously desired to put him in his place, but something bigger than his obvious annoyance prevented him from doing so.

"I am contacting you because there has been an important development."

"Oh?" Rafe was suddenly interested.

"It seems that Ragna is missing."

He was happy the communicator was not set to visual because Einar would have surely spotted his lack of surprise.

"What does this have to do with me?" He simply asked.

"Well, it's obvious, don't you think?" When there was no response, Einar continued in a whisper as if someone else was present. "Sigur, your hatred of Ragna is no secret. And after what she did, it would not surprise anyone if you had decided to take matters into your own hands since the Interplanetary Collective has done nothing. And you understand that I was not in agreement with that. An unsanctioned attack in the public eye should have been met with swift and meaningful punishment." Rafe still didn't respond, and Einar continued to fill the empty spaces.

"Look, Rafe, if you've had anything to do with Ragna's disappearance—"

"My wife and I have been busy securing an interviewer, safe locations, and proper questions. I have no time for kidnapping Ragna —and had I wanted to do so, I could have achieved that months ago," came Rafe's smooth response. Again, he was happy there were no visuals. "And as for her disappearance, perhaps she has seen my wife's interview and understands that the tides have gone against her and her cause."

Rafe had been following the news as much as possible—and not simply the news broadcast to the public, but the insider information from top government workers to the common man and women on the street. Most importantly, after the video showing the murder of his family, a wave of Galatian fighters vowed allegiance to his fight for freedom.

The rich had attempted to discredit Karma based on her meager origins, but that had only made her more popular with the people on the streets.

Over the course of the last day, humans from across the world were vocalizing their viewpoints in a way that hadn't been done for many years.

Maybe that was the real reason the Queens wanted to talk to him. They could go to hell.

"Rafe. Lt. Sigur," Commander Einar continued. "I fear that The Collective will get involved if you don't agree to this parley."

It was the Commander who had always seemed more intimidated by The Collective. But that would make sense if he had to be careful of which missions he assigned to them so as not to step on the toes of various interest groups.

Rafe stroked his chin as he considered several possibilities that might help his cause. "Commander, I obviously don't trust the Queen's Council. They support the actions of the Black Masks. But I will agree to a virtual parley as long as my wife is invited. It must also include the Bound-mates of my crew members as well as their current partners, the current head of the Black Mask war council, and each member of the Queen's Council. I also want a Japoxillian delegate from The Interplanetary Collective present. And finally, I want Mayva Heath available to face my wife."

"Yes!" Einar replied happily. "I will return your list of requirements to The Most Exalted."

Hearing Einar say that phrase with such ease sent a chill of disgust down Rafe's spine. He disconnected without another word and resumed his course to the flight deck. Soon, all humans that would be placed in stasis would be in their chambers, and he would be at the helm to get everyone safely to their new home—at least for the foreseeable future.

And by everyone, that included Haru and Tamsyn. If he could get the key players preoccupied with a meeting, then it would be easier to have Haru slip away from Caeda and the guards she had watching him.

If all went as planned, then Haru and Tam would be joining them on EX-112.

The PN/157-SOP Interplanetary Communicator was the top-of-the-line mini-computer translator.

Developed by a network of scientists during the deadly Congotz Battles fifty years prior, the communicators were spy-proof and could perform a plethora of necessary actions from strategic to medical.

Only used by the highest-ranking members of several universal military units, the PN/157-SOP Interplanetary Communicator had one nifty trick. It could provide a correct mixture of breathable air as long as it was dispensed within a small space—such as a hyperbolic chamber. It also had the ability to cleanse any unnatural poisons or gasses for at least 12 hours. For prolonged use as a respiratory, it would need the PN/98Z replaceable filter.

While not many people knew the many uses of the communicator assigned to the military elite who wore them like old-fashioned wristwatches, M Sigur had made it her business to understand the seemingly insignificant trinket's many valuable uses.

Chapter Thirty-Five

Rafe bent and placed a kiss on Karma's lips. Like sleeping beauty, Karma was now in a deathlike sleep. Soon, the glass dome would encase her, and the chamber would feed her air that would essentially send her body functions into a state of hibernation.

He had no fear of malfunctions or any other technical issues. But seeing her as she had lain when comatose for so many weeks made him both angry and sad. He was once again reminded why they had to go to such lengths just to live.

Ragna.

"I promise you Ragna will beg at our feet in agony before I take her final breath. Not one second before she is fully aware of the pain we inflict on her will she be released from her mortal existence."

He touched her cheek with the tip of a finger, careful not to graze her tender flesh with a razor-sharp talon. Rafe finally pressed the control to close the dome and watched as his sleeping beauty fell back into a coma-like state.

He turned away and looked over M's dome and then finally Runnar's. The babe was swaddled because Nanny worried that he might scratch himself in his sleep, and even at barely three months, his claws could do a great deal of damage.

But even at his son's young age, Runnar seemed to be aware he could cause pain—perhaps because he had scratched his own human flesh. He didn't purposely inflict pain on Nanny or his mother, although he had, on occasion, left a pretty bad scratch on M. And that was most likely because she couldn't speak to cry out in pain. She just took it. And still, she never shied away from an opportunity to hold and play with the babe.

Rafe left the room feeling the weight of his fortune at being a member of such a perfect family.

As he headed back to the medical bay, he contacted Drago using his communicator.

"Yes, Rafe?"

"Has your family been put under?"

Drago exhaled a long breath. "It is done."

Rafe grunted. It had likely been an equally joyless task for him as well. "Gather the others, and we will meet in simulator four. I need to update you on my latest conversation with the Commander."

"Eh, and I have an update on Haru and Tamsyn. We will meet at the quarter hour."

Drago rose from his seat in their quarters. There was one chamber that contained his Maddie. A smaller one was beside her that contained his son. She had asked to hold him in her arms as she slept, but he advised that the special mixture of gasses had to be a perfect cocktail for a babe and, therefore, it wasn't advisable for them to stay together. Maddie's disappointment felt like a physical blow to him. He would have to work overtime to make up for these last few months.

He reached down and picked up Rex's toys, placing each lovingly into his toy bin. They had to be successful with their goals, or six years from now, the law would see him bound to Isyss and Maddie, and Rex whisked away to lead their lives without him.

He could no longer imagine a meaningless existence with his

Galatian Bound-mate. Their couplings and interactions had never filled him with exquisite joy the way Maddie made him feel. He supposed he cared for Isyss, but now he knew love, Drago also knew he could never feel this strongly for any other person—Galatian or human.

He contacted Kendrick first as the door to his quarters closed behind him.

"Kendrick. We are to meet Rafe—brother? What are you doing?"

Kendrick swept off the baseball cap. He'd forgotten he was still wearing it. He was so accustomed to living alone and doing what he wanted without the eyes and judgment of others that sometimes he became too comfortable.

"Is there a problem?" Kendrick asked, sidestepping the question.

"There are some new developments that we need to discuss," Drago replied slowly. He was looking at Kendrick's living space. He had chosen human accommodations instead of a Galatian den, which would have been much more comfortable.

There was a poster hanging on the wall of a human playing basketball. And another holographic image of a musician who rapped lyrics to fast-beat music. The television was on in the background and showed a sports game being played.

"What are you doing, Kendrick?" He had no human to cater to, so why was he living like this?

"Don't worry about it," came his response. "I'll see you in Sim four shortly." He disconnected the connection, and Drago scratched his head.

Kendrick looked around his room and cursed when he saw how visible the human paraphernalia had been. For a long time, he'd used it to decorate his living space. After Auras's death, he'd found solace in the human objects that decorated his home. Soon, he began to collect items he appreciated, beginning with music and trinkets. And then it moved on to items of clothing: a cool jacket he'd seen a movie star wearing. He'd even had a jogging suit tailored for his extra tall form. There was even an opening to accommodate his tail.

He loved it so much he now had more than twenty items of clothing from jeans to a vintage leather jacket.

Kendrick had taken on the speech pattern of the humans he observed. And when he was in the privacy of his own home, he often times pretended he was human.

It was a secret he didn't want to share with anyone—well, maybe Justina. She didn't judge but spoke freely. He liked she was supportive while still speaking her mind. Auras had always spoken her mind, but he seldom found anything of interest in her thoughts. She knew how to pleasure him with food and sex, but there wasn't much else she could do for him.

Justina was different. They spoke like real human friends. When she asked how he was doing in light of his consort's death, he knew she expected a true answer. With her, he could admit that, at times, he became lonely. She had reached out and gripped his hand, and he knew then she was a kindred soul.

And since Paris had released her, he thought about taking her on as his replacement consort. The only thing that had prevented him from talking to Paris about it—not that it was any of his business after he'd taken up with Daya Porter, but what held him back was the outdated idea of consorts.

He and Justina were friends. And that is what they were fighting for, after all: the ability for one to choose whom to spend the rest of your life with—even if that was with a human.

He picked up his baseball cap from the floor, dusted it off, and then placed it back on his head.

Paris was dining between the thighs of Daya with great fervor. They had gotten used to making a comfortable pallet on the floor to make love, but there had been some major changes.

Daya no longer feared removing her clothing during the act. And

Paris appreciated tonguing her delectable lady parts as he gazed up the long lines of her body: over the bend of her knee, the dip in her belly, the sway of her breasts, the delicate curve of her collarbone, and finally to her upturned face that whipped back and forth in pleasure.

The pulse in his prick sped up at the sight of her ecstasy, magnified by her keening cries of pleasure.

Paris elongated his tongue and tenderly filled her pussy. Her hips rose to meet him as her body writhed. He felt her fingers gripping the smooth dome of his head. He kept the fine scales there clamped down so she felt nothing but softness against her hands.

She was calling out for more as she pressed him against her, forcing his tongue deeper.

One day, this will be my prick...

He tongue-fucked her roughly as this was one of the few areas of her body undamaged by fire, and he could give it to her hard.

"Yes, YES, YES!" Daya screeched as she moved to grip the comforter within her clenched fists.

A pool of her delicious essence began to flood his tongue, and he slurped it down like a delicacy. He reached up to lightly pinch her nipple as if it was a lever to produce more of her cum—and perhaps it was because next, a watery gush filled his mouth.

Her words became a garbled sound of groans and whimpers as she orgasmed spasmodically against Paris's face.

When she was spent, she peered at him from half-hooded eyes. "Give it to me now."

He sat up on his haunches between her legs, his prick as hard and thick as a club. He stroked himself lightly.

"No. We agreed that this would be a quicky. And if I cum on you, you'll have to take a full-on shower or else you'll wake up three days from now with my seed stuck all over your face and body. And you know I'll shower you with buckets of it."

Despite her fatigue, Daya laughed uproariously. She reached for the head of his prick, and he sucked in a sharp breath.

"I need my dessert, babe." Daya milked him with quick, expert strokes, and within a minute, Paris did indeed cover her with his seed.

They were in the shower about to begin round two when Paris's communicator sounded.

"Who the fuck-?" he cursed. He sighed and then leaned forward to flick Daya's nipple one last time before he stepped out of the shower and answered.

"Drago? What?" he snapped.

"Catch you at the wrong time?" Drago asked. "I've been doing that a lot."

"Uh...no." Paris stepped out of the bathroom, closing the door behind him. He obviously didn't care if Drago saw him nude, but he didn't think Daya would appreciate stepping out of the shower only to be caught on hologram by Drago Engström.

"Apologies. Daya and I were just...saying our goodbyes."

Drago took in Paris's semi-erection and moved on. "There is a meeting in Simulator 4. Meet after you've... said all of your goodbyes."

Paris's brow dipped. "Is something wrong?"

"I think Rafe just wants to fill us in on information. And I, too, have things to share."

Paris's expression became grim. "As do I. I will meet you shortly." After powering off his communicator, he looked down at his hungry prick.

"Later," he promised.

Rafe had manufactured a replica of a Galatian meeting chamber in the ship's simulator. The four current members of his Galatian Guards were sitting on tall, throne-like stones smoothed perfectly to accommodate the size and tail of a Galatian. The stones were in a circular formation, while the remainder of the large chamber looked like Rafe's den back in Galatia.

Even the sound of a nearby pool and waterfall gave the impression of a grotto—except that those items were just simulations. With the exception of the thrones, everything would disappear with the press of a button. The thrones would be absorbed back into the organic compound that awaited the next command to mimic an organic substance.

"I miss Galatia," Drago said as he looked around the simulator.

"I don't," Kendrick replied with a sneer. "Earth has so much more entertainment."

"If only we can get to a point where we enjoy Earth's entertainment," Paris replied.

"Some of us may enjoy it more than others..." Drago didn't look at Kendrick, but the other man felt a jolt of panic, which he tried to quickly mask.

"Brothers," Rafe spoke. "I gathered you here today because there has been a new development. Commander Einar contacted me."

Drago blew out a long breath. "You should have blocked him like I did. He is just a spy for The Collective."

"Yes," Rafe agreed. "But I need to know where *he* and, therefore, *they* stand on matters. Einar has confirmed that the Queens are aware that Ragna is missing."

Kendrick cursed. "Do they suspect us?"

"Of course," Rafe replied. "But there hasn't been an accusation... yet."

"Then we won't talk to him again," Paris stated plainly.

"That might be difficult. I've agreed to a meeting with the Queen's council."

"Why would you do something like that?" Paris shot back in alarm.

"Because as long as I control the meeting, we can better facilitate our needs."

"It was eventually going to happen," Drago replied. "The Collective has made a great show of allowing us to 'work things out.'" Rafe's eye widened when Drago made air quotes. "But they will need to make their decision about our emancipation sooner than later."

Kendrick snorted. "The last time they deliberated on an important matter, it took over five Earth cycles. The Collective's 'sooner' is not in alignment with human longevity.

"Then it is a good thing we are not awaiting their decisions," Rafe replied. "Daily, our forces grow."

"Yes," Drago agreed. "Reports show that since Karma's interview, there has been a spike in both human and Galatian warrior support. Of course, by the same token, the human conservatives are treating Karma as the scapegoat for all discontent between the rich and poor. In fact, there has been a significant bump in rebel funding. And although it's not possible to know exactly how great, our intelligence shows that new membership in various rebel groups is at an all-time high. I have prepared a report."

Rafe stroked his chin. "I hate to remove Tamsyn from her assignment. She has been a great source of information. But their facial recognition programs will discover her—if it already hasn't been done."

"No, she is out and on her way to safety," Drago said. "It's Haru that I worry about. "Caeda is no fool. She has him watched like a hawk despite the fact he has played his part well. He's made no attempt to leave her even when the opportunities to do so were very blatant."

"He is being tested," Paris stated.

"Yes," Drago confirmed. "But Haru has made no attempt to touch her communicator, even when she 'mysteriously' leaves it at his disposal. He has obviously passed her various tests."

"Well, that is because she believes he is there to spy on *her*," Paris added while crossing one leg over the other, sending the pleats of his skirt to fall to either side of his legs. "But he isn't there to listen to her but to her servants, to the people in the market, the everyday people that important individuals tend to forget about."

"Yes," Drago sighed. "But it won't be quite as easy to extract him as it was to deposit him. He needs access to a pod, and his has been confiscated by the Queen's war council."

Rafe smiled. "Let me tell you about my idea to rescue Haru. We're going to have that meeting with Amalia and her council. But I told them only if all of the Bound-mates were present, the two Japox-illian delegates from The Interplanetary Collective, Mayva Heath, and, of course, our own mates."

Everyone made sounds of surprise. Rafe continued to smile. "With Caeda out of the way, and all the key players scrambling to accommodate my demands, Haru should be able to take advantage of an opening."

"Good deal," Drago smiled.

Paris wasn't smiling. "I have another matter to discuss. As you know, I had my own prisoner. There has been a new development that I haven't even spoken to Daya about."

Chapter Thirty-Six

Rafe tensed at Paris's words. Paris said nothing lightly. When he disclosed something of importance, it was on a need-to-know basis. Rafe didn't even want to learn all the things Paris had done without his knowledge. But to mention it at this point was more than likely significant.

"What development?"

Paris leaned back on his throne. "The human I placed in the dungeon lives."

"And was that not the reason you kept him in the dungeon? To amplify his suffering?"

Paris nodded coolly. "Yes, but there came a time when keeping him a prisoner was no longer productive to anyone." He stared pointedly at Rafe. "Nonetheless, it was Daya's decision to keep him when I was ready to dispense of him. When that was no longer conducive, I had to take the control."

Paris wasn't apologetic about that. He respected Daya's needs and wants. But if it came to the better good, he had no qualms about taking matters into his own hands. He understood her moral compass and the limitations that it placed on her when dealing with his alien standards. But in the end, he would never allow her to fail—even if that meant taking over that control.

The fact Paris didn't agree with his decision to bring Ragna with them wasn't lost on Rafe. But he wasn't asking permission. However, when it was all said and done, he knew his brothers would support him in whatever decisions he made.

Good. As he had every intention of torturing his ex-mate before he allowed her the relief of death.

"I went back to the school with every intention of putting the human out of his misery," Paris continued. "But when I placed him in the incinerator to give him a taste of the pain he had inflicted on my mate, he begged for his meager life, a life that included a small cold cell and barely edible food.

"I decided then that his suffering hadn't been great enough. He should have been grateful for the prospect of death."

Rafe was reminded of Ragna's words, begging for mercy, begging for death. He instantly understood what Paris meant.

"So, I pulled him out of the incinerator, and I dumped him near the worst hospital in the city—the one designated for the poorest of the poor. He should have died. But it seems that we took much better care of him than he had ever attempted to care for anyone else." He figured Daya was behind that. She fed him too well and cared whether he had enough water to drink on a daily basis.

"You just let him go..." Kendrick spoke in surprise.

"With some safeguards. I have given Merrick instructions to keep tabs on him. He should have died suffering within a short time of being dumped. However, the hospital was able to stabilize him. They placed him in a medically induced coma." ...where he wasn't suffering. He should be suffering!

Drago stared at Paris as if daggers could fly from his eyes. "This could adversely affect the school. If he wakes up—"

"*If* he wakes up, Merrick will end him."

"If he wakes up," Drago continued, "it will take only seconds for him to explain where he's been all this time. It takes moments to reveal what is located in the basement of a school that we control. Paris, he can point fingers at you, but more importantly, at Daya Porter, a teacher in a school that our team has been protecting. In the wrong hands—"

"I understand," Paris snapped. He sighed and spoke calmer. "I understand. This is why I bring this to you now."

Rafe interrupted the impending argument. "Well, I can tell you what I want you to do to handle this, but what do you want to do?"

Paris didn't pause in his response. "I want him to suffer. But...I need for him to die."

"Then it is settled. Have Merrick carry out the deed as soon as feasible." Rafe turned to Kendrick. "Reach out to your law enforcement contacts to confirm that nothing has been reported and that no one is investigating the school." He looked at Drago, "Make sure the Galatian guards assigned to the school are aware of the threat. At this time, don't bring the humans into the fold. Matters are too touchy to risk our military turning against us."

"Ai," Drago and Kendrick said in unison.

Rafe drummed his fingers across his knee as he thought. If someone had done to Karma what had been done to Paris's lover, he would have done the same to the man. The idea of it nearly sent him into a rage.

"I understand why you did this, Paris," he growled. "He hurt your woman, and he was unapologetic about it until you took matters into your own hands." Paris nodded once. "There is no difference with my decision to keep Ragna. She killed my son. My son!" No one spoke for a long while before Rafe continued. "And she killed someone that each of us cared for: Titus, Auras, Pogo, LayLay, and our other Japoxillian comrades."

Rafe's eyes moved to those of each of his brothers. "I need each of you to understand how much I hate that *itchnol* and how badly I need her to suffer. Death is too good for her."

"I understand, brother," Paris replied quietly. "My hatred of Ragna knows no bounds." He leaned forward. "But let us agree to make this ending swift despite our hatred, in the best interest of our family, who are struggling with renewed trauma and fear."

Rafe inhaled heavily, his chest moving up and down. His friend was right.

"When we arrive, I will have Dr. Brookstone revive Ragna. I will then dispense her and send her corpse to flames."

Drago, Kendrick, and Paris nodded in agreement.

Rafe was tired of the topic. He moved on. "Reports state that James Chambers has left the compound. Our military team is on high alert for any retaliation. The remainder of the soldiers and guards will vacate the premises by sundown."

There would be very few remnants of those who had called the place home for the last few months.

Rafe stood, and the others followed suit. "Let us disperse. We each have a great deal to accomplish." He left the room without another word.

Mayva was sound asleep despite the fact that the mattress was flimsy and the blankets course. She felt a slight chill and pulled them up to her chin.

"Pod," she mumbled sleepily. "It's cold." She drifted back into a restless sleep until, a few moments later, she realized that the room hadn't warmed up at all.

"Pod!" she called sharply and then rolled over onto her back where she looked around the darkened room. It was still night and the shades were drawn tight which didn't allow for even the slightest bit of light, even from the moon and stars.

She rubbed her eyes and yawned. "Pod?" Damnit, where was he —it. She wasn't even sure creatures like him had true genders. They could 'become' whatever they wanted to become. She didn't want to think about that. It had her feel disgusted.

She reached over to the bedside table where the light controls were located and then illuminated the room in a warm yellow light—which only highlighted the drab and dingy conditions.

Pod said that this was a safehouse operated for the use of the Queens on the rare occasions that they ventured to Earth. It was more like a dump. She wasn't even surprised to learn that the Queens didn't use the small cabin any longer because it was so outdated—or what he described as rustic.

As she looked around the bedroom, she confirmed he wasn't in sight. Hopefully, he had gone out for more supplies. He had brought meat and bread for sandwiches. Sandwiches as if she were a street urchin!

Ugh, she hated him. He was so stupid. How did you escape with the head of the North American Galatian Exchange without preparing proper accommodations?! She climbed out of bed, making sure her fur slippers were right at her feet. If she accidentally touched the questionable floor with her bare skin she might scream. Again.

He hated it when she screamed, so she did it often. She screamed when he didn't do something right. She screamed when he asked her questions about unimportant things like her thoughts or feelings, as if she would tell something like *it* the thoughts that went through her mind.

First and foremost, she regretted giving Ragna so much power over her. She should possess all the power in their relationship. Without her, the rebellion wouldn't be the well-organized machine she had created. Those bunch of good ol' boys hated what they didn't even understand. Her speeches had pinpointed a true target for their rhetoric; that whore that had stolen her position.

Of course, she had every intention of making Karma pay for leaving her on the outskirts of relationships that had taken her years to hone. The girls were supposed to be hers to control, but they fell all over themselves to please that imposter. She spared a thought about Auras and Polat and felt an inkling of regret.

Suppressing it she moved to the next room and turned on the

light where it was clear to see that it too was empty. Pod had left without stoking the fire in the fireplace?

Ohhh, when he returned, she was going to give him hell. She cursed and walked into the kitchen to make herself a cup of tea. He made it pretty good and she couldn't replicate the tarty sweetness he added to it. She searched the refrigerator for the likely piece of fruit he surely added to it, but it was all strange and alien.

Slamming the door shut she added sugar wishing that it wasn't the processed white stuff. She needed to trade Pod in for an upgraded version.

She carried her tea into the bathroom and began her morning routine. She bathed with the poor-quality soap and then conditioned her long hair the best she could with the over-the-counter conditioner. She hoped he remembered to get another bottle. Her long hair needed every drop, and since she washed it every other day, she needed plenty.

She moisturized her skin, checked for wrinkles and blemishes and then applied her makeup with care. She wasn't doing this for Pod, but to make sure she maintained her beauty. Just because she was struggling now didn't give her an excuse to let herself go. One day she would meet the man that matched her in looks and status.

At the moment, that man was Rafe Sigur. A throb of longing shot through her. Damn, Pod, where was he to satisfy her?!

She stormed to the window where the sun had risen as it was well into the morning and heading towards afternoon. There was nothing to see but trees.

They were in the middle of nowhere. No...*she* was in the middle of nowhere.

She allowed her brow to crease (momentarily forgetting her fear of developing age lines).

"Who is going to make my breakfast?" she whispered aloud.

The next morning when Mayva woke up, her anger had dissolved. She had flipped over a cocktail table and broken a lamp the night before when she'd grown hungry and there was no vendor to create her meals or ingredients for her to cook something she could bear to eat. She had eventually scrambled two eggs. In the very back of her mind she kept tabs on her provisions.

Just in case.

Mayva reached into her bedside table drawer where her communicator was located. But who would she use it to call? Ragna had to be frantically searching for her. And those horrible guards would certainly mistreat her if they had the slightest opportunity.

She thought about her mom and dad, but it was their fault that... Mayva just shook her head. She loved them about as much as they loved her which was zero.

She couldn't allow herself to be returned to Ragna. That monster had treated her atrociously—and after all she'd done!

Hmmm. When you didn't like your boss the best thing to do was to go over their head... That would be to The Most Exalted. Mayva knew for a fact that Ragna hated that one. She took pot shots whenever the topic of the high-ranking Queen ever came up.

If the head of the Queens knew the abuse Ragna had subjected her to, *and* she was reminded of her importance to the cause then she might be returned to her prized position—all while deposing that bitch Ragna.

Mayva stared at the communicator. Once she turned it on they would track her. She might wait another day, just in case Pod dragged his sorry ass back to her.

Not once did she consider he might be somewhere hurt, fighting to return to her.

But he wasn't. Pod had cleared out realizing he had dodged something he feared more than the Queens.

Chapter Thirty Seven

When M's eyes opened, she had no residual sleepiness, she did not wonder where she was and there was no fear or trepidation. All she knew was a sense of purpose.

Kill the Black Mask.

She turned her head to make sure she was alone. Well Mama and baby brother were there, but sleeping in their own glass sleeping chambers. Besides them she was alone in the room. She looked down and saw she was just wearing her black Galatian clothing. That meant either Mama or Papa had discovered them beneath her real clothes. That didn't matter half as much as the fact she still felt the blade of the hunting knife strapped to her ankle.

Good. Mama and papa had accepted her role as a protector.

She looked at the communicator strapped to her wrist. It was releasing a proper mixture of breathable air. She wasn't sure exactly what would happen to her once she opened her chamber—she didn't think it was the air that would hurt her outside of it. It had to do with the speed doing things to her insides—like when uncle Paris would take her back and forth in his pod. They would fly in the sky so fast she could sometimes feel herself being sucked back into her chair before he let the craft go into auto pilot.

M pressed the emergency lever that would open the chamber from the inside. It only made sense that there was a way to escape the chamber and papa had confirmed it. When the door lifted, M acted quickly. She sat up until she was in a crouch and then quickly leaped from the platform.

It instantly became apparent why a human wouldn't want to travel for any length of time during warp speed without a sleeping chamber.

First, it seemed as if she moved in fast speed despite the fact her body felt heavier. Her heart thumped louder and she could hear the blood rushing throughout her veins. It was almost like she wanted to explode from the inside out! The sensation wasn't painful, but it certainly wasn't comfortable.

She eyed the closet situated at the far side of the room. Papa had said not all the humans would be put to sleep. The important people would wear special suits that would equalize the pressure—special people like the doctor who was taking care of the Black Mask.

M reached the closet before she realized it—and very nearly ran right into the door! She opened the closet and saw what she had seen while they had toured their quarters: two white air suits.

She had reasoned that if there was a lever to open the chamber for emergency purposes, then there had to be spare suits for everyone.

M wasted no time retrieving and then slipping into the suit. Her tummy was beginning to ache and she suddenly had a strong urge to go to the toilet for a big poop. But that was just a fake feeling. She had a scary idea that if she didn't get into this suit straight away, then it wouldn't be poop coming out of her body, but maybe her insides.

A soft alarm sounded that made her jerk as she quickly zipped the oversized fabric together. But it was coming from her communicator and not from the suit or some other detection device warning someone she'd escaped her chamber.

Unstable environment detected

She quickly hit the sound off button, quieting the tattle tale alarm and faltered as she remembered to retrieve the knife.

The pressure in her tummy grew and she could have ripped a nice solid fart only she wasn't going to chance that it would just begin a landslide of intestines!

She quickly grabbed the knife, not worrying about the makeshift holster and dropped it to the floor, practically flinging it so she could grab one of the huge helmets to slip over her head. It was a glass dome with 365-degree visibility and once it attached to the neck of the suit, there was a swoosh of air and the safety engaged securing it to the suit. A moment later the arms and legs began to draw up and like a band it snapped to fit her perfectly—well except the gloves. They were still too big. For now, she didn't care about the gloves because the pressure to make a poop was thankfully ebbing away.

She reached up to swipe the sweat from her forehead, remembering she was in a space suit when the back of her hand struck the dome. Yeah, her brain was rattled. She forced herself to sit down and catch her breath. As she spared a precious-few-moments to clear her head, she thought about uncle Haru.

"Back when the world had wars, there were people from Japan that were called Kamikaze."

That's a funny word, but I like the way it sounds. M and Haru were taking a break from her *wakizashi* and *katana* training. He said the training should go hand in hand, just as the swords would.

He was crouched on the floor with his back to the wall, his tail was almost like a little chair, coiled beneath his bottom.

Trying to mimic him the best she could, M had to be satisfied with just crouching low with her butt just shy of touching the floor.

Her uncle passed her a water bottle and after she took a long swig, he drank the rest. She watched him in admiration at the way he drained it in one gulp.

"Some of the most terrible words have beautiful meanings," her uncle continued. "Kamikaze means divine wind."

What's so terrible about that?

"The actual name was the Divine Wind Special Attack Unit. Like the Galatian Guards, they were military aviators. Unlike us, their job was to die." She had given him a look of disbelief. "The job of these pilots were to aim their planes at their opponents and kill them in the resulting explosion."

Uncle Haru… that seems silly. They wouldn't even get to see the end of their battle!

Haru clasped his hands before him as he spoke. "They, like us, live by a code. They called it the Bushido code. We call it____." And then he made a sound that no human tongue could recreate. It came from his chest and stomach and gushed from his mouth like a soft whisper.

"Honor until death. Being a Galatian Guard means we would rather accept death before defeat."

I would rather live so that I can keep fighting

Haru laughed. "We would too, young one. We would, too."

M's communicator vibrated softly, pulling her from her reverie. It was probably indicating that the environment was stabilized again. She couldn't see the communicator now that it was inside of the suit with her, but she could still control it even it if was covered. For now, she wanted it quiet.

She picked up the hunting knife happy she had it, but knew where she could get something better.

M crept out of the closet. Her body still moved too fast, but it no longer felt like she had rocks chained to her. But she still felt like she was in an old-fashioned cartoon that moved in fast forward.

Papa had a large weapons case which was currently in the storage unit of the ship. But no Protector would go completely weaponless. She went to the crates that were stacked neatly in the room. It wasn't all of their belongings, just what Mama said were the essentials. She located papa's satchel and in it were the weapons she had seen him pack while back on Earth. There were two laser guns, a pistol and the thing she needed; an electrical baton.

There was no holster so she couldn't carry everything. She returned the hunting knife and grabbed the baton and laser gun. Standing, she grabbed one of Mama's bags and slipped her weapons inside. Then she took a deep breath and opened the door.

The space craft was huge. Uncle Drago had told them the stats, but she hadn't cared about any of that. What she did find interesting is that there weren't just human and Galatian's on the craft. Earth was a restricted planet and aliens weren't allowed there unless they had military clearance—like Dorf and a few others.

But here on the space ship, aliens moved freely and comfortably. There were short ones, tall ones, round ones and some that weren't shaped like humanoids at all. Papa had explained that they were here to do a job and to not bother them as they didn't have the same sense of propriety as humans.

M didn't know exactly what that meant, but got the feeling that if she pissed off someone, she might get smacked.

Once the door opened, part of her fully expected to see Papa standing just on the other side with darkening scales and a severe look on his face. But the coast was clear. No one was even in the corridor. But she decided that even if there was, it wouldn't matter. No one knew her business just like she didn't know theirs. To those still walking around, she would just be another alien allowed to stay awake because she had an 'essential' clearance.

M moved to the elevator and got her first test when the door opened and an alien was standing there. It was somewhat humanoid, meaning that it had arms, legs, a torso and head. After that the resemblance ended. The alien had skin like a pig; pink and beige and in some places there were coarse tufts of hair. The alien had a face like a troll with tusks that thrust out its bottom lip. It wore a gladiator helmet, a leather jacket and blue jeans. It would have been scary if it wasn't shorter than her.

The alien nodded and moved aside to give her room. She nodded in return, entered and then pressed the control for the sick bay.

Once the doors opened, she saw that this level was busy with people moving about. M knew she would have to rely on her wits. Sometimes the best plans were none at all, because sometimes you just had to improvise.

She saw the sick bay up ahead with the two Galatian Guards from earlier still stationed outside the doors. That was good. They would remember her. It was the one part of it all she had planned. She walked toward them and that's when someone spoke to her.

"Hey, little girl? Are you okay?"

M looked at the youngish woman who wore a suit similar to hers. The only difference is she had a medical cross over her heart indicating she was part of the medical staff.

M's mind leaped into overdrive. She wrinkled her face and gave the woman the most woeful look.

I want my mommy

"Aww." The lady crouched before her. "Who is your mommy?"

My tummy hurts, M continued.

The woman's expression grew worried. "We need to get you back into a chamber. Come on, honey. I'll get you to sick bay." She took M's hand and led her to where the guards were standing.

Well, this was much easier than she had thought it would be! But instead of going into the room that the two Galatian's guarded, she was being led to a different room, which was next door to it.

M stared at the guards as she was made to walk past them. They didn't move, their eyes were trained straight ahead, but she knew that their tails observed them.

I want my daddy. I want Rafe Sigur! she cried.

Just in case they hadn't recognized her before, they would now. And all they would see was a nurse that was familiar to them, and a little girl that belonged to their commander.

M slipped her hand into the satchel, bypassing the laser gun and gripped the baton. Using the fast motion of the warp speed to assist her, she released the woman's hand and withdrew the baton in one fluid motion. She flung herself at the two Guards while in a tight spin, catching one of them in the torso with the hard electrified metal. He was barely able to make a pained 'huff' sound before the momentum of her spin allowed her to kick the second guard high on his neck which knocked him off balance.

Months of training with her papa and uncles had taught her that surprise move. M had always been fast, but the warp speed of the ship made her even faster. She envisioned herself slapping the control to open the bay door because you had to see it in your mind in order to make it happen in the real world. And just as she landed lightly to her feet her hand did engage the control to open the door!

M sprang forward even while the electrocuted Guard reached for where she had been, not expecting her to have reflexes like a Galatian. M wasn't where he grabbed. She was now inside the secure room.

M spun again knowing that the spin allowed her swing to carry much more force. She didn't have to actually see that one of the guards had also sprung forward close behind her because it's what Uncle Paris would have done—had done many times in practice. The arc of the electric baton struck the guard hard in the face.

M's head whipped around to see how close the pool was.

"What the-?" Dr. Brookstone yelled. He was standing by a scanner, also wearing a white medical suit. M ignored him and darted forward, her eyes trained on the prize. The cocoon floated in the center of the large pool, concealing, protecting the murderous bad lady.

Something tripped her. It was the tail of one of the guards! She stumbled, barreling forward, her eyes still trained on the cocoon. M flung the baton forward praying she was close enough for it to land in the pool of water where it would electrocute the Galatian again. Just one more time.

Please...

Chapter Thirty-Eight

"Lt. Sigur, there is an electrical surge coming from Sick Bay one."

Rafe looked over at the control panel and opened a virtual map where he could see that something was going on where Magna was housed.

He opened the communicator to the ship's main medical floor. "Dr. Brookside." There was no response. Rafe moved quickly to the bay's door while he pulled up information on the guard's station. Before he could call one of them, he got an incoming.

"Lt. Sigur." The image of a stunned looking guard appeared before him. "There's been an incident." Rafe could see the man staggering to his feet. "Your daughter..."

"M? What about my daughter?!"

"She's here, sir."

What in the hell? Rafe was now moving as quickly as he could while wearing boots, running at break neck speed to the bay's door. He moved so quickly that non-Galatian's looked behind them in shock in his wake. He bounded off the walls when other individuals were in his way, his body twisting in acrobatic moves while he maneuvered around his crew.

His daughter was in the sick bay and his mind was going wild wondering what could have happened to her. Was there a malfunction within her Chamber? What could have caused such a big outage that it was detected on the main deck.

By the time Rafe reached the elevators, his heart was racing. When the doors closed too slowly, he wanted to pound it with his fists! There was a *Greginarian* and *Bablibash* within the relatively small compartment; both were very small aliens that could easily be squashed by someone of his size and strength.

He drew his tail close as he reached out to M's communicator. He growled when there was no response. Rafe returned his attention back to the monitor where the Galatian Guard was now standing with his laser gun trained on an individual. Rafe made the hologram stationary and then widened the perspective.

M, who was wearing a white anti-gravity suit, was knelt on her knees, her dome covered head lowered to her chest. Her back was to two of the Galatians with her hands crossed behind her! Even with the suit and helmet he knew her because of her wild hair haloed within the large 360-degree glass.

"What in the fuck do you think you're doing?!" he roared. His daughter looked so tiny being flanked by the two huge armed Galatians, especially within the suit that had shrank down to better fit her. What alarmed him was the position she was in was one of execution. Prisoners in that position were given the honorable death of beheading.

"STAND THE FUCK DOWN!" He yelled.

The two Guards didn't hesitate to lower their weapons. But they continued to watch his little one warily. M didn't move.

The doors to the elevators finally opened and Rafe could see the sick bays just ahead. A crowd was beginning to gather around the opened door of bay one. He was there within a second, sweeping people out of his way—mostly humans who hadn't realized that danger was barreling their way. Those unfortunates went flying through the air! One was knocked unconscious when he hit the adjacent wall, another went crumbling with crushing force when his airborne body came to a sudden stop against a metal counter.

"Little One!" He yelled and lifted the little girl into his arms. He held her at arm's length after the brief hug and saw her lip was swollen and split. A scant amount of blood was visible. But her eyes lit up at the sight of him.

Rafe roared and spun to the two Guards. They were trained to stand at attention before their Commander, but both looked uncertain and prepared themselves to take a blow from him.

"Who did this?!"

"She fell," came a voice that didn't belong to either guard.

Rafe turned and saw Dr. Brookside in the water of the pool. He was doing a scan of Ragna's cocoon using a handheld wand. The doctor didn't look at Rafe as he continued with his examination.

"Your daughter will be okay." Dr. Brookside finally looked up and over to Rafe. "She managed to wage an attack against your prisoner here."

M clung to her father. When he looked at her, she met his eyes. They flinched a bit but she met his gaze unapologetically, and with courage. Her expression seemed to say; *I did what I did...*

Rafe gestured to the Guards. "Dismissed." His attention then returned to Dr. Brookstone who was wading out of the water towards them. His white suit amplified the lack of melanin in his equally white skin and hair. Even in his anger, Rafe recognized the man's uniqueness.

When he eventually stood before them, Rafe saw that the doctor's expression was completely unreadable. He was very good, because Rafe was quite proficient at reading humans. He set his daughter to her feet and M immediately moved to reach for a baton that lay on the floor.

Wait, Rafe thought. That was one of his weapons!

Garry moved quickly and grabbed the baton before M could

reach it. The doctor put his hands on his hips, not in anger but in amazement.

"Ah ah ah, Little One," he chided. Garry's eyes met Rafe's again.

"Your daughter managed to best two of your Galatian Guards to get in here. She then threw this weapon at the pool while the barrier was activated. Luckily, we had enacted the electrical sphere as you had ordered." Garry dared not take his eyes off the little girl as he continued to explain, although he did want to point out what had saved the prisoner's life.

"When this baton hit the electrified sphere that encased the pool, it shorted it out. As you know, if your prisoner would have managed to awaken and attempted to touch the electrical barrier, it would have cooked her instantly. By the same token, if that baton had made contact with the pool, it would have done the same." His expression became earnest as he looked at Rafe. "The barrier protecting your prisoner has been destroyed. Had your daughter gotten hold of this baton and tossed it into the pool, then that Black Mask would have been annihilated."

Garry then looked at the little girl with surprising admiration. The Queen's death would have been swift had the child achieved her goal. There was none of this 'healing her so they could torture her to death.' How could any of them think that a physician would be okay with that, regardless of how much he condemned her actions? He had even considered giving her an injection that would put her out of her misery. But in the end, he knew that it wasn't his place—more so, it wasn't his decision to make.

If her life was to end, then it would be someone else's decision to make. He wanted nothing to do with it. His hands were dirty enough.

He thought of the little boy he'd treated in Tanzania. Oskar was a Black African with skin as white as snow. He'd never seen a doctor that had the same condition as him and he'd shyly touched his skin and hair, marveling at the similarities.

Garry had taken him and several other children stricken with Albinism to the local eye surgeon where their sight was surgically corrected. He provided up to date skin care products which would only need to be taken once daily to protect them from the harsh African sun. His team was to remain there for two months to treat as many children as possible—and yet he chose to spend most of it with the small group of children that had initially garnered his attention—among them was Oskar.

The other children were grateful and celebratory at the attention and gifts, but Oskar, who was only about ten years old, didn't find joy in any of it.

'*What happened to your teeth Oskar?*' He was missing too many for even a child of his age.

'*My Da sold them to pay the rent...*'

Garry had just stared at him in horror. But Oskar smiled—not because he was happy, but because he wanted to comfort his new friend.

'*It is okay, Dr. Garry. My Da says that even though I am bad, at least I am good for something...*' Garry's attention returned to the present at the sound of Rafe's angry voice.

"M," Rafe finally spoke, his tail rigid while his color moved from dark to green and then back again. He was trying hard to hold his temper. "What were you thinking? You could have been killed! My Guards would have been well within their rights to take your life to prevent you from killing our prisoner! And then I would have been in the wrong for ripping them to shreds! Their blood would have been on your hands, M!"

Dr. Brookstone took a step in front of the little girl, creating a barrier between the two.

"Don't you dare hurt her!"

Rafe's eyes rested on the doctor's colorless ones. He was a tall one, only about a head shorter than Rafe. There was fearlessness within this strangely colored human. Paris had said he was a mercenary and Rafe could see that Garry Brookstone had seen and done a great deal of dangerous and reckless things. This obviously wasn't the first.

Rafe could have killed him with one swipe of one finger, and this doctor surely knew this. And still, he stood up for his daughter. But Rafe could hurt no one who would offer his life to protect his child.

"She is my daughter and I would never hurt her. If you know anything about Galatians, you know that much."

Garry watched him warily for another moment. Indecision flashed in his eyes.

'Where is Oskar?' Garry had demanded when the little boy hadn't shown up to the doctor's office earlier in the day. Garry was at the door of the little shack that housed the boy's mother, father, and seven siblings. Oskar never missed an opportunity to visit the center in order to get away from home and his abusive father.

Garry had only known the child for two weeks and he was already asking about adopting him. He was certain his father would sign away his rights to the child for the right price, and his mother did nothing to step in for the sake of her son.

'Where is Oskar?!' Garry had demanded again. No one would answer, no matter how angry he got.

He eventually had no choice but to return to the center. Later, he learned that the child had been dismembered and his body parts sold to various witch doctors to help line the pockets of his wretched mother and father. It was the first time that Garry had killed someone...

He finally moved to the side. The Galatian's words were true. They would never hurt a child. It was probably the only thing that had saved this one from the two Galatian Guards. They had held back, but she had been amazing! She fought with an instinct that came only from someone who was used to fighting for survival.

I'm sorry Papa. M said.

Rafe's jaw clenched when M looked up at him with her big brown eyes. But she could have been killed! But she was his little warrior. She had done what warriors do. He inhaled a long breath. She would be punished as a warrior.

"You are to return to your sleep chamber and this time, a Guard will be stationed by your side for the remainder of this trip. I see that it wasn't that Black Mask who should have been guarded, but you! You went against my wishes; your Commander. Your Papa! And you will be punished."

Rafe held out his hand for hers and M didn't hesitate to place her little hand in his. His heart began to melt.

I must punish her, but this will be hell on me...

Garry watched them leave the sick bay. A feeling fell over him that he was making a huge mistake.

The End...

Sneak Peek: Book 6, Eden

Chapter One

"Wait. Lt. Sigur," Garry called after them.

Rafe paused to look at the doctor.

"You can't put her back to sleep so close to the last injection. She's simply too young to take another dose right now." He glanced behind him at the cocoon floating in the swirling Galatian waters.

"I can monitor her vitals here. She can stay in her suit until it's safe to put her back to sleep."

"Are you suggesting that you guard my daughter—here, in the same room with the very same prisoner she's already tried to kill?"

"I'm suggesting that your daughter not be banished to a small chamber for twenty hours while she's wide awake." He gave M an amused look at her shocked expression. Some of the strongest warriors had completely lost it if they awakened while still encased in what would quickly begin to feel like a tomb.

"And, no," Garry continued. "It's not safe for the prisoner to be left unprotected—and by that, I mean the *prisoner* isn't safe. I'm returning her to the transport where the electrical dome in that pool will keep her secured until we arrive in Eden.

"In the meantime, your daughter can remain in her suit and do some chores around here to help work off some of this damage she created."

Rafe considered this non-violent type of punishment. Not that he had ever intended to physically punish her. But since punishing children in any way went against the beliefs of a Galatian, he felt instant relief at this idea.

But then he looked at the doctor dubiously. Perhaps this man underestimates his daughter. It would be unwise to do so. Ragna was a testament to that.

"Or," Garry shrugged. "Just be sure to monitor her vitals—or bring her back here every few hours for me to do it." The doctor turned with a sigh and lifted his wand to continue his work with the prisoner.

Rafe looked at his daughter. "You will stay with Dr. Brookstone. And you will do as he says. For now, he is your Commander, but my eyes will still be on you, Little One. Your monitor is to remain on visual."

Yes, Papa.

He clenched his teeth and then gave her a brief hug before exiting the bay without her. He called out his final instructions over his shoulders, allowing his tail to observe them. "I expect you to be on your best behavior, M. I will send two Galatian Guards to escort Ragna." And then he was gone.

Garry looked at the child. She looked so sweet and innocent, and yet he had seen with his very own eyes what she was capable of. She had whipped the tar out of two full-grown Galatian males!

"Well, you can start by cleaning the specimen containers and pipettes before we recycle them. Everyone tends to complain about the smell of urine and blood in the incinerator."

M's nose went up, but she wasn't complaining. She knew she'd have to face her punishment head-on. The problem is that it would have been worth it to have the bad lady dead. She had hurt her papa, was being punished, and she hadn't even achieved her goal.

~*~

They were sitting on rolling stools several hours later, having a meal break. Just as Rafe stated, two Galatian Guards had taken Ragna away, and he was able to confirm through the ship's controls she was secure and her vitals were stable.

There was no eating in the regular way when wearing the full suit. Therefore, they had to take their nourishment through ports in the suit which secreted nutritional enzymes against the flesh. It was only a short-term solution to starvation. But no one had factored in the food cravings while considering the logistics of building the life-sustaining device.

"You're not feeling hungry, are you?"

The little girl shook her head.

"Good, because this suit is equipped to nourish you in every way." He whispered the next. "There's even a flap in the back if you have to use the toilet. But the suit slows all of that down, so you shouldn't need to do any of that."

M tried to look over her shoulder at the back of the suit for this flap. She couldn't see it if it was there. She looked back at the doctor again for her next task.

So far, she had washed like a hundred clear little cups in a solution that was supposed to kill the stink before they were recycled. Her big gloves had made the task hard, but she did it. Afterward, she had to wipe down all the furniture. Dr. Brookside had claimed she had made a mess of things, but it wasn't true. The only thing a mess was the electrical cage that had protected the Black Mask.

At first, she was mad at the doctor. But then he told her that if she had reached the pool and touched the electrical barrier, she would have died instantly. Then he had fussed at her a little.

'I told you about the barrier and that no one could get in or out. Didn't you understand what that meant... ?'

He had been right. Her plan had been to get close enough to

throw the electricity into the pool. She would have touched the barrier to do it. She would have died. She had been stupid about her need to get rid of the threat against her family. That is why a true warrior made plans, but was open to change. A warrior didn't just hope for the best!

'*Look,*' he had said. '*I understand why you did what you did. I even see by that Galatian suit you want to be a warrior.*' Her chest had puffed out. She *was* a warrior. Garry continued as if he understood her expression. '*I have fought for my beliefs—killed for my beliefs. But I make a plan, so I can live to fight another day.*'

Afterwards, M wanted to hear him talk. And talk he did. He talked about his travels, about why he had no pigment, and even about the kids he worked with. What he didn't like talking about was fighting. But she learned that he fought with the Galatians, specifically with Uncle Paris!

But he wouldn't give her details. Still, M decided she liked Dr. Garry.

"You ready for your scan, kiddo?" He asked while standing.

She made a face. She would rather stay awake with the doctor.

Garry sighed when he looked at her monitor. Per her father's requirement, it remained stationary so that he could visually monitor her, but it also meant she had to walk across the room to use the controls to speak to him.

He wished he could take a look at why she was unable to speak. He was sure that Lt. Sigur had gotten the best of the best in physicians, which didn't always mean they were the best in pediatrics. Children's injuries and disabilities often changed with the onset of puberty but definitely as they grew. M's case could use another look.

He felt bad that it wouldn't be him to do it.

Garry scanned her vitals and then nodded in approval. "Yes. You're ready."

She looked distrustfully at one of the chambers.

"Sorry that I can't give you your communicator back, but since you know how to use it as an escape mechanism..."

M shook her head as if to tell him it was okay. She didn't need it.

Garry used her communicator to speak to Rafe. The visual only went one way, but there was no audio unless it was activated. He assumed Rafe was too busy to listen to their idle chatter.

"Lt. Sigur, your daughter is ready to enter the chamber. I will be administering the sedative now."

"M," Rafe's voice came through the communicator. "I am unable to return to the sick bay. Things are very hectic. But I am watching, so I am here with you." M nodded. "You aren't afraid, are you, Little One?" M shook her head adamantly. "Good. We will talk when you wake up." His voice had become a mixture of stern yet filled with love and concern.

M nodded again.

The protocol was to leave her in her suit within the chamber and after making sure she was comfortable; he input a tube into one of the suit's ports and administered the sedative.

She looked a bit lost in the large suit, and Garry's heart went out to her. What life had this little girl led to cause her to do such a thing?

"M. Count backward from ten. You'll be asleep before you reach zero," Garry said.

M gestured for the communicator who was on a rolling cart. She probably wanted to tell her dad bye before she went under. He retrieved it and handed it to her.

But he saw her turn the audio to only be heard in this room. So, it was him she wanted to speak to.

You think I stupid for what I did. I not. Grown-ups think they know best, but they know too much. When you know too much, you have too many choices. And the most important thing is not important anymore.

My daddy say he gonna kill Black Mask. He wants to kill Black Mask. But something will happen that he thinks is more important. And he will say I'll do it later. Then she will heal and get stronger. There is nothing more important than her dying.

Garry thought about her words and then he nodded. "I agree with you M. I do. I saw what she did and I know terrible people like her; people who kill babies... " He looked away as if he wanted to exorcise distant memories. With a sigh, he looked at her again. "Your father is consumed with hatred and the need for revenge. When the little boy I wanted to adopt was murdered by his father, I annihilated that man. I took his arms, then his legs, and finally his heart—and I kept him alive while I did it.

"I thought it would make me feel better. But it made me into a monster because deep down I knew there was another side to that story. I know he made himself and then Oskar believe that he was evil in order to do what he did. And then he had that child murdered... and he did it because his other children were starving. He didn't take the money and run, he bought food. I saw..."

M watched the doctor, not completely understanding the story, but understanding enough.

Garry let out a soft breath. "That's a road I can't and won't travel down again. I just... want you to know why I'm doing this. You will never have to worry about that lady again. But right is right and wrong is wrong."

M frowned in confusion. But Dr. Garry was already administering the sedative.

TGE MASTER KEY
THE GALATIAN GUARDS

NAME	FAMILY	EARTH'S ORIGIN	BOUND MATE	JAPOXILLIAN
RAFE SIGUR	-WIFE: KARMA CHAMBERS -CHILDREN: RUNNAR, ELIJAH JAMES, M (EMMY) -MOTHER: JADORITY -BROTHER: GILA	ICELAND	RAGNA	SIR DORF (KNIGHTED)
DRAGO ENGSTRÖM	-WIFE: MADELINE (MADDIE -CHILD: REX -MOTHER: BIRTA	ICELAND	ISYSS	KEMISTRY
TITUS GRAYSON	-MATE: POLAT -MOTHER: NO HUMAN NAME	SCOTLAND	FILENE	BROMHILD
KENDRICK WASHINGTON	-MATE: AURAS -GIRLFRIEND: ? -PARENTS: NO HUMAN NAMD	NORTH AMERICA	EVORA	POGO
LEOLO SANCHEZ	MATE: JAYNE (REJECTED) -MOTHER: NO HUMAN NAME	SOUTH AMERICA	NOT NAMED	SOLOMAR
PARIS FRENCHMAN	-MATE: JUSTINA -WIFE: -MOTHER: URSA	FRANCE (EU)	THALIA	LAYLAY
HARU BANO	-WIFE: TAMSYN (TAM) FELICIDAD HERNANDEZ-BANO -MOTHER: LEPHORA	JAPAN	CAEDA	NAO

GALATIAN EMOTIONAL COLORS

COLOR	EMOTION
GREEN	NEUTRAL STATE
WHITE	FEAR FOR SOMEON THEY CARE ABOUT (NO COLOR FOR SELF-FEAR)
YELLOW	AMUSED
PINK	SMILE. AMUSEMENT
ORANGE	LAUGHTER. EXTREME PLAYFULNESS
PURPLE	ANNOYANCE
BLACK	DISAPPOINTED ANGER
RED	RAGE
BLUE	SEXUAL AROUSAL
KALEIDESCOPE	ALARM. ANXIETY

Pepper Pace Books

STRANDED!
Juicy
Love Intertwined Vol. 1
Love Intertwined Vol. 2
Urban Vampire; The Turning
Urban Vampire; Creature of the Night
Urban Vampire; The Return of Alexis
Urban Vampire; The Final Battle
Wheels of Steel Book 1
Wheels of Steel Book 2
Wheels of Steel Book 3
Wheels of Steel Book 4
Angel Over My Shoulder
CRASH
Miscegenist Sabishii
They Say Love Is Blind
The Throwaway Year
Beast
A Seal Upon Your Heart

Everything is Everything Book 1
Everything is Everything Book 2
Adaptation book 1
Adaptation book 2
About Coco's Room
The Witch's Demon book 1
A Bubble of Time
Awakening
1954
The Galatian Exchange Book 1: Karma and Rafe
The Galatian Exchange Book 2: The Family
The Galatian Exchange Book 3: The Enemies
The Galatian Exchange Book 4: Strike of the Black Masks!

SHORT STORIES/NOVELLAS
~~***~~
The Way Home
MILF
Blair and the Emoboy
Emoboy the Submissive Dom
1-900-BrownSugar
Someone To Love
My Special Friend
Baby Girl and the Mean Boss
A Wrong Turn Towards Love (An Estill County Mountain Man
Romance)
True's Love (An Estill County Mountain Man Romance)
The Miseducation of Riley Pranger (An Estill County Mountain
Man Romance)
Christmas Redemption (An Estill County Mountain Man Romance)
The Delicate Sadness
The Shadow People
The Love Unexpected
The Vinyl Man

Punishment Island
Super G

COLLABORATIONS
~~***~~

Sexy Southern Hometown Heroes
Seduction: An Interracial Romance Anthology Vol. 1
Scandalous Heroes Box set
Secrets of the Elite

WRITTEN UNDER BETH JO ANDERSEN
~~***~~

Snatched by Bigfoot!
Bigfoot's Sidepiece
Mated to the Bigfoot!

WRITTEN UNDER KIM CHAMBERS
~~***~~

The Purple World book 1

About the Author

Pepper Pace creates a unique brand of Interracial/multicultural erotic romance. While her stories span the gamut from humorous to heartfelt, the common theme is crossing racial boundaries. She writes in the genres of science fiction, youth, horror, urban lit and poetry.

For More Information From the Author

Sign-up to the Pepper Pace Newsletter!

http://eepurl.com/bGV4tb